A Timely Elopement

Joana Starnes

Chapter 1

The room was small and received precious little daylight – it was on the wrong side of the house – and the walls covered in dark and absurdly pretentious paper-hangings seemed to close in on him as Fitzwilliam Darcy dropped his hat and gloves on the nearest table and strode towards the fireplace.

He frowned. Many would say that the step he was about to take was ill-judged in the extreme. Madness, they would call it, sheer madness. Yet it could not be helped. Nay, it could not be helped.

He ran his hand over his mouth and chin, drew a deep breath and turned around to face the only sunlit corner of the parlour, where Elizabeth sat bathed in a golden glow, at the table by the window. His eyes warmed as he took in the enticing sight.

'Fitting, the soft light which through yonder window breaks – for she is the sun,' he thought, and a hint of a smile tugged at the corner of his lips when he found himself paraphrasing the Bard like a besotted youth. Nevertheless, she *was* a ray of sunshine. He had thought as much from the earliest days of their acquaintance. She was all that was bright and good. Her cheerful disposition – the warmth of her love – the heat of passion: she stood to bring all that into his life, and more besides. True companionship. A blissful and rewarding union. A life with her would undoubtedly provide more than ample compensation for the censure that his choice would hasten to attract.

Lips tightened, Darcy banished all thought of naysayers and the forthcoming storm. He was his own man after all, and nobody's fool. And who but a weak-minded fool would be swayed from his course of action in something quite so personal as this? Of course, he would do his duty – he always had and always would – but henceforth he would do it as *he* saw it. With Elizabeth beside him. He *would* secure his heart's desire – secure *her* – and if the world at large could not understand that happy men did their duty better, then the world could go hang!

All of a sudden, the words were out, as though of their own volition:

"In vain I have struggled. It will not do. My feelings will not be repressed. You must allow me to tell you how ardently I admire and love you."

His lungs filled with air and a blessed sense of peace washed over him, now that the deed was done and the long-withheld avowal was out into the open. Every trace of doubt and all his natural and just misgivings fell away like a discarded coat, leaving him almost giddy with relief, and his heart lighter than a feather. He gave a faint, dismissive little shrug as he continued:

"In declaring myself thus, I am fully aware that I will be going expressly against the wishes of my family, my friends, and – I hardly need add! – my—"

'Damnation!'

The expletive was held back more by luck than judgement, and instead of giving full vent to his displeasure at the interruption, Darcy merely turned around to glare at the opening door. The young maid – blameless recipient of his vexation – dared not say a word, but bobbed a flustered curtsy and stepped out of the way to make room for Colonel Fitzwilliam.

All that the newcomer was allowed to offer was a brief greeting, before Darcy forestalled him:

"This is not a good time," he said crisply. "I would appreciate it if you gave us a moment."

The flash of apologetic comprehension in the colonel's eyes told Darcy that, although he had not taken his cousin into confidence, not fully, Fitzwilliam had astutely grasped precisely what it was that he had interrupted. Yet, instead of making himself scarce with due haste, he grimaced and advanced into the room.

"I hope you will forgive me," he said to both, his mien suitably contrite, "but you are needed at Rosings, Cousin. I thought I might find you here—"

"And so you have," Darcy cut him off. "Pray let Lady Catherine know I will attend her as soon as—"

It was his turn to be unceremoniously interrupted:

"It cannot wait," Fitzwilliam declared without equivocation. "We have reason to fear that Anne has eloped. To own the truth, with Wickham."

ஒ௦ ௦ஒ

"*What?*" Darcy hissed, his voice deathly quiet – so much so that, by comparison, Elizabeth's exclamation was almost shrill:

"Mr Wickham? Mr *George* Wickham?"

"The very one," Fitzwilliam confirmed, a grim set to his jaw. "You know of him, then. I could not ascertain whether my cousin told you—"

"I have not," Darcy intervened, but the terse warning was for naught. Elizabeth's wary glance was already darting from one to the other.

"Told me what?"

Fitzwilliam held his peace. '*As well he should,*' Darcy inwardly grumbled with a fresh flare of vexation. It was not his cousin's place to answer. It was his, and both of them knew it. So he squared his shoulders and gave her the unvarnished truth:

"Last summer Wickham had made the same designs upon my sister – or rather, upon her substantial dowry. He had worked to persuade her to consent to an elopement. He was foiled, thank goodness, but..."

Darcy broke off, concerned in no small measure by the host of unreadable emotions that played on Elizabeth's countenance as she slumped back in her chair with a quiet, "Oh."

He frowned. He had no way of knowing what it was that she was thinking, but she could not be allowed to form an ill opinion of his sister!

"Georgiana was but fifteen at the time, which must be a fair excuse for her imprudence," he added swiftly. "She had no notion of his mercenary and deceitful nature, nor could she guess the full extent of his depravity. Her tender heart had kept fond recollections of him from her girlhood, so she believed herself in love," Darcy elaborated, and was about to defend his sister further by disclosing that the dear girl had confessed the scheme to him of her own accord, when Fitzwilliam cut in, his fists clenched and his eyes shooting daggers.

"You should have let me run him through and pay him back for all the grief he caused us!" the colonel spat through gritted teeth, and much as he understood that the reminder of Georgiana's heartbreak was sufficient provocation for his cousin's outburst, Darcy gave a gesture of impatience.

"Do cease bringing that up, will you?" he said with uncompromising firmness. "You saw sense and agreed that it was for the best. Had you been harmed, it would have destroyed her."

Fitzwilliam's jaw tightened.

"The wretch would not have stood a chance. And he would not be alive today to injure us again."

"Yes, well, that is as may be, but dwelling on *'if only'* is not helping matters," Darcy pointed out, insensitive as it might have been to say so. His pragmatic nature coming to the fore in times of crisis, just as it always did, he pressed on with the salient question: "What do you know of Anne?"

Fitzwilliam rubbed his jaw and took a deep breath as if to calm himself, then proceeded to relate with as much coherence as he could muster:

"She was not missed until the time when we were meant to congregate for dinner. When she was tardy in making an appearance, our aunt grew impatient and sent up for tidings. Anne's lady's maid must have been acting on express instructions, for she tergiversated to the best of her abilities, but the woman is no match for Lady Catherine. When it could no longer be concealed that Anne was not in her chambers, the lady's maid had to come down and face the inquisition. Needless to say, she crumbled, and in due course confessed everything. Namely, that for the best part of two months, Anne had been exchanging illicit correspondence with a man who, judging from her description, bears an uncannily close resemblance to Wickham. Also, that a case crammed full with essential apparel as well as sundry jewels and personal possessions was tucked into the phaeton at Anne's feet when she and Mrs Jenkinson left the house for their daily outing."

Darcy pressed his lips together upon the oath that threatened to burst out.

"And what has been done, what has been attempted to recover her?" he forcefully asked instead.

"The phaeton is ill-suited to carry her over any great distance, so I dispatched riders towards the nearest turnpike inns to trace her. I know not what their success has been. I left the house at the same time in search of you."

Darcy grimaced.

"You had better go back to make preparations for departure and let Lady Catherine know I shall return directly. That is to say, as soon as possible," he amended, settling a long look upon his cousin, which would hopefully convey his meaning.

Never obtuse, the other nodded in understanding and acceptance, yet still cautioned:

"Do not tarry long. As you can imagine, our aunt is frantic. Besides, once she recovers from the shock, she might begin to wonder what is keeping you."

Darcy rolled his eyes and shrugged. At this point in time, the risk of rousing Lady Catherine's suspicions as to his motives and intentions was the least of his concerns.

"I trust you will pacify her as best you can," he muttered, then urged, "Go, Cousin. I will see you shortly."

With a bow to Elizabeth and a solemn glance encompassing them both, as if to wordlessly beg pardon for bursting in to bring grave tidings at the worst of times, the colonel finally complied.

⋅⊙⊙ ⊙⊙⋅

The sound of the closing door drew Elizabeth from her musings with a start. She glanced up with belated contrition when it occurred to her that she had not even acknowledged the colonel's leave-taking. Oh, well. He deserved better, but he would not mind. Today of all days, he had far more pressing matters vying for his attention.

And so did she – which was the reason why she had barely attended to the gentlemen as they had spoken of the staggering developments at Rosings. Truth be told, she had registered less than one word in ten, while she had endeavoured to come to terms with a fair number of shocking revelations. Namely that Mr Wickham – the amiable and charming Mr Wickham – was a cad. That he had worked his wiles upon an innocent and trusting girl – his benefactor's daughter – Mr Darcy's sister. That, once foiled, he had been quick to make designs upon another dowry – Miss King's – only to abandon that quest in favour of a better catch and elope with the heiress of Rosings. Moreover, that he had made a fool of *her*. He had stood before her, looked her in the eye, and kept a straight face as he had told her that the only reason for the manifest bad blood between him and Mr Darcy was the latter's jealousy and his own unguarded temper.

'I may perhaps have spoken my opinion of him, and to him, too freely. I can recall nothing worse,' he had declared. Nothing worse! He had brazenly claimed he could recall nothing worse, yet mere months prior he had sought to ruin the man's sister!

And she had believed him implicitly – had commiserated with him – had credited his deceit – had indulged him like the veriest of simpletons! That rankled the most. It ought not, Elizabeth knew full well. His trespasses against his benefactor's kin were a vast deal worse – they were despicable. Spinning a falsehood or two was trifling in comparison. Yet her anger swelled; she could not help it. Mr Wickham had made a fool of her – and she had suffered him to do so. Nay, she had aided and abetted him!

Elizabeth cringed when another galling notion struck her: had Colonel Fitzwilliam not burst into Charlotte's parlour with his shocking tidings, by now she might have told Mr Darcy that she had not lost her senses to the point of consenting to marry a man who would treat his boyhood companion with no humanity. She might have taken him to task in defence of the vile rogue and reproached him for withholding the living stipulated in his father's will. That fragment of Mr Wickham's tales of woe might well be true – and why not? In the light of the day's disclosures, Mr Darcy was more than justified in his resentment. Mr Wickham should count himself fortunate that a more severe punishment had not been meted out to him. The blackguard! Had he sought to harm one of *her* sisters—!

Elizabeth took a deep breath to subdue the anger that surged at the mere thought. She had to own that she was of the same mind as Colonel Fitzwilliam: the repulsive creature deserved to be run through. Nay, worse – he deserved to be drawn and quartered!

"I need not tell you how distraught I am that everything has gone so dreadfully awry," Mr Darcy suddenly said from across the room, and in a flash Elizabeth's murderous intentions vanished, leaving her to the realisation that she had given precious little thought to his singular avowal. Nor had she reflected on the fact that he had professed his love and ardent admiration, yet he had dissuaded Mr Bingley from offering for Jane on account of *'strong objections against the lady,'* as Colonel Fitzwilliam had inadvertently disclosed that very morning on their walk.

Elizabeth pursed her lips. Had she not been so incensed by Wickham's treachery, she might have dwelt with bemused indignation on how little Mr Darcy understood the bonds of sisterly affection, and likewise wondered how he could reconcile advocating one course of action to his friend, while for himself he chose the very opposite.

She was not afforded the leisure to ponder on either of those subjects. In a few long strides, Mr Darcy crossed the expanse of floor between them and resumed with fierce determination:

"You have my word that I will work to bring this to the speediest conclusion – to the least damaging conclusion that could be reached under the circumstances. I stayed behind to assure you of this. There is nothing else for me to say. Not now. I—" He bit his lip and after the briefest pause he solemnly spoke again, "You must be in no doubt of my hopes and wishes, but there is nothing I can ask of you at present. It would be ungentlemanly and moreover unfair to expect you to connect yourself with a family tainted by a scandalous elopement. Good God, this is beyond everything!" he burst out, his voice laden with the acutest bitterness, and spun on his heel to pace away from her. "I would have offered for you within weeks of our acquaintance, were it not for the inferiority of your connections – and now I am thwarted by one of *my* relations! Farcical, I would call it, had this happened to any other man."

Elizabeth arched a brow at the last remark. Inconsiderate and instinctively self-centred, it promptly did away with the stirrings of compassion that had crept upon her at the thought of his unrequited love and the severe blow of Miss de Bourgh's disgrace at the hands of his foe.

"Remarkable – is it not? – how the difference between farce and tragedy is but a matter of perspective," Elizabeth observed but, to her consternation, her reproachful sarcasm was entirely lost on him.

An ardent glow stole upon Mr Darcy's countenance as he earnestly replied, "Have faith, my love. Believe me, tragedy is not to be our lot."

Elizabeth opened her lips to speak, but before she could retract or clarify her flippant comment, he strode to her side and, instead of towering over her as he had done of late, he pulled up a chair and sat, then reached to clasp her hand and spoke again with a staggering depth of feeling:

"There is nothing that I will not do to bring about our union, Elizabeth, you must know that! Anne's misjudgement and Wickham's scheming shall not keep us apart a moment longer than strictly necessary. He will be apprehended and banished, and Anne's false step will be hushed up. This business *will* be set to rights one way or another. And I will follow you to Longbourn as soon as the deed is done," he vowed and brought her hand to his lips. Not a faint brush over the back of her fingers, but a burning kiss pressed into her palm.

Breath caught in her throat at the unaccountably heady sensation that quickened her pulse and sent a thrill coursing through her veins. The missish response shocked and vexed her in equal measure. She had no business to sit there quivering like a witless damsel – nor he to take such liberties. She had not accepted his offer of marriage, and had no intention of doing so.

With a quiet sigh, Elizabeth drew her hand away, uncomfortably aware that she must tell him that. It would be cruel to let him labour under a misconception. She flinched. It would also be unconscionably cruel to deal a fresh blow to one who had already been pained by bad tidings from another quarter. The prospect sat ill with her – it was not her way to deliberately injure anyone. But it must be done. There were no two ways about it.

"Mr Darcy, I—" Elizabeth haltingly began, only to see him pushing his chair back and rising to his feet with an exasperated, "Oh, for goodness' sake! A few moments' peace – is that so much to ask for?"

She stared, at a loss to grasp the reason for his display of temper, until her cousin's voice reached her through the open window:

"Come along, my dear Charlotte – come, Maria, do make haste! Let us go within. I can scarce breathe. This is in every way dreadful! Do make haste. We must sit… talk… find a way out of this calamity! This is not to be borne. Disgrace, woeful disgrace, and undeserved to boot. No malice on my part, I acted in the best of faiths, and yet I reap nothing but ruin. Who could have possibly imagined…! Gracious, they do say that the road to perdition is paved with good intentions, and truer words were never spoken. May the good Lord have mercy and deliver us from this predicament!"

The front door was slammed shut, soon followed by another one somewhere in the house. With a steadying breath, Elizabeth stood from her seat and braced herself for the pandemonium which, she could scarce doubt, would burst into the parlour in no time at all.

Chapter 2

"How was I to know? *Who* could have possibly imagined?" Mr Collins spluttered yet again, and Elizabeth clasped her hands together in her lap, at pains to stop herself from growling in irritation. Her cousin's incessant pacing and the same two questions – repeated almost word for word at least a dozen times in as many minutes – were already driving her to distraction.

She shuffled in her seat as she grudgingly acknowledged that she really ought to be more charitable. Mr Collins had reason enough to be distressed. Apparently, he was no longer in Lady Catherine's favour. The blame for bringing Mr Wickham to Miss de Bourgh's notice had been laid squarely at his door, and for once Elizabeth found herself in agreement with her cousin: how was he to know what would come of it?

"All I did was convey the man's regards!" Mr Collins pointlessly sought to explain himself – at least to his wife and cousin, since his patroness had refused point-blank to listen. "As for mentioning Miss de Bourgh and her ladyship to Mr Wickham, I could have done no less once I had learned of their prior acquaintance. I thought it only proper to inform the officer that the ladies were in good health when I last saw them and we sat at quadrille together, just as I deemed it my privilege and duty to give the same good tidings to her ladyship's nephew…"

The reference to that gentleman put a deeper crease in Elizabeth's furrowed brow. Her cousin's ill-timed return to Hunsford had blasted every hope of a forthright conversation with Mr Darcy. Unsurprisingly, the commotion had sent him on his way. As soon as Mr Collins had made his tempestuous entrance into the parlour with Charlotte and Maria on his heels, Mr Darcy had bid his terse adieus and, with a meaningful and deeply unsettling, "Until we meet again, Miss Bennet," had quitted the parsonage and left her to her unresolved conundrum: however was she to disabuse him of the notion that she would bestow a favourable answer when they met again?

Elizabeth still had no solution in mind and, to her increased discomfort, Mr Collins' passing reference to Mr Darcy seemed to awaken Charlotte's curiosity as to the *tête-à-tête* that she, her spouse and Maria had just interrupted.

It was little wonder that Charlotte's interest should be piqued. Her friend had already remarked on Mr Darcy's frequent visits at the parsonage and, direct as always, had voiced the belief that *she* was the inducement. Elizabeth suppressed a grimace as she wished she had paid heed to Charlotte's comments. But nay, she had foolishly laughed them off, and his avowals had caught her so woefully unprepared.

'*Well, too late now,*' Elizabeth peevishly told herself and affected not to notice the questioning look that her friend had sent her way when Lady Catherine's nephew was mentioned, safe in the knowledge that Charlotte had more sense than to quiz her on the inflammatory subject in Mr Collins' presence.

Sadly, that was not the end of the matter. The troublesome question came from the man himself:

"By the bye, Cousin Elizabeth, why was Mr Darcy here?"

"He must have come to enquire after her health, once he had learned that she was too ill to dine at Rosings," Charlotte intervened, and with a small nod of gratitude towards her tactful friend, Elizabeth hastened to lend support to the convenient excuse.

"Aye, just so," she swiftly said and, to her relief, Mr Collins was prompt in crediting the deception.

"So considerate of him! Such gentlemanly condescension, quite on the par with his noble aunt's generosity of spirit—" he proceeded to enthuse, only to gasp when a new notion occurred to him. "My goodness, I wager that he would have been disposed to aid me in my plight! Her ladyship was too overcome by grief to spare me a moment of her precious time at this dreadful juncture, but Mr Darcy would have listened. Oh, why had I not thought of this before? What a golden opportunity – so wretchedly missed! It must have been the shock, else I would have seen sense and asked him to present my case to his aunt. If he came all this way for something so trifling as my cousin's headache, he would have been prevailed upon to come to my assistance in this distressing and delicate matter. And

Lady Catherine might have lent a more sympathetic ear to my protestations of regret and innocence, had they been conveyed by her own nephew," he lamented. Yet all of a sudden, he darted across the room in a fresh burst of energy. "There is still time!" he breathlessly declared. "I shall follow him to Rosings forthwith. If I make haste, I might catch up with him on the way."

For her part, Elizabeth doubted it, just as she severely doubted the wisdom of the scheme. She made to say as much, but Charlotte was there before her:

"Pray allow me to urge caution, my dear," she said, her voice even and quietly persuasive, yet confidently so – a clear indication that this was not the first time she had successfully guided her husband in like manner. "I fear Lady Catherine would be most severely displeased, should you delay her nephew in joining her and offering consolation. Besides, a matter of such delicacy requires more than a few words hastily exchanged on the lane to Rosings. To my way of thinking, this calls for a proper communication formulated with as much care and attention as your sermons. I have every reason to believe that Mr Darcy will not absent himself from Rosings for too long," she added, her gaze studiously averted from Elizabeth, "and when he does return, there must be a far more auspicious moment than this to speak to him and beg his assistance."

Mr Collins frowned as he listened to her with the mulish air of one determined to follow his own counsel. No sooner had she finished speaking than he sternly replied:

"My dear Charlotte, you know that I rely on your opinion in all things within the scope of your understanding, but I will thank you to return the compliment and defer to me in matters of import. Frankly, I am baffled that you fail to grasp the severity of our situation. Even a lesser woman should have seen that our welfare is threatened – why, our very livelihood! Need I spell it out that her ladyship might change her mind regarding my preferment?"

"No, sir, you need not," Charlotte said tersely, her countenance taut, while Elizabeth held her peace with great difficulty and Maria shuffled uncomfortably in her seat. "I have already grasped that, I assure you."

"Then why would you advocate delay?" her husband retorted. "Nay, nay, the circumstance is too dire to admit procrastination. It must be addressed at once, and with the greatest circumspection!"

Nevertheless, Charlotte's disparaged opinion must have given him pause, for Mr Collins did not burst out of the parlour, but paced back towards the middle of the room, his mien clouded with the visible effort at anxious contemplation. Then his air brightened, and he exclaimed with triumphant satisfaction:

"Ah, now I have it! I shall write to him. This is the way forward: a well-thought-out and carefully worded letter. I shall write it directly, then hasten to the turnpike inn to send it express to Mr Darcy's house in town. He will have it tonight – and read it tonight too, I wager, as soon as he goes home to request his people's assistance in the search for Miss de Bourgh, as he surely must. Nay, my dear, not another word!" he peremptorily forestalled his wife when she made to speak. His hand raised in a request for silence, he added smugly, "See? Did I not tell you that I would find the best solution?" he boasted, as if *he* had been the one who had argued all along that there was merit in structuring one's thoughts on paper rather than blurting them out on the lane to Rosings.

By the looks of it, Charlotte's contentment in the married state came both from her ability to guide her husband and from the wisdom of biding her time and choosing her battles, Elizabeth inwardly observed as her friend made no further effort to dissuade Mr Collins from his purpose. Charlotte merely gave a weary little sigh as her other half strode out of the parlour.

෴

Once the room had grown quiet, Elizabeth lost every inclination to ponder on her friend's marital contentment – or, in this case, lack thereof – as a sudden notion struck her: she might have found the answer to her conundrum and, strangely, she was indebted to her cousin for that.

A letter would serve – a well-thought-out and carefully worded letter. Not from *her*, naturally. She could not possibly write to Mr Darcy! But her father could. Aye, her father could write to him with impunity. She could learn the address of his townhouse from Charlotte, then enlist her papa's aid. He would not like it in the least, but he would assist her. Little as he cared for letter-writing and moreover for penning one as difficult as that, her dear papa would bow to the necessity. Mr Darcy must learn that he had no reason whatsoever to travel into Hertfordshire.

She flinched. Heaven forbid that he should arrive at Longbourn as her professed suitor and make it known to all and sundry that they had an understanding. If this should reach her neighbours and acquaintances – and, worse still, *her mother…!*

Goodness, he must be dissuaded at all cost from coming to Longbourn, however cowardly and callous it might be to convey such a message in a letter from her father. No doubt, the matter should have been addressed in private, face to face. Mr Darcy would be mortified by her father's involvement. Yet even he would see that this was preferable to having the rest of Meryton in the know as well. For all her justified resentment for his role in ruining Jane's hopes and for his prideful manner throughout the course of their acquaintance, she was not so petty as to extract revenge in so contemptible a fashion and humiliate him with a public rejection of his suit. Not to mention that, once her mother learned that she would reject *'ten thousand a year, and very likely more,'* life at Longbourn would become unbearable.

The very notion made her cringe.

"Wretched, wretched business," she whispered in acute frustration – and realised that she had voiced her thoughts aloud only when Charlotte reached out and pressed her arm.

Elizabeth darted her eyes towards her friend and met Charlotte's glance of wistful gratitude.

"Thank you, Lizzy. Aye, it is a wretched business indeed," Charlotte nodded, patently under the misapprehension that Elizabeth had referred to Mr Collins' unmerited disgrace.

With a twinge of her conscience at having spared no thought for her friend's troubles, Elizabeth covered Charlotte's hand with hers.

"Surely this will be set to rights," she said with energy. "Lady Catherine must have spoken in the heat of anger. Eventually, she is bound to see how senseless and unjust it is to make a scapegoat of your husband."

Charlotte winced and sat up in her seat.

"That reminds me," she said blandly, turning towards her sister. "He will appreciate a cup of tea as he writes his letter. Will you see to it, Maria dear? Pray find Hodges and ask her to take some tea to Mr Collins in his study. And perhaps some buttered fruit-bread would not go amiss."

Obligingly, Maria left the room to seek her sister's housekeeper, without pausing to ask why Charlotte had not rung the bell. Elizabeth did wonder, but not for long. As soon as the door closed behind the younger girl, Charlotte spoke swiftly, her voice low and anxious:

"This wretched business, as you called it, is far more dreadful than you know! Oh, Lizzy, I did not dare confess the worst of it to Mr Collins, and I did not wish Maria to hear either. She will fret on my account and, unlike you, she cannot be trusted to guard her tongue. But I must speak to someone. I— *I* am to blame for all this! I colluded with Miss de Bourgh and agreed to convey her first message to Mr Wickham. I enclosed her sealed note in a letter to my brother and asked him to deliver it discreetly into Mr Wickham's hands."

"Oh dear," Elizabeth whispered, then inwardly chastised herself for her foolishly unhelpful reaction. She squared her shoulders and cut straight to the heart of the matter: "So, you think that this is the reason for Lady Catherine's—"

"No. By now, you must be familiar with Lady Catherine's ways. Her ladyship does not mince her words, nor skirt any issue. If she knew of it, she would have said so in no uncertain terms. She has not learned of my role in the affair as yet, but if she does – *when* she does – we shall be ruined. Ruined!"

Elizabeth released a heavy sigh, overcome with compassion for her friend. Charlotte's fears were more than justified. If Lady Catherine had vented her anger on her parson for merely mentioning Mr Wickham's name in Miss de Bourgh's hearing, she would surely throw Mr Collins out on his ear if she should ever be informed that Charlotte had gone behind her back and lent assistance in this manner.

"But you did not convey the other letters, did you?" she offered in mitigation.

"Lord, no! In truth, I never knew that there were others. Not until Lady Catherine had extracted that information from Teague – that is to say, from Miss de Bourgh's lady's maid. It appears that Teague was the one asked to convey the secret correspondence by post or in person, once I had foolishly made a beginning. But I could not refuse her. Anne – Miss de Bourgh – begged me most fervently, and I could not bring myself to turn away. You saw yourself what sort of a life she leads here – no company, no diversions, no escape from scrutiny. After a while, we became quite close. She said I was a great comfort… And when she learned that Mr Wickham had taken a commission in Hertfordshire, she told me that she needed to ask him a favour. That was all: a favour. There never was anything to suggest that she held him in particular regard, nor that she contemplated an elopement. I am prepared to wager that Mrs Jenkinson knew nothing either. She is so fretful and transparent that she would have betrayed herself by now, and betrayed Anne's secrets too, if she had the slightest inkling. She must have been informed of Anne's plans no sooner than this morning. I should imagine she was all too willing – grateful, even – to abscond with Miss de Bourgh, rather than stay behind to weather the storm. And now I am the one left to face Lady Catherine's wrath when everything is brought into the open. Goodness, Lizzy, what am I to do?"

This was the first time in living memory that Charlotte – cool, collected and level-headed Charlotte – had utterly lost her composure. With mounting concern, Elizabeth clasped her friend's hand in both of hers and racked her mind for words of reassurance. Eventually, she found some:

"No one knows of your involvement save Miss de Bourgh," she sensibly said. "Had she disclosed it to her lady's maid, by now the woman would have revealed it to Lady Catherine. I understood from Colonel Fitzwilliam that she was browbeaten into confessing everything she knew. I think we can safely assume that Miss de Bourgh will have the kindness to keep your secret—"

"Aye. This is my only hope," Charlotte bitterly exclaimed. "Clinging by a thread—"

She did not have the chance to say anything further. The door opened to admit Maria. But before Charlotte could think of yet another excuse to gain them a few more moments of privacy, fresh commotion burst into the little room. Just like the last time, the one responsible for it was Mr Collins:

"Cousin Elizabeth, you are wanted at once! Her ladyship has sent word. She requests your company on her journey. You must escort her to her brother's townhouse. A man has just come in a gig. There is not a moment to lose. We must grasp this olive branch! So very generous of her ladyship to extend it and ask a relation of mine to attend her! Make haste and change, pray. I have already sent Peggy up to lay out suitable travelling apparel and pack your trunk. What rotten luck that the letter to Mr Darcy is unfinished – indeed, 'tis barely begun.

But you must speak with him, Cousin, as soon as the opportunity arises. While you are readying yourself, I shall pen a list of subjects you should touch upon when you speak with him and, above all, her ladyship. You must make use of every moment spent in Lady Catherine's company to tactfully impress upon her that I am innocent. This is your chance to show your loyalty to me, Cousin, and indeed your gratitude for my welcoming you into my home despite the awkwardness subsisting between us ever since you refused my most honourable offer—"

"Really, Mr Collins!" Charlotte cut in, turning beet-red at her husband's crassness. "Elizabeth will do as best she can, even without… hm!… such exhortations."

She might as well have said *'despite such exhortations,'* Elizabeth thought, affronted by her cousin's appalling lack of manners. So, Mr Collins thought her in his debt for allowing her to set foot at Hunsford, did he? She pursed her lips. Were it not for Charlotte, she would know how to answer. As for dancing attendance on Lady Catherine…

But then common sense settled in and did away with the instinctive response born from anger. Nay, she *should* attend her. For Charlotte's sake, and likewise her own. A stay at Lord Malvern's townhouse might provide her with the opportunity to set matters straight with Mr Darcy in person, not by letter, and without her father's involvement.

Her lengthy silence must have unsettled Charlotte, for she wistfully said, "Lizzy, pray do not distress yourself. You need not go, if you dislike the prospect so very much."

"Madam!" Mr Collins cried in horror. "Mind what you are saying, will you? She cannot possibly refuse to oblige Lady Catherine!"

Resisting the urge to dart her eyes heavenward, Elizabeth rose to her feet.

"Rest easy. I shall go," she spoke up to reassure her friend and silence her obnoxious cousin.

Distress warring with gratitude in her countenance, Charlotte quietly thanked her, while Mr Collins gave a forceful nod and declared, "Aye, of course you shall. This is just as it should be."

⁓இ ஐ⁓

The preparations and the short journey to Rosings took no time at all. As the small, unprepossessing vehicle sent to collect her rounded the last bend in the road and rushed through the imposing gateway, Elizabeth caught her first glimpse of the hustle and bustle at the entrance. The elegant drive that wound in a wide circle before the porticoed *façade* now bore a stark resemblance to the courtyard of a busy hostelry. A large barouche was waiting, with the coachman, footmen and postillions at the ready. Servants were scurrying to and fro, one with an armful of carriage rugs and cushions, another with a wicker basket and six more with an assortment of trunks and cases, which they proceeded to secure at the back of the conveyance under the butler's supervision. The harnessed horses stomped and snorted, and beyond them two saddled mounts were barely held in check by a pair of grooms, while a nervous-looking lad sought to strap a set of saddlebags in place without being trampled.

The gig drew to a halt behind Lady Catherine's barouche, and Elizabeth stepped out without waiting for assistance. It would have been long in coming anyway. The man who had brought her there took his time in leaving his seat, then hesitantly offered, "Mayhap you'd care to make your way within, ma'am? Or sit yourself in Lady Catherine's carriage till her ladyship is ready to depart?"

Elizabeth's lips quirked in wry amusement at this indication of the sort of treatment she should expect in Lady Catherine's sphere – and not only from the great lady herself. Wait in the carriage, indeed! Whatever next? Was she perchance expected to carry her own trunk to the barouche as well?

A fresh burst of activity at the entrance drew her from her arch reflections. A footman emerged, carrying a second pair of saddlebags. Hard on his heels were Colonel Fitzwilliam and Mr Darcy.

"Miss Bennet!" exclaimed the latter. He gestured the others to continue on their way but, for his part, he changed course and hastened down the stone steps towards her. "What brings you here?" he swiftly asked. "Not further trouble, I hope!"

Despite herself, Elizabeth gave a quiet little snort as she waited for him to join her. Trouble? Ha! It was both fitting and ironic that he should speak of further trouble, since *that* was the main reason she was here, about to embark on an unplanned journey: the vast amount of trouble he stood to cause her with his abrupt offer and his declared intention to follow her to Longbourn.

Sadly, at this point in time she could not speak of it and seek to prevent it – not on Lady Catherine's doorstep and with a host of servants milling about. So Elizabeth merely said, "No. Just your aunt's request. She wishes me to escort her to town."

"And you would comply?"

Why he should be displeased at her compliance, Elizabeth could not begin to fathom. Unless he took objection to yet another interruption, for he aimed his scowl at Lady Catherine's butler as the man approached with a half-bow and a very formal, "Good evening, ma'am. Just in time, if I may say so. Lady Catherine wishes to be gone at fifteen minutes to the hour. Her ladyship bids you to wait in the great hall. If you would follow me… Oh, and Jonah, be sure to strap the young lady's trunk to her ladyship's carriage."

Well, at least they had established who was to move the trunk, Elizabeth airily thought. But a moment later, the groom was forestalled.

"Leave that for now, Jonah. I thank you, Ormerod, you may return to your duties," Mr Darcy spoke with much less ceremony and nothing of the old butler's sedateness. Then, without so much as a *'by your leave,'* he took possession of her elbow and steered her away from the two men and the rest of the swarming crowd.

His presumption could not fail to antagonise her. So, he already imagined that he could direct her every move. Of course. The misguided soul who would accept his offer of marriage would be expected to obey him without demur, just as Ormerod and Jonah had.

It would not do to make a scene, so Elizabeth did not. Nevertheless, she bristled:

"Your cousin is waiting," she pointed out. "I thought you were about to set off."

"We are," came Mr Darcy's terse agreement. "But I would speak with you."

"And I with you. But this is not the time."

"No. A pity. Still, this scheme of my aunt's – I must say that I do not like it. I would strongly suggest you make your excuses and return to Hunsford."

Elizabeth arched a brow. He was charm personified and no mistake. Heaven forbid that she should wander into Lord Malvern's hallowed halls tonight and let it slip that he aimed to align himself with a little nobody from Hertfordshire.

"You need not harbour any concerns on that score," she said crisply. "In fact, I—"

"But I do," he cut her off, in blatant disregard for the most basic requirements of civility. "My aunt is not at her most congenial at the moment. I fear she will make for a demanding and irascible companion, and I would much rather she did not vent her ire on you. Not while I am not there to deflect it."

"Oh."

That was... unexpected. He had scarce given himself the trouble to deflect her ladyship's unmannerly remarks before. The startling change of stance surprised her into a nervous little chuckle. So, Lady Catherine was not congenial at the moment. Hm! Was she ever? Well, at least now she had good reason to be as unpleasant as she chose.

"She is a distraught mother," Elizabeth saw fit to share the charitable reflection with Mr Darcy, her voice and manner softened by an inborn sense of justice which prompted her to make some amends for suspecting him of self-absorbed and prideful motives. For the same reason, she continued, "I shall not take it to heart, whatever her ladyship might choose to say or do today. I flatter myself that I can weather it."

All of a sudden, his mien warmed into a disarmingly open smile.

"If anyone can, that would be you," he said, distracting her from the unprofitable exercise of warily staring at the novel turn of his countenance that altered his expression almost beyond recognition. By the looks of it, the dour Mr Darcy could sport a smile if fancy took him. Astonishing! Until now, he had given no evidence of it.

But that was neither here nor there. He must have smiled in unholy satisfaction when he had persuaded spineless Mr Bingley that he could do better than Jane. Elizabeth glanced away as she welcomed the reminder of his unpardonable interference. It was a very good defence against the recollection of the feel of his lips pressed to the palm of her hand. Inopportune and treacherous, that bothersome memory had just resurfaced a few moments ago, when Mr Darcy's hand had slipped from her elbow to close around her fingers, and his thumb had begun to brush back and forth over her knuckles.

She could still sense the light caress despite the double barrier of gloves, and it might have occurred to her to wonder why she had not withdrawn her hand as yet, had he not distracted her further with a softly spoken, "Thank you. You are generous and kind, as always. My aunt might not be able to show due appreciation, not today, but I am very grateful for your patience with her. Your company will be a comfort. And it will be very good to see you sooner than I might have expected." Briefly, the clasp of his fingers tightened and he whispered, "Safe travels, and I hope your journey is not overly taxing."

Elizabeth did withdraw her hand at last, but thought it only proper to say, "And yours likewise. God willing, you will find Miss de Bourgh before too long, and keep her safe."

Mr Darcy nodded, and his air grew sombre as he spoke again:

"This reminds me: I must appeal once more to your kindness and ask you to keep my disclosures about Georgiana's error to yourself."

Her shoulders stiff, Elizabeth tossed her head back.

"You may be assured of my secrecy," she retorted, rather offended that he should think her prone to gossip. "I would not jeopardise anyone's good name with careless talk."

"No, of course not. I was speaking of keeping that information from my aunt and the rest of my family."

Her eyes widened.

"They do not know?"

"None of them knows, except Fitzwilliam. We are very close and I trust him without question. Even if he can be alarmingly hot-headed under severe provocation, as you must have gathered from his outburst at the parsonage. But as for the others, it would be best for Georgiana if they remained in ignorance."

"I understand. They will not hear of it from me," Elizabeth replied without hesitation, and saw his tense countenance smoothing into relief.

Mr Darcy clasped her hand again – in silent thanks, no doubt – then bid his farewells and hastened on his way.

The solemn promise was easily made. And it would be easily kept, Elizabeth determined as she watched him weave across the busy drive. Of course she would not breathe a word of the sad business. She would not endanger anyone's good name, as she had already told him. Besides, she of all people could see the need of keeping damaging disclosures from one's meddlesome relations. Miss Darcy's secret would be safe with her.

But the fact that he had chosen to trust her with it — trust her without question after a short and fraught acquaintance — was as astounding as it was illogical.

A man who, by his own admission, prided himself on his superiority of mind should have paid more heed to the dictates of logic. Likewise, a sensible young woman should know better than to ponder on confounding gentlemen and their irrational choices.

Vexingly, it was easier said than done.

Chapter 3

"You are very dull this evening, Miss Elizabeth Bennet," Lady Catherine testily observed as the large and unwieldy carriage negotiated the tight bend into the turnpike road. "You have scarce spoken two words together since we set off. What reason have *you* to be out of spirits?"

"My apologies, ma'am," Elizabeth replied, her voice even. "I was lost in thought. Is there anything you need?"

"Tranquillity in my old age," Lady Catherine snorted. "You shan't find *that* in the wicker basket."

"Sadly not," Elizabeth agreed. "But I might find a thing or two that would make up for your missed dinner."

Lady Catherine gave a dismissive flick of her hand.

"Food by way of consolation?" she scoffed. "You should know better. I am not the sort. But go ahead, make free if it pleases you."

Elizabeth shook her head. She might not have Lady Catherine's troubles, nor her fiery disposition, but at the moment the wicker basket held no appeal to her either.

"I thank you, no. Perhaps later."

Her companion released a high-pitched, "Hmph!", then resumed prodding, "So, you have no appetite and you were lost in thought. What were you ruminating on, pray tell, that was so engrossing?"

Elizabeth suppressed a smile. Seemingly, Mr Darcy knew his aunt well. The lady *was* given to pestering and harassing when she felt the need to take her mind off her own woes. What would Lady Catherine say, should she learn that she was travelling to town with the inconsequential duckling who had been singled out by the prize drake long intended for her ladyship's own daughter?

But then Elizabeth silently chastised herself for her too playful spirits and, in this case, her downright cruel wit. Poor Miss de Bourgh! She had been duped like many others, and hers would be a grim fate indeed, unless she was found and restored to her family. Tied for life to a cad like Wickham! No one deserved so harsh a punishment for a temporary lapse in judgement.

"Am I to have a reply this side of midnight, Miss Bennet, or would I have been better advised to bring along my housekeeper's cat for company?"

Elizabeth looked up and sought to give a kindly answer, for all her ladyship's foul temper, and do her best by Charlotte too, if she could.

"I was thinking of Miss de Bourgh, ma'am, and hoping for a happy conclusion for her. And also for my cousin."

"Your *cousin?* What has he to do with anything?"

"Precious little, your ladyship. My point entirely."

"I see," Lady Catherine sneered. "If you are about to plague me with a misguided show of loyalty, you had better go back to keeping silent. Your cousin is a fool."

Elizabeth gave a quiet chuckle.

"In good conscience, I cannot dispute that. Yet, however foolish, he is devoted to you. And so is my friend Charlotte. Not foolish, I mean, but devoted to you."

"Bah! Devoted to the living at Hunsford, more like, and the many favours I might be cajoled into bestowing upon the pair of them and the Lucas brood. I was not born yesterday, Miss Bennet. Kindly remember that."

"I would never presume to forget it," Elizabeth said with a little smile. "Nevertheless, my cousin and his—"

"Enough, Miss Bennet!" her ladyship commanded, her hand cutting through the air in an angry gesture. "I brought *you* along because I could not bear their company. I shall not have my journey into town bedevilled with talk of Collins and his wife. Frankly," she peevishly added, "if you are so attached to your cousin, I wonder that you had not married him yourself when you had the opportunity."

"Ah. He told you?"

"He tells me more than I wish to hear," Lady Catherine snapped. "But he had been oddly economical with words on that score. Why did you reject such an advantageous offer?"

Nothing was beneath the great lady's notice, was there? And no private affair into which she would scruple to pry, Elizabeth thought with some impatience and no little resentment. But she was determined to keep her sense of humour, so she airily replied, "Precisely because my cousin is a fool."

"And you fancy yourself clever? Hmph. Take it from me, you are mistaken. A clever girl would have kept her father's estate in the family. She would have married Mr Collins and made the best of it. Much like your friend Charlotte does."

"There is no doubt about it, my friend is far more equal to the task than I."

"Sarcasm, Miss Bennet? Born from spite, I should imagine."

"I will plead guilty to a touch of sarcasm, ma'am," Elizabeth said with a wry smile. "But there is no spite."

"Hm. You will tell me next that you do not resent her for standing to become the mistress of your girlhood home."

"Just so. I do not."

"Saintly as well, are we? You disappoint me, Miss Bennet. I was under the impression that you had no qualms about giving your frank views on everything."

"Then I shall endeavour to fulfil your expectations, ma'am. My frank view on my friend's union is that Mr Collins was exceedingly fortunate to have met with one of the few sensible women who would have accepted him, then made him happy once she had. My friend has an excellent understanding – although I might not consider her marrying Mr Collins as the wisest thing she ever did. But she is happy to devote herself to making a good home for him, and assisting him in his duties to you and the parish. She is most grateful for your kind attentions, and has grown deeply attached to your daughter. I believe there is nothing that Charlotte would not do for Miss de Bourgh," she said, choosing her words with care, so as to give substance to her friend's generous motives, should Charlotte's full involvement ever come to light.

She suppressed a sigh as she hoped against hope that it would serve the purpose. But sound reasoning and fairness were by no means certain in the case of one as volatile as Lady Catherine.

"Your friend had better give proof of her deep attachment when Anne is returned home," her ladyship muttered darkly, "since she had been of no use whatever in ascertaining what Miss de Bourgh was contemplating. All saints preserve us! A steward's son! What was the girl thinking?" she suddenly cried, throwing her hands in the air, then rounded on Elizabeth. "If you are about to say '*She fell in love,*' I will not answer for the consequences! Love is a sop for fools and a honed blade in the hands of fortune hunters. He *is* a fortune hunter, is he not? What do you know of him? Myself, I know nothing of the cursed man, save that he is the son of my late brother-in-law's steward. He *must* be a fortune hunter. His descent attests to his guilt."

Not long ago, Miss Bingley had made a very similar indictment. How very like her to spout the same aristocratic views as Lady Catherine, even though she had no blood ties to an earldom to support them, Elizabeth inwardly scoffed. But then she dismissed all thoughts of Miss Bingley. She had no wish to dwell on the Netherfield ball, when she had made such a fool of herself before Mr Darcy by championing that unmitigated rogue.

Nor was she about to further distress Lady Catherine with a confirmation of Wickham's unscrupulous nature, even if Mr Darcy had not sworn her to secrecy on the subject of his sister and the cad's designs on her. So, instead of the frank views that her ladyship expected, Elizabeth merely offered, "Ours was a very short acquaintance, ma'am. I scarce know Mr Wickham."

For all her dissembling by omission, that much was true: she scarce knew him. Yet she had believed his every word simply because he was plausible and charming and cut a dashing figure. A harsh lesson, that: how foolish of her – beyond foolish – to be swayed by first impressions. Given the keen wits that her papa had often praised her for, she should have known better!

"I hope and pray that Miss de Bourgh will be found soon," Elizabeth was compelled to add, and was moved towards sympathy rather than indignation when Lady Catherine snorted in response.

"My daughter requires more substantial assistance than empty hopes and prayers. Thank goodness that Darcy and the colonel were at hand to provide it," she brusquely remarked. Still, she reached out in the now darkened carriage to find Elizabeth's arm, and pressed it firmly in something that might be construed as gratitude.

⁙

They changed horses in Bromley, at the *Bell*. Lady Catherine sent one of the footmen to make enquiries, and thus discovered that her nephews had preceded her by the best part of an hour, but no one answering Miss de Bourgh's or Wickham's description had been seen to pass through. Once it became quite clear that there was nothing else to learn, her ladyship refused the offer of tea and refreshments and rejected the suggestion that she rest within. Instead, she requested the support of Elizabeth's arm and leaned heavily on it as she walked back and forth around the edges of the busy courtyard. Before long, they were once more on their way.

The drive through the southern part of town reminded Elizabeth of Cheapside. All manner of vehicles, from humble traps and handcarts to heavily laden coaches, milled to and fro. Bustle, noise and clamour still reigned supreme, despite the lateness of the hour.

A different sort of bustle reigned over the fashionable quarter, and Elizabeth looked about her with undisguised interest. She had rarely driven through the West End at night – only when her dear aunt and uncle had kindly regaled her with an evening at the theatre. Even now, a flurry of people in elegant apparel swirled before the Little Theatre, and Piccadilly thronged with stylish carriages. Burlington House was all lit up as though for a large and fashionable gathering, and strains of music could be heard over the rumbling of countless wheels upon the cobbles.

Strains of music likewise came through the open windows of one of the imposing residences ahead, when Lady Catherine's barouche drew to a halt on a lamplit street off Hanover Square, behind a long line of emblazoned carriages. Impeccably dressed gentlemen emerged from each vehicle in turn, escorting ladies swathed in silks and satins. Feathers bobbed, jewels glittered, and the hum of cheerful voices punctuated with the odd peal of laughter rose and ebbed like the murmur of the sea.

Lady Catherine groaned in deep vexation.

"My brother is entertaining. Marvellous! This is precisely what I needed: a host of busybodies prying into my concerns." She gave a weary sigh, then called out to her coachman, "Take me to Berkeley Square, Burton. At least I can be assured of privacy at Darcy's house tonight."

♦♦♦

The mews were shrouded in darkness, with only the faint glimmer of the waning moon to show him the way, as Darcy nudged his exhausted post horse towards the stables. In due course, the lanky lad who slept in a small room beyond the stalls – or in the hayloft in the summer – made a bleary-eyed appearance to greet him and see to the poor beast's comforts.

As for himself, Darcy walked along the passage that skirted the gardens and let himself in through the rear entrance with the key that he always kept about his person whenever he was in or near town.

The house was dark and quiet and no one was about, which was little wonder at one hour after midnight. He briefly considered walking into his study in search of a glass of brandy, but that notion was dismissed almost as soon as it came. A wink of sleep would serve him a vast deal better.

He made his way up the great staircase in the dim light of the sole Argand lamp that was always left to burn right through the night, and would have ambled quietly towards his bedchamber, but the thin sliver beneath the door of his sister's sitting room gave him pause. A faint quirk tugged at the corner of his lips as Darcy shook his head and tutted. It was far too late for Georgiana to be up. Still, he would not chide her for reading long into the night. It would be good to see her.

He approached, gave the door a light tap, and was asked within. And, in one glorious instant, the unimagined, sweet reward that he beheld made up for all the trials of the day. Georgiana was not reading, and she was not alone. In the wing-chair next to hers sat Elizabeth.

Chapter 4

Elizabeth straightened in her seat, just as her companion leapt from hers with a joyful, "Brother! You have returned!"

Miss Darcy rushed across the room to greet him with a peck on the cheek and nestled briefly into his embrace, then urged, "Come, come in. Do come and join us."

"Gladly. I thank you, yes, I believe I shall," Mr Darcy readily agreed, closing the door behind him. But the smile brought by his sister's fond welcome changed into something very different as he followed her towards the fireplace. It grew conspicuously intimate, and every brotherly undertone was gone by the time he stopped before Elizabeth and bowed. "Miss Bennet. What a wonderful surprise!" he said, and she blushed despite herself, nettled to discover that the unconcealed delight in his voice and countenance – so blatant and so out of character – had the uncanny power to fluster her even more than his sudden appearance.

"There has been a change of plans," Elizabeth felt compelled to explain. "Your uncle was hosting a large gathering tonight, and Lady Catherine had no taste for company."

"Of course," Darcy concurred and, the dire nature of his aunt's motives notwithstanding, his gaze still held Elizabeth's and lost nothing of its brightness as he added, "I am very happy she chose to come here instead."

"Do take a seat, Brother, while I see to fresh tea," Miss Darcy suggested, and proceeded to busy herself with the caddy and the now-empty teapot.

He silently complied. For her part, Elizabeth held her peace as well and forbore to ask if he and the colonel had had any success in tracing the runaways. There was every chance that he would not wish to distress his sister with talk of Mr Wickham.

Yet as soon as she had finished spooning the tea leaves and carefully refilled the pot with hot water from the urn, Miss Darcy resumed her seat and bravely opened the difficult subject of her own accord.

"Any news of them?" she quietly asked.

Her brother glanced towards her.

"You heard, then."

Before Elizabeth could begin to wonder if she would be suspected of speaking out of turn, Miss Darcy replied with a little shrug, "Of course. Our aunt was very… vocal in her distress and disappointment."

"I see." He sighed. "Sadly, I bring no good tidings. A fair amount of time was lost with a fruitless search along the road to Bromley, but Fitzwilliam and I eventually traced them to Croydon, then to Clapham. An elderly lady travelling with two attendants. The woman answered Mrs Jenkinson's description, and there is good reason to believe that Anne was posing as her maid and Wickham as a footman. But from Clapham onwards there was no sign of them. They dismissed the chaise that had brought them thither, and were last seen removing to a hackney-coach. Were it not for the wild goose chase to Bromley, we might have caught up with them on the way. As it stands, the roundabout route served them better, which must have been what they had envisaged all along."

"And then?" Miss Darcy prompted, once her brother had fallen silent.

He shrugged.

"It was very dark by the time we reached Clapham and, as you can imagine, that did not help matters. Nevertheless, we made enquiries at every coaching inn on that side of town, but to no avail."

"What of the ones in Hatfield and Barnet?" his sister asked, but Mr Darcy shook his head.

"No. No need. They are not headed for Gretna."

Puzzled, Miss Darcy arched a brow.

"How do you know?"

Her brother reached out to hold and press her hand.

"Anne is of age," he said gently.

So Wickham had no reason to spirit his prey to Scotland, as the rogue had meant to do the previous summer, Elizabeth readily concluded. Naturally, Mr Darcy forbore to put it in quite so many words. Not that there was any need for him to do so.

"Oh yes, of course," his sister said. "I did not think of that."

"So, do you suppose them to be still in town?" Elizabeth spoke for the first time in many minutes.

"Yes," he confirmed, a sombre expression stealing upon his countenance. "No other scheme would offer better chances of concealment until a marriage could take place."

"How are we to learn where they might plan to marry?" Miss Darcy asked with growing agitation. "If they have procured a special licence, there are scores of churches and chapels they can choose from – hundreds of them!"

The firmest conviction rang in Mr Darcy's voice when he replied, "The Archbishop would never favour the likes of Wickham with a special licence. Men of much higher standing have seen their petitions rejected."

He must have known whereof he spoke, but that was not enough to reassure his sister.

"What of a common licence?" she insisted. "That can be obtained with greater ease…"

Elizabeth held her peace. It would have served no purpose to observe that, to the best of her knowledge, Miss Darcy's concern was well founded. When the cost was no object, a common licence could be very easily obtained. Worse still, it might have been obtained already. Yet her thoughtful silence was for naught. The younger girl was quick to arrive at the same dispiriting conclusion that she herself had reached:

"There is not much hope of preventing the marriage, is there?" Miss Darcy mournfully said.

A steely glint shone in her brother's eyes as he clasped her hand.

"That creature will not worm his way into this family!" he declared with unparalleled sternness. "They will be found. Fitzwilliam has already set the wheels in motion. He knows just the sort of men who can apply themselves discreetly and efficiently to the task. We called upon the principal figures tonight. Their people will set out at dawn. Wickham shan't have the last laugh, I promise. Even if the worst should happen, a life of luxury at Rosings will not be his lot. I know more than enough of him to ensure he is granted free passage to Botany Bay; but, for Anne's sake, he will be permitted to choose some other distant shores. Either way, he will not be suffered to benefit from his runaway marriage. And, in due course, that will be dissolved."

"Anne will not thank you for this," Miss Darcy whispered.

Her brother grimaced in regretful agreement.

"No. Not for a while yet, I imagine. But once Fitzwilliam and I can make her see what sort of a man he is, she might."

"So what are the pair of you proposing to do now?" Miss Darcy tentatively enquired.

"First thing in the morning, Fitzwilliam will ask Lord Malvern to use his influence with the bishop or any of his acquaintances at the Prerogative Court to learn if a marriage licence was issued already, and for which church—"

"Have you considered Mrs Younge's parish?" Miss Darcy suggested with obvious displeasure.

"We have," he said, his mien and the brevity of his reply leaving Elizabeth in no doubt that speaking of this Mrs Younge, whoever she might be, was as distasteful to him as it was to his sister. Nonetheless, he continued: "In fact, we stopped in Edward Street as well, little as she appreciated unexpected callers in the middle of the night. But they were not there. Nor could we learn where they are staying."

"She did not know – or would not say?" Miss Darcy differentiated.

"I am inclined to think she had no notion. She seemed exceedingly put out that she could reap no profit from this, so I am prepared to wager that she would have gladly bartered with us if she had anything to sell. Even so, we took no chances. Her doorstep is to be guarded day and night and her servants' comings and goings likewise watched, in case she does have knowledge of Wickham's whereabouts and aims to send word to warn him – or negotiate the price of her silence. Come morning, men will also be sent to keep an eye out for him around the Prerogative Court, the *Horn Tavern* in Godliman Street and other such locales where expectant bridegrooms are known to wait for their licence to be issued."

"You thought of everything," Miss Darcy said, awed sisterly pride and deep affection in her voice.

"In truth, I can claim precious little credit," her brother owned. "It was mostly Richard's doing. I could not have cast so wide a net in mere hours. Having said that," he added with a grimace, "I cannot pretend I am quite so eager to follow his advice in all respects and sit twiddling my thumbs while we wait for Wickham to be caught in it."

Her own questioning look must have matched his sister's, Elizabeth assumed, once Mr Darcy had glanced from one to the other and proceeded to elaborate.

"Fitzwilliam is of the opinion that a host of inobtrusive characters would be vastly more effective than the pair of us searching blindly and drawing attention to ourselves with our very presence in places where we would generally have no business to be. He pointed out that Wickham will go to ground if he has any reason to suspect we are closing in on him."

Whereas luring him into a false sense of security would be a better choice by far, Elizabeth inwardly acknowledged, impressed in no small measure with the colonel's tactical skills. Then the rogue would be more likely to venture out and about, and could be spotted, trailed and apprehended. But it must be devilishly hard for men of action to content themselves with lying in wait. Particularly when the two gentlemen in question had sufficient reason to follow the blackguard to the ends of the earth and tear him limb from limb.

When Mr Darcy spoke again, it was to show that he bowed to his cousin's wisdom with the greatest reluctance:

"Unfortunately, he is not wrong there. So we had better brook keeping out of sight and leaving it to his men to root Wickham out. We shall go to meet with them again in the morning – discover how many people they could dispatch to coax information from innkeepers and vicars and what have you. And then we shall determine what else is to be done."

"Is Richard at Malvern House now?" Miss Darcy asked.

Her brother nodded.

"Aye, he has taken himself home for a few hours' sleep. He was of a mind to stay here at first, but then thought better of it. He needs to speak to his father and enlist Lord Malvern's aid as soon as may be."

Miss Darcy reached out and stroked his cheek, as though she had forgotten that they were not alone – a tender gesture which seemed to have come as second nature.

"A wink of sleep will serve you too," she whispered.

"It will. But not just yet. If anything, this is even better."

Out of the corner of her eye, Elizabeth saw him glancing at her as he said that, but his sister did not seem to notice.

"The tea must be infused by now," Miss Darcy casually observed, then filled the cups and distributed them.

Her brother took a sip of his and asked, "How is Lady Catherine bearing up?"

The question might have also been for her, Elizabeth suspected, yet it was Miss Darcy who replied:

"As well as can be imagined. She will not be defeated, but she is very shaken."

"She is asleep, I take it?"

"Yes, but only just. She spent a great many hours pacing in the drawing room and in her bedchamber. Miss Bennet, Mrs Annesley and I kept her company, of course, and sought to comfort her, but she would not be soothed by vain assurances. Who would? Sadly, all we had to offer were empty words and laudanum. She steadily refused the drops, but at long last Miss Bennet prevailed upon her to change her mind. Our aunt fell asleep some three quarters of an hour ago, so we left her resting peacefully. Mrs Annesley chose to retire too, but the pair of us came here first for a cup of tea," Miss Darcy elaborated. However, a quick glance at the clock on the mantelpiece compelled her to amend. "Oh, is it twenty past one already? Then we left Lady Catherine's bedchamber nigh on an hour and a half ago. I lost track of time while Miss Bennet and I sat here chatting," she concluded with a dainty little shrug.

The turn of her brother's countenance showed that he would have dearly liked to know of what they had been speaking. Yet he voiced no question of the kind. His eyes sought Elizabeth's and held them in a long, smiling gaze as he asked instead:

"You have prevailed upon *Lady Catherine* to change her mind?" He gave a faint chuckle, then shook his head. "I have long suspected you of weaving enchantments. Now I have proof of it."

The heat of a fierce blush flared in Elizabeth's cheeks. This cheerfully teasing manner was nothing short of flirtation. She had no other name for it. Overt flirtation – and in his sister's presence, too! Whatever possessed him?

She dropped her eyes to her cup of tea and took a sip in an effort to conceal her discomposure, and likewise the sharp surge of vexation at finding herself so easily flustered. She did not look up, but feigned great interest in the pattern on the china as she airily remarked, "Stranger things have happened."

She pursed her lips as she heard him concur, "Indeed," but refused to oblige him with a glance or, perish the thought, another sign of discomposure. At least not until the sound of a log suddenly falling in the grate made her start so badly that she nearly spilled her tea onto her lap.

"Fitzwilliam, really!" Miss Darcy mildly chided, and that alone might have added to Elizabeth's confusion and made her wonder what the colonel had to do with it, had she not learned by now that this was also Mr Darcy's Christian name.

Unconventional and bordering on the eccentric, the appellation had not failed to surprise her the first time that the young lady had referred to Mr Darcy in this manner. But then the singularly uncommon name had been mentioned in Elizabeth's hearing again and again – had effortlessly and fondly rolled off his sister's lips during their long, engaging, yet often perplexing conversation. Their deeply perplexing conversation, truth be told.

How could it be otherwise? Bewilderment and more than a touch of incredulity had been the overriding sentiments while Elizabeth had listened to the younger girl painting an astonishing picture of Mr Darcy as a devoted and openly affectionate brother; the fair master of a large household and a vast estate; diligent; dutiful; good-natured; attentive; supportive; the soul of kindness and generous to a fault. There seemed to be no end to the praise that Miss Darcy would lavishly heap upon him.

Elizabeth could not tell why his sister had chided him just now, but when she glanced up, she found him fire-iron in hand, eyeing her with concern and contrition. Ah. Then he must have poked the fire and caused the log to drop.

"You have not scalded yourself, I hope?" he asked.

Elizabeth shook her head.

"No. The tea is still safely in the cup." But she thought it prudent to relegate the delicate receptacle to the greater safety of the table.

"Thank goodness," Miss Darcy said. "Pray forgive my brother, Miss Bennet. He tends to amuse himself by poking and prodding the fire when he is at leisure."

Elizabeth arched a brow.

"Does he?"

"So it seems," the younger girl replied, casting him a little smile. "I have noticed as much on many an occasion. In fact, he often chooses to sit closer, on the floor. I hope you will not think too ill of me if I confess that I am partial to sitting on the floor as well when the pair of us are spending our evenings here together, chatting or reading. Almost as a rule, I find myself a cushion and join him. It reminds me of the picnics we used to have in my nursery when I was a little girl. Still, some decorum is in order, now that I am grown up."

"Oh, aye, quite grown up. A veritable matron," Mr Darcy chuckled as he leaned forward to restore the fire-iron to its place.

Despite herself, Elizabeth stared. Who *was* this man who cheerfully teased – had picnicked on the nursery floor with his little sister – still spent his evenings with her, chatting or reading – flirted openly – played with fire – and bore a mere physical resemblance to the aloof and prideful gentleman she knew?

Miss Darcy's sudden gasp startled her out of her reflections.

"Brother, you must be famished! It had completely slipped my mind, but now this talk of picnics… Let me ring for something, a cold collation of sorts," she eagerly offered, yet Mr Darcy made a small gesture of protest, then reached out and pressed her hand.

"Not at this time of night. Leave them be, the poor souls. Come morning, they will have their hands full," he said with a wry quirk in his lips.

A considerate master, then. Just as his sister said he was. And in all likelihood, he was in the right about his people having their hands full on the morrow. As soon as Lady Catherine awoke, the entire household was bound to know about it.

"Even so…" Miss Darcy murmured, unconvinced. But then her pensive countenance brightened. "Wait. There is something I might have for you," she said and stood.

Her brother chortled.

"Do not tell me you are still replenishing your secret reserve."

Her sheepish smile must have given him the answer, for he leaned back in his seat and laughed.

"One of these days, the mice will get to it, you know," he affectionately teased, "and you will squeal in the middle of the night and frighten us all out of our wits."

Miss Darcy flashed him a little grin.

"If that should come to pass, I shall endeavour to remember I only have myself to blame, so I had better not squeal," she retorted. "Let me fetch my secret reserve, as you call it. I shall return directly."

And with that, she scurried into the adjoining bedchamber – and for the first time since their fraught encounter at the Hunsford parsonage, Elizabeth found herself alone with Mr Darcy.

How strange that the experience should unnerve her so! He had never unnerved her. He had antagonised her, aye, and vexed her on more than one occasion. But she had never felt so ludicrously discomfited by their *tête-à-tête*, nor so acutely aware – even without looking – that he was watching her. Staring at her.

He had always stared. And she had always laughed it off – had laughed at him too, under the thinnest veneer of civility. Now she could only laugh at herself for her foolish unease and the bizarre sensation that her every nerve was tingling.

And then he spoke, and his low whisper perturbed her all the more.

"Will you not look at me?"

She did. There was nothing to it. Or so she thought, until she met his eyes. Yet his next words were incongruously prosaic.

"How was your journey?" Mr Darcy wished to know.

"Fine. It was absolutely fine."

"And my aunt? I hope she was not too difficult."

"No, she was not."

Not *too* difficult, anyway.

The corner of his lips curled up into that sort of incandescent smile which had flustered her within seconds of his arrival.

"I have never found myself quite so much in Lady Catherine's debt – nor Lord Malvern's, for that matter. I thought that, if I had very good luck, I might catch a glimpse of you at my uncle's house tomorrow. Amid half a dozen people laying plans and talking all at once. Not for a moment did it cross my mind to hope for anything like this. Yet here you are – and it makes amends for everything: for this wretched day; for the frustrating affair at Hunsford. I wonder if you can imagine what joy it is to see you in my home. I wish you never had to leave."

Elizabeth blinked – once… twice – and said nothing. The reversal was uncanny: she, lost for words – he, more communicative than ever. Uncanny and bordering on the alarming. Finding herself lost for words was a profoundly alien sensation. She did not like it in the slightest.

At her continued silence, he said softly, "I see I am making you uncomfortable. I should beg your pardon for speaking too freely, both now and a few minutes ago. But I have longed to speak my mind for a fair while. And it is a vast relief to do so."

Elizabeth dropped her gaze. Now was the time for her to speak *her* mind – have the conversation she had come to town for. Or at least make a beginning, while Miss Darcy was out of the room.

A deep furrow creased her brow. It would be easy work to speak her mind, if her mind were not in such a hopeless muddle. She *had* come to town – and found a great deal more than she had bargained for. Had seen a side of him she never knew existed. Countless new facets, rather. New – and intriguing – and more than a little pleasing. And above all, she had seen him in his home. No ceremony. No reserve. No trace of the despot she expected. Not his sister's keeper, but her whole world; her protector and succour. The manifest affection between the pair of them gave new depth and meaning to the fact that he had chosen to trust her with Miss Darcy's damaging secret. And seeing what he was to someone he loved gave substance to the avowal that he admired and loved her.

Somewhere in the course of this extraordinary day, he had ceased to be the last man in the world whom she could be prevailed upon to marry. What else he had become or stood to be, she could not tell. But before she could even begin to apply herself to that particular subject, she had to speak her mind in one regard – and ask one crucial question. So she looked up and spoke:

"What of the strong objections to my family? I expect they apply to me as much as Jane."

She had caught him off guard, it was plain to see. The warm glow in his eyes gave way to discomfort.

"Oh," he said, shifting in his seat. He ran his hand over his chin and drew the obvious conclusion: "Fitzwilliam told you."

It was not a question, but she answered it nevertheless.

"Yes. This morning, on our walk. Yesterday morning, rather," she amended, remembering that it was past midnight – in the first hours of a brand-new day. Yet even as she said so, Elizabeth found it hard to believe that her conversation with Colonel Fitzwilliam had taken place no further than the previous morning. Somehow, it seemed a long time ago.

"I see," Mr Darcy said and stood. With a terse, "Excuse me," he spun round and made his way into his sister's chamber, leaving Elizabeth wide-eyed and baffled, staring after him.

ೋಲ ೨ಎ

In mere moments, he returned. He carefully closed the door behind him and rejoined her by the fire. But this time he sat closer, in the wing-chair that had been his sister's, and leaned forward, elbows on his knees.

"I asked Georgiana to give us some time. I hope you do not mind," he said, and reached for her hand. He clasped it between both of his as he resumed, "I am sorry that you have been informed of something which, viewed in a mistaken light, may have given you uneasiness. I wish Fitzwilliam were not so loose-tongued," he muttered, eyes narrowed in vexation.

"You must not blame your cousin. He named no names. The inference was mine," Elizabeth replied crisply as she withdrew her hand.

Mr Darcy grimaced.

"May I know what he said?" he pressed on, his displeasure scarce abated.

Without preamble, she gave him what he asked for:

"That you congratulated yourself on lately saving a friend from the inconveniences of a most imprudent marriage. On account of very strong objections against the lady, as he put it." She made no effort to attenuate the bitterness of the reproach, nor strip away the note of sarcasm from the words that followed: "I wonder that you should have endeavoured to make such a mystery of it. I rather imagined that disguise of every sort is your abhorrence."

"It is," Mr Darcy confirmed grimly. "I had no intention to conceal any of this from you, nor claim that I did not rejoice in my success once I had persuaded myself to keep my distance from Longbourn, and urged Bingley to do likewise. But I wish you had heard everything from *me*, not in this roundabout and careless manner. Damn Wickham! And, frankly, damn my cousin too," he muttered through gritted teeth. "If I had the chance to say my piece at the parsonage, you would have gained a clear understanding of my reasons."

The arrogant assumption, so reminiscent of his Hertfordshire persona, and above all the stark admission that he rejoiced in his success, could not fail to provoke her. So Elizabeth shot back, "If you had the chance to say your piece at the parsonage, I would have refused you."

His shock was readily apparent. A good many seconds passed in frozen silence, until he finally asked, "*Why?*"

Elizabeth gave an irritable little shrug. Yesterday, in Kent, she could have presented him with a well-ordered set of reasons. Not much was left of that neat arrangement now. A host of revelations had jumbled nearly everything she thought she knew of him. Longstanding grounds for dislike had been shown up as a web of distortion and deceit, and would henceforth inspire not contempt but compassion. Other causes for complaint had been nudged out of place by his sister's account of him, and were now blurred – softened – altered. But she was not about to tell him that; not when, clearly, his pride had not been softened. So she answered his question with another:

"Does it matter? After all, a narrow escape from objectionable circumstances should give you further reason to rejoice."

"I might have thought so at one time," Mr Darcy soberly acknowledged. "But not any longer," he declared with no little emphasis. He sought her hand again, and his tone grew earnest when he resumed in a warm, persuasive manner that made him sound nothing like himself. "I was about to say that my rejoicing was short-lived. Keeping my distance was a hollow victory. There was no joy in it. Quite the opposite. I missed you. And all efforts to remind myself of my objections to some of your relations were of no use at all. I found that improprieties were easily forgot when they were not immediately before me. But the same could not be said of you. Much as I tried, I could not forget you. In fact, I could scarce put you out of my mind for longer than one waking hour at a time," he said, shocking her with the unreserved avowal.

It was not the sort of thing a prideful man would say.

Elizabeth bit her lip and left her hand in his, even as she chastised herself for finding his words gratifying. She should know better. Words were cheap.

Aye. So they were. But actions spoke louder.

He had come to Hunsford to offer for her.

She was not of a mind to thank him for deigning to conquer his prejudices against her relations, but she *was* compelled to privately own that the conduct of some did leave much to be desired.

The honest admission of their shortcomings might not go a very long way towards excusing Mr Darcy for standing in judgement but, on the whole, she found that his choices cast a most unflattering light on his friend's. Mr Bingley had no noble kin, no grand estate, and much less reason to spurn a connection with the Bennets. If Mr Darcy had seen the error of his ways, then surely Mr Bingley had no grounds to proudly cling to prejudices. Yet he had given no sign of setting foot at Netherfield anytime soon, if ever – and that did not speak in his favour.

'*Men!*' Elizabeth inwardly scoffed in exasperation. They had all the freedom in the world to come and overset a quiet, unsuspecting neighbourhood; spark involuntary admiration and the flare of attraction with their fine bearing and their handsome features; blast favourable impressions with uncivil remarks or, worse still, give rise to expectations with unguarded displays of partiality – and then vanish, never to be seen. Until recently, that is, when Mr Darcy had burst into her peaceful existence yet again, by turns to vex, astound and mystify her.

What was she to make of his avowals?

And what store was she to set by them?

When he suddenly disrupted her train of thought with a most inopportune, "Would you tell me now why you might have refused me?", Elizabeth's exasperation got the better of her.

It was this more than anything that prodded her into retorting, "What reason had I to accept you, apart from your notable estate in Derbyshire?"

He flinched, and a shade of the old hauteur crept into his eyes. It rang in his voice too, when he retaliated, "I would have thought that ardent admiration and regard might count for something."

Elizabeth dropped her gaze to their hands – still joined. She had offended him, and was rather sorry for it. She softened her voice when she replied, "They generally do. Or at least they should. But until yesterday you gave no sign of either."

"No sign!" Mr Darcy exclaimed in disbelief. "I could scarce tear my eyes away from you whenever we were in company together."

"You fixed me with dark and brooding stares. I was convinced you looked only to find fault."

"Nothing was further from my thoughts! Besides, there is no fault in you for me to find."

"I thank you for this pretty speech, but no one is a picture of perfection. Least of all myself. For one thing, not long ago you were of the opinion that my greatest defect is the propensity to misunderstand."

Darcy's lips twitched.

"Ah, that. I think you will find it was *'to wilfully misunderstand'*," he teasingly observed. "And, by your own admission, I was right."

Elizabeth could not forbear a chuckle and darted her eyes heavenward in mock despair.

"It is a matter of great astonishment to me that you can be so infuriating even when you are flirting. Pray tell me, how do you achieve that feat?"

"I fear I cannot say. I have not had a great deal of experience in that regard."

"In being infuriating? I find that very hard to credit."

"No, that comes naturally, I am told. I was speaking of not having had much experience in flirting."

She arched a brow, quite taken with their game of quick-fire banter, and no less with his jocular manner. So she gave him his due:

"From what I saw of late, that comes naturally too."

"Thank you. I am glad to hear it," Mr Darcy chuckled softly, and said nothing further. Instead, he stroked her hand, then raised it to his lips and brushed a light kiss on the back of her fingers. "With the risk of being censured for boasting," he added with an unapologetic smile, "I will point out that I was right about us too."

"Were you? In what way?"

"This — you and I — the repartee — the connection — the spark, if you will — is just as it should be," he said, making her wonder if he spoke thus because he had sensed her pulse quickening in response to his ministrations. Either way, he continued, "In this, we are well-matched, regardless of our different stations in life and the irksome trouble we can expect from our relations. Admittedly, mine will present less of a challenge now. There will be no more talk of family obstacles or marrying for duty. As for your relations' improprieties…" He shrugged. "As I said — easily forgot. Besides, at this point I would be the worst sort of hypocrite to cast aspersions, since my cousin's elopement is so much worse."

Elizabeth might have bristled at the mention of their different stations in life, had she not seen the evidence for herself. His elegant townhouse. His uncle's imposing mansion. His uncle's fashionable guests – a far cry from the populace of Meryton.

She did not bristle. In good conscience, nor could she agree that Miss de Bourgh's false step was worse than Lydia's hoydenish ways or her mother's ill-breeding. Miss de Bourgh – an heiress with a sheltered upbringing – had been deceived by a practised seducer. What excuse did her mother and sister have? None at all. They deserved to be censured – and her father likewise, truth be told, for not curbing their excesses. But Jane did not deserve any censure of the kind. There could be no objections to her – she was all sweetness and goodness. And if Mr Bingley could be so easily persuaded to abandon her – if he had not understood her worth, but walked away and never looked back – then he did not deserve her. In time, Jane might find someone who would see her for the jewel that she was. Perhaps, after a fashion, Mr Darcy had done her a favour.

Elizabeth raised her head to share some of her reflections – the ones pertaining to Miss de Bourgh, at least – only to find him leaning closer and his eyes burning into hers.

"I am not in the habit of going back on my word," Mr Darcy began with the greatest urgency, "but given everything we have already said tonight, we have gone too far beyond equivocations. I promised I would wait until this wretched business of Anne's is set right, but I cannot. Not once I learned that you might have refused me. And yet you said that admiration and regard do count for something. So where does that leave us?"

She gasped, not so much at the question as at the feel of his thumb brushing over her lower lip, once his hand had curved around her cheek. She saw him swallow hard and unwittingly did likewise, her throat suddenly dry. For all the admirable traits she had discovered in him, she was reminded in a flash that he was strong-willed, often domineering, and patently accustomed to having his own way. Everything about this unnerving moment worked to confirm it. His hand on her cheek – an almost proprietary gesture, and far too intimate for a proposal that had not been accepted. His demand for an answer – insistent and so very premature. His eyes flicking to her lips time and again, as if any moment now he would forget himself and kiss her. The very fact that his face was hovering over hers and his whole frame exuded an intimidating and highly volatile admixture of impatience and barely harnessed power – so much so that she leaned back and faltered, "I… I do not know."

He leaned away too, and his hand dropped from her cheek to close around his knee. And then he raised it to press his eyes shut as he forcefully exhaled.

Elizabeth bit the corner of her lip and murmured, "I should retire now. If you would excuse me…"

She started – quite noticeably, too – when his hand shot out towards hers. But he had the good sense to stop mid-gesture and entreated, "Will you not stay for a little while longer? Ten minutes – five. For Georgiana's sake. It will distress her if she has reason to suspect that something is amiss."

Elizabeth nodded. She shuffled back into her seat and smoothed her skirts with a quiet, "Very well."

"Thank you," Mr Darcy said, his voice subdued, and vanished into his sister's room to fetch her.

The pair of them returned in no time at all.

"I am all anticipation. What have you in store for us?" he asked as he ushered Miss Darcy within, his cheerful air exceedingly convincing. He must value his sister's comfort very highly indeed.

Seemingly, he also valued hers. Seven minutes later – almost to the second – he helped himself to two more almond macaroons from the delicate jasperware box that Miss Darcy had brought into the sitting room and rose to his feet.

"My apologies, but now I must beg to be excused. Chances are that Fitzwilliam will be up with the lark as always, and make an appearance in the earliest hours. Good night, Georgiana. Thank you for sharing your secret reserve – it was just the thing. Do not stay up too late and sleep well. Good night, Miss Bennet."

He dropped a kiss on his sister's cheek and gave Elizabeth a restrained bow. By the time he had straightened up, an impulse she could not regret prompted her to leave her seat and offer him her hand instead of a bland curtsy.

"Good night, sir. And I wish you Godspeed if we do not meet at breakfast."

"Thank you. You are very kind," Mr Darcy said and bowed again, this time very deeply, to press his lips to the back of her hand after the continental fashion – although she was quite certain that he had thanked her for more than her good wishes, and that the continental fashion had naught to do with anything.

Three quarters of an hour later, when she was abed, Elizabeth tucked the corner of the pillow under her chin, released a long breath that sounded like a sigh and steadfastly refused to ponder any longer on an idle and most inconvenient question: what if he *had* kissed her after all?

She could not know that, at the same point in time, one of Darcy's pillows was faring a great deal worse. It was pummelled thrice, then flung to the floor as he growled a few choice words about cursed halfwits who had lost their brains into their breeches, had no *finesse*, no patience, and not one miserable ounce of self-control!

Chapter 5

It had not been a good night. In fact, were it not for the sheer exhaustion brought by the many hours in the saddle, Darcy doubted that he would have slept at all. And every waking second had been a torment. Because she was in his house. For once, that was not yet another all-too-vivid dream. Nor was it a deliberate immersion into wildly arousing fantasies. She truly was under his roof this time... but a few doors down... *abed*, for goodness' sake! And nothing was resolved between them.

The only comfort was the unprompted offer of her hand when she had bid him good night. A sign that he was forgiven for cornering her in such an ill-judged manner? Or a mere act of kindness? After all, she *was* very kind.

He had propped himself up on one elbow and sought to pummel the second pillow into shape, then dropped his head back down with an oath. She was everything he had ever wanted, and not knowing where he stood drove him to the edge of reason.

Not that reason was of much assistance in the matter. It brought no certainties – just pointed out the obvious: namely, that she should have leapt at the opportunity of becoming Mrs Darcy. Yet she had not. And, truth be told, he could not but take offence at her reluctance – and moreover at her extraordinary declaration that she had contemplated a refusal. Still did, for all he knew.

It was positively baffling that one as astute as she could fail to grasp the magnitude of the compliment he had paid her, and likewise the full breadth of vexations he was prepared to endure for her sake. How had it escaped her that, given the relative situation of their families, nearly everyone in his circle would regard the union as a degradation? As a highly reprehensible connection? Indeed, as a rational man, he could not but see it as such himself – and rightly so. Of course he would shudder at the prospect of close ties with Mrs Bennet, her vulgar sister and their Cheapside relations. Nothing but the utmost force of passion could induce him to link his name with theirs.

At Hunsford, he had begun to explain as much to Elizabeth when he had been interrupted – but, upon reflection, perhaps it was just as well that he had been prevented from expressing his views in such blunt terms. If she had not seen his offer of marriage for the tribute that it was – a heartfelt homage to her delightful person – then she might have also failed to find due proof of his devotion in his honest recitation of the impediments he had brought himself to overlook in order to have her beside him. Perhaps his need for her ought to be couched in different words next time. In better words.

But what better words *were* there? He had already told her that he admired and loved her and that, despite everything, he could not forget her. As for the depth of his devotion, what greater proof of it was he to give than his willingness to align himself with indecorous country bumpkins and a number of tradespeople?

The restless vigil had supplied no answers, and the fitful sleep had brought no rest. Darcy awoke with a headache and in a far from jovial temper. The prospect of enforced inaction did nothing to improve it. The need to wait went sorely against the grain – wait for time alone with Elizabeth – for his cousin to make an appearance – for Wickham to be apprehended. Patience had never been his forte and, now more than ever, he was chafing at the bit to act. Yet, much as it rankled to entrust nameless strangers with the task of hunting Wickham down, there *was* comfort to be found in not having to hasten out of the house, now that he had his own fresh troubles to address.

How soon would Elizabeth come down?

And what was he to say to her this time?

Rehearsing speeches was a ludicrous notion, so Darcy instantly dismissed it. He readied himself for the day and made his way into the breakfast room – only to discover that a pleasant surprise was in store for him: Georgiana was already there, despite the early hour. She cast him a smile and greeted him brightly:

"Good morning, Brother. Come, do sit. Shall I pour your tea?"

"I thank you, yes." He took a seat beside her and draped the napkin over his lap, seeking to keep his tone neutral as he asked, "Miss Bennet is still abed, I take it?" And, with any luck, so was Lady Catherine, he thought, but kept that to himself.

"I imagine so," Georgiana said. "Still, I hope she comes down before our aunt. Then perhaps I could persuade her to take a turn in Green Park with me. Would you like to join us?"

"Very much," Darcy answered truthfully, yet was compelled to add with great reluctance, "But I should stay behind and wait for Richard. Not to mention that I should be here when Lady Catherine awakens."

His sister reached out to press his hand in sympathy and silent acknowledgement that there was truth in that, then proceeded to prepare his tea just as he took it, quietly humming to herself as she poured a splash of milk into his cup, and then the steaming brew.

"'Tis so very good to hear you sing. I missed it," Darcy remarked with a warm smile – and then cursed his foolish tongue, lest his unguarded comment remind her of the reason why she had not felt inclined to hum over the breakfast table for such a length of time.

Yet, thankfully, the shadow of old – the dreaded pall of misery – did not return to cloud his sister's features.

"Was I singing? I had not noticed," Georgiana replied as she placed his cup of tea before him. "I do feel at peace with myself this morning." And then her mien sobered as her eyes sought his. "I think I know the reason. And I believe you will be pleased to hear it too."

"Oh?" he cautiously prompted.

"I can believe you at long last, Fitzwilliam," she whispered. "Time and again you said that I was not to blame for... Ramsgate – and now I can believe you. 'Tis so... liberating!" Georgiana declared with quiet intensity, and her vibrantly earnest tones brought the sting of tears to her brother's eyes.

Darcy reached for her hand and squeezed it.

"My darling girl, I cannot tell you what a relief it is to hear you speak thus. I am so happy for you – for us both," he said with feeling. "But... would you mind telling me, why now?"

He had to ask; he could not help it, unwise as it might have been to look too closely – probe too deep. But true, lasting healing lay in openness. He had to know what she was thinking, so that he would stand a better chance to nurture and support her, if the need arose.

Under his wary eyes, his sister's demeanour grew contrite.

"This will sound awfully self-absorbed, I fear," she confessed. "It *is* monstrously selfish of me to find a measure of solace in Anne's error, but... I do. She is six years my senior, and a great deal wiser than I could have hoped to be last summer, yet she was just as easily deceived. I blamed myself for so very long, Fitzwilliam," she haltingly resumed, "for being so foolish, so *naïve* and unworldly as to agree to an elopement, but now it seems to me that I need not have been quite so severe on myself. If Anne was lured — and she scarce knew him — what chance had I to see deceit where I thought I would find nothing but affection and goodwill? You said all along that I was not to blame, I know," she murmured, reaching up to stroke his face. "'Tis just that... after yesterday, I find it easier to believe that it was not just your extreme kindness speaking." When she raised her eyes to his, they were glistening with tears. "Will you forgive me for not taking you at your word for such a length of time?"

Deeply moved, Darcy whispered back, "There is nothing to forgive. Thank goodness you can put all this behind you."

"And about time, too," she fervently replied, turning in her seat to wrap one arm around his waist — but she inadvertently caught the tablecloth and gave it a sharp tug that sent their cups rattling in their saucers.

"Careful now, or you will have the tea in our laps," Darcy chuckled, then produced his handkerchief from an inner pocket to dab at the tears that had spilled over her cheek. "I trust I need not blow your nose as well," he teased, making her burst into a shaky giggle as she took the square of linen from him to dry her tears rather more effectively.

"I thank you, no. I imagine I have mastered the skill by now," she said, and his eyes softened at fond recollections of the ruddy-cheeked imp that she had been, back in the days when she *had* required his occasional assistance in that mundane task, or others like it.

He leaned towards her to press his lips to her temple.

"Come now, behave yourself and eat your toasted muffin, there's a good girl," he cajoled, just as he must have done all those years ago.

He could not see that the door had opened quietly behind him. It was Georgiana who caught a glimpse of their guest over her brother's shoulder and drew back to offer a welcome and a conscious little smile.

"Good morning, Miss Bennet. I beg your pardon, you will find me in a prodigiously silly frame of mind today. But pray pay me no heed and join us. I hope you had a good rest. Such a fine morning, is it not? I wonder, would you be inclined to take a short stroll in Green Park with me after breakfast?"

"Raspberry jam, Miss Bennet?"

"I thank you, sir. I find I cannot resist that particular preserve," Elizabeth airily replied with a little smile.

Darcy returned it as he moved the small lidded dish closer to her plate, and forbore to mention that he already knew as much – just as he knew that she favoured plain toast over warm rolls and muffins, and crab apple jelly over marmalade. He likewise forbore to interfere in Elizabeth's conversation with his sister, but returned to buttering his own slice of toast and left the two ladies dearest to his heart to speak at leisure of Green Park and the proposed outing.

The intimacy of the shared breakfast was a delightful illustration of how each day would begin, if – nay, not *if*, by Jove, but *when* – Elizabeth came to stay and share his life. This gratifying glimpse into the future brought a much-needed sense of tranquil joy that could even reconcile him to his inability to join them on their walk, and easily appeased all his concerns over the unsatisfying end to the exchange in Georgiana's sitting room. All would be well. Of course. It must be.

He was not surprised, just mildly vexed, when – unavoidably – an interruption came and did away with the peaceful interlude. The sound of hurried footsteps out in the hallway heralded the regrettable intrusion, and a moment later Mrs Annesley tumbled into the quiet room.

Darcy grimaced. His sister's elderly companion was a model of impeccable deportment. A firm proponent of *festina lente*, she always made haste slowly and in the most ladylike manner, and never allowed herself to get into a state. He had no need to be told who was responsible for Mrs Annesley's departure from the norm, but when the dear soul spoke, Darcy discovered that Lady Catherine was well on her way to discomposing more than one member of his well-ordered household.

"My apologies for coming down so late, but there was a great to-do upstairs," Mrs Annesley faltered. "Martha is utterly distraught. It seems that she, Gemma and Hannah were darting hither and thither to fulfil her ladyship's requests with due haste. Poor Martha had to step out of the way to make room for Gemma, who rushed in pell-mell with another pitcher of hot water, and unfortunately Martha stumbled backwards, right into one of the pedestals by the fireplace. The glass candelabrum that stood on it fell off, and is now broken quite beyond repair," she mumbled with an apologetic glance towards Darcy, then his sister. "I understand that it was one of Lady Anne's dearest pieces. One of a matching pair – a fine example of early English rococo, and a gift from Lady Catherine herself. Martha dissolved into a flood of tears when her ladyship imparted all that information. I hastened her out of Lady Catherine's chamber and sought to comfort her as best I could, but she is disconsolate. I sent her down to inform the housekeeper of the unfortunate breakage and undertook to present the matter to you myself, beg your pardon on the poor girl's behalf and endeavour to persuade you to keep her on. Of course, she understands that her wages will be docked——"

Darcy shook his head.

"No, that will not be necessary," he said as he pulled up a chair for the fretful lady. "Do sit, Mrs Annesley, and catch your breath. Would you care for some tea, perhaps?"

Georgiana selected a fresh cup and began to pour the soothing beverage, but her companion stopped her with a flourish of her hand and a swift, "Thank you, my dear, but I should allay Martha's fears first. I will send word and return directly. But, Mr Darcy, are you quite certain, sir? About the girl's wages, that is to say? I was hoping you would have the kindness to keep her in her post, but writing off the loss is exceedingly generous."

"Not at all. And yes, I am quite certain, as long as she does not make a habit of it," Darcy said, and left it at that.

He was not of a mind to inform Mrs Annesley – and least of all Martha – that the item in question had never been one of his mother's favourites, although Lady Anne had kindly refrained from sharing that view with her elder sister.

The candelabra suited Lady Catherine's tastes, which had always veered towards the elaborate and the heavily ornate – a decorative style his mother had scrupulously avoided. This was presumably the reason why, for as long as Darcy could remember, the ostentatious pieces had been kept out of sight, in the bedchamber that Lady Catherine had always occupied during her infrequent visits to Berkeley Square – a choice which, in his aunt's eyes, must have had all the markings of a most thoughtful gesture.

In all likelihood, the breakage pained Lady Catherine a great deal more than it did him. So no, he was not about to dock Martha's wages. Not to mention that the girl would have needed longer than a lifetime to cover the artefact's monetary value in full.

With a few more hurried words, Mrs Annesley excused herself and left them. Thus, Darcy could speak more openly than he would have deemed proper in that lady's presence:

"Well, duty calls – for me, at least. The pair of you might still have your walk, if you hasten on your way."

Georgiana flashed him a quick glance as though she was seriously considering the suggestion, yet she said nothing. In the end, Elizabeth was the one who spoke:

"Tempting, but perhaps I should resist the impulse. It would not be fair on Lady Catherine – nor, I daresay, on you."

Darcy settled a warm look upon her in unreserved appreciation of both the sentiment and her willingness to express it.

"Thank you," he said, buoyed by renewed hope that the day would end on a happier note than it had begun. She was in his home – and everything was possible. They *would* find the time to speak again in private and set everything on the right course, once he and his cousin had returned from their mission.

The corner of his lips curled up at the enticing prospect of a second late-night interlude in Georgiana's sitting room – better than the first, God willing – yet the smile gave way to an impatient grimace when his glance alighted upon the clock on the mantelpiece. Fitzwilliam should have been there by now. What on earth was keeping him?

⁂

The answer to that question was soon brought by Simon, the first footman. Within minutes of Lady Catherine making an appearance on the heels of a still fretful Mrs Annesley, the man came into the breakfast room to announce the colonel, and also Lord and Lady Malvern.

"There you are! Thank goodness," Lady Catherine welcomed her brother. "What news? Have you learned anything? Darcy just told me that you were meant to enquire if a licence was issued. Oh, you may speak freely in present company," she impatiently added in response to Lord Malvern's wary glance towards those unconnected to the family. "Mrs Annesley is already informed of the sad business, and so is Miss Bennet, my parson's cousin. She has come to town for the express purpose of supporting me at this trying time."

and my butler. And perhaps my wife's lady's maid. As for the others, they would be sure to drop a word or two in the ears of their friends in other households, and by tomorrow night our troubles will be made known to our acquaintances – served up as salacious titbits in dressing rooms all over town."

"So what is your answer?" Lady Catherine spluttered.

"Richard here has the right of it" Lord Malvern said with a nod towards his second son. "Not only that the servants cannot be trusted to keep silent, but they would not even know where to look. They are strangers to obscure guest-houses, secluded coaching inns and whatnot, and the same can be said of him and Darcy. Employing a set of inconspicuous people is likely to serve us a great deal better."

"What inconspicuous people?" Lady Catherine suspiciously asked, her eyes darting from her brother to her nephew.

Lord Malvern gestured the colonel to make his case.

"A couple of men I know and their army of street urchins, church-door beggars and tavern loiterers," Fitzwilliam concisely enumerated.

Darcy frowned. He had not seen the need for such bluntness when he had explained the matter to Elizabeth and Georgiana the night before, and his cousin should have been at least as tactful in his dealings with Lady Catherine. True enough, street urchins, church-door beggars and tavern loiterers had the unassailable advantage of being both unobtrusive and perfectly positioned in the sort of locales where snippets of information could be garnered, but Lady Catherine was bound to take exception to Fitzwilliam's ill-judged candour.

She did not disappoint.

"Are you telling me that I should entrust my daughter's reputation to street urchins, church-door beggars and tavern loiterers?" she fulminated, her voice rising with every unsavoury category she listed.

"They do not know precisely whom they are seeking," the colonel pointed out. "No names – neither Anne's, nor Wickham's. Such revelations would have served no purpose anyway. It stands to reason that false names will be given at every turn, or no names at all. The scouts have nothing but physical descriptions."

"And what of the heads?" Lady Catherine argued. "Will they not put two and two together?"

"Perhaps," Fitzwilliam conceded. "But they will keep their mouths shut."

"Your confidence is touching," Lady Catherine sneered. "You will tell me next that these people understand decency and honour."

The colonel's reply was brief and to the point:

"They understand that they owe me their lives. For those two, that is enough."

"Well, then," Lord Malvern spoke in the ensuing silence, "we had better go into Darcy's study and go over the finer points of this wretched business. Not you, Georgiana," he sternly told his niece, who had dutifully made to stand. "You should remain here with your companion and Lady Catherine's. You are too young for this kind of talk."

Darcy grimaced at the blatantly dismissive reference to Elizabeth as Lady Catherine's companion. But before he could attempt to repair the damage his confounded aunt had wrought, his other aunt claimed her share in the conversation:

"I would beg to differ," Lady Malvern said, largely to her husband. "Georgiana is no longer a child. She has just turned sixteen. A most fitting age for her to become aware of the dangers that lurk in the path of young ladies of fortune. She must be taught how to protect herself from fortune hunters. Although it would have been vastly preferable, of course, if she did not have to learn that most valuable lesson from her own cousin's errors," she sniffed with a sidelong glance towards her sister by marriage, whom she could not abide.

Lady Catherine's nostrils flared and her chest swelled in indignation, but Darcy paid little heed to the telltale signs of the coming storm, too concerned by the look of deep discomfort that had just settled upon Georgiana's countenance. To his relief and renewed gratitude, he saw Elizabeth reaching out to press his sister's hand – yet another sign of her thoughtful nature. Doubtlessly, now she had a better understanding of his reasons in urging her to keep Georgiana's youthful indiscretion from the overbearing members of his family.

But the storm he had purposely ignored was quick to command his full attention:

"Or indeed from her own brother's failings," Lady Catherine shot back. "None of this would have happened if Darcy had given Anne due consequence and married her when she was old enough – as he knew full well that he was destined to, ever since the pair of them were in their cradles. But I shall not see us waste any more time with fruitless talk," she declared, and spun round to bear down on her nephew. "There is not a moment to lose. You must find Anne before she takes an irreparable step, and then you must marry her at once!"

Darcy skewered her with a look of disbelieving outrage, but he would not say a word. Across the room, Colonel Fitzwilliam tossed his head back and snorted. The only articulate protest came from Lord Malvern:

"Come now, Catherine, that is beyond the pale! Aye, it would have been an excellent match. Eminently sensible. The pair of them were formed for each other. I was in favour of the union, and never made a secret of my disappointment that matters were held in abeyance for such a length of time," he said, glaring at his nephew. But when he spoke again, it was his sister whom he fixed with an unwavering stare. "That being said, none of us can expect Darcy to go through with it *now*, and run the risk of Pemberley going to Wickham's by-blow."

"My dear sir!" his lady cried. "Pray mind what you are saying. This is no language for young ears."

"Which is precisely why I wished Georgiana to have no part in it," her husband retorted. "I am in no humour to choose my words today."

And neither was he, Darcy thought, a grim set to his jaw. With the greatest effort he had held himself in check so far, and had not given Lady Catherine a stern piece of his mind in response to her preposterous demand. Finding his uncle on his side for a change had been of scant assistance in the matter. It was only Elizabeth's and Georgiana's presence in the room that had kept him from exploding and setting Lady Catherine to rights once and for all. He would not mortify them with an unbridled display of temper – although he was quite certain that Elizabeth would have witnessed it with far more aplomb than his timorous sister, and would have understood his reasons in full.

Nevertheless, it was highly advisable to shelter them both from open confrontation on the distasteful subject, so he said crisply, "Georgiana, you and Miss Bennet were about to take a stroll in Green Park. I believe now would be a good time to do so. Pray ask Simon to escort you. And Mrs Annesley, would you be so kind as to accompany my sister and our guest?" he added, purposely pointing out Elizabeth's standing in his house and in his eyes – so very different from Mrs Annesley's own.

"An excellent notion," Fitzwilliam agreed.

"Oh, very well," his aunt muttered. "I suppose you may go, Miss Bennet. But do not tarry long. I wish to remove to my brother's house by noon."

Lady Catherine's assumed right to regulate Elizabeth's comings and goings vexed Darcy quite as much as her ladyship's claim on Lord Malvern's hospitality seemed to have irked Lady Malvern. A sharp look of marital displeasure was cast his lordship's way when he distractedly indulged his sister:

"What was that? Oh. Yes, of course. You are welcome to come. And the young lady likewise, if you wish."

To Darcy's chagrin, a moment later he was presented with a fresh reason for vexation. It came from the least expected quarter:

"I am honoured, but I feel I must decline," Elizabeth said – the very first time she had spoken directly to his uncle, and of all the things she might have said, she had opted for a refusal of Lord Malvern's invitation! Oblivious to the implications, she continued, "I should not intrude upon your family circle, but go to stay with my own relations."

Lord Malvern arched a brow.

"Oh. You have family in town, have you?" he drawled, his air uncannily alike his sister's when Lady Catherine had loftily expressed surprise at the intelligence that Mr Gardiner could afford to keep a manservant.

Lips tightened into a severe line, Darcy could only hope that Mr Collins had not given Lady Catherine a full account of the Bennets' connections and their whereabouts – or that she would not hasten to bandy it about if he had. He flinched when the information came from Elizabeth herself:

"I do, yes. In Gracechurch Street."

Darcy rolled his eyes in exasperation. What in God's name possessed her to volunteer quite so much? For goodness' sake, she was one of the brightest ladies of his acquaintance! Yet only a simpleton could be excused for such a blunder as to blithely show herself in the least flattering light.

It was unlikely that Lord and Lady Malvern would not know in which part of London Gracechurch Street was. Nevertheless, Lady Catherine spoke up and removed every shade of doubt in that regard.

"But that is in *Cheapside!*" she sneered. "Who in their right mind would choose to lodge in Cheapside and not at the Earl of Malvern's townhouse?"

"To each their own," his lordship said with a dismissive shrug.

Darcy was not of a mind to stand about and learn what response Elizabeth would make – if any. With a terse, "Excuse us," towards the assembled company, he strode to the door and ushered her, his sister and Mrs Annesley out.

ఆలి ఆ

"My dear Georgiana, I had no notion that you were thinking of walking out this morning, and now I fear I shall have to delay you," Mrs Annesley said as soon as they had gained the hallway. "I should go and change into something more suitable for the outdoors. Unless you would prefer to leave as soon as possible?" She darted her eyes towards Darcy as she added, clearly for his benefit, "I expect your brother will not mind if you were to leave me behind and walk with Miss Bennet. And with Simon to attend you, naturally…"

"Oh, no, we can certainly wait for you," Georgiana was quick to reassure her. "I was thinking of going up myself to choose a warmer shawl, and sturdy boots as well. They shall not go amiss if we decide to veer off the gravelled paths," she told Elizabeth, who acknowledged the common sense of it with a slight nod.

"Yes, I expect sturdy boots are in order at this time of year," Elizabeth replied, and made to follow Georgiana and Mrs Annesley towards the great staircase.

But Darcy had different thoughts on the matter. He stopped her with a light touch on her arm.

"Miss Bennet, might I have a word?"

She cast him a quick glance and blandly agreed.

"If you wish."

Darcy's brow furrowed as he chose his words. His first impulse was to discuss the Gracechurch Street *faux pas*, but there was every reason to believe that, with her ready wit, she would grasp her error ere long. Besides, what was done was done. He would rather make a better use of the few available moments of privacy, and address a more pressing matter – one that could still be changed.

"I was hoping you might reconsider and accept my uncle's invitation," he said softly.

His tactful approach was ill rewarded with a terse, "Were you?"

"Yes. It was kindly meant." He stopped himself at the last moment from adding *'and it deserved to be courteously accepted.'* It would not do to censure her in Georgiana and Mrs Annesley's hearing – the sound of their footsteps still reached him from halfway up the stairs. Worse than that, he could be overheard by Simon or one of the other footmen who might be returning to their posts at any time. So he said instead, "Moreover, it would afford them the perfect opportunity to know you for who you are."

"And not as Lady Catherine's companion, you mean," Elizabeth retorted coldly.

Her almost scathing tone could not surprise him. Of course she would be as displeased as he about his aunt's condescending manner. He gave a gesture of irritable resignation.

"Her presumption is beyond galling, I know," he candidly acknowledged. "Fortunately, Lady Malvern is cut from a different cloth. For all her quiet ways, she is a force to be reckoned with, both within the family and in society. I would have liked her to get to know you better," he said simply, not quite certain whether he should finish his thought or hold his peace, lest she resent feeling cornered yet again if he spoke of their union as a foregone conclusion.

Still, he would have liked her to grasp how matters stood. No, he most certainly did not require anyone's consent to wed, nor anyone's blessing. Not even Lord and Lady Malvern's. But the support of his most influential relations would doubtlessly ease her way into his world. He was still trying to decide how best to phrase it, when she spoke again:

"Whereas I was thinking that if I stayed in Gracechurch Street, *you* might become acquainted with some of my relations, for whom—"

She broke off and bit her lip.

"For whom…?" he gently prompted.

Elizabeth gave a swift wave of her hand.

"No matter. It was a fanciful notion. After all, Cheapside is a long way from here."

"So it is – in every sense," Darcy said with energy, encouraged by her understanding. "It would be infinitely preferable to have you just around the corner."

A Timely Elopement

The look she cast him was odd, to say the least. A blank stare tinged with something akin to disappointment. Or whatever else it might have been. He could not tell. The indefinable emotion was suddenly consumed by a flare of vexation which was a great deal easier to recognise, however unaccountable.

"No doubt," Elizabeth replied in a clipped tone. "But I must abide by my original plan. Excuse me. I should not keep your sister waiting."

And with that she spun round and hastened up the stairs, leaving him prey to his own surge of unconquerable vexation. She was the most infuriating slip of a girl he had ever beheld! The most desirable too, which was the other half of the acutely frustrating problem. He ached for her – and there was no turning back. Forsaking her was out of the question if he ached for her even now, when she had just brought him closer to losing his temper than his infernal aunt had achieved earlier, in the breakfast room. No mean feat, that! Elizabeth's confounded stubbornness would be a frightful challenge to his equanimity and no less of a threat to their daily comforts. Even so, as he followed her lithe form with his eyes, his overriding thought was that their disagreement would have had a vastly different end – if they were already married.

There was every chance that for the best part of their life together she would render him wild with anger and wild with desire by turns – or both at the same time. Very well. So be it. They *would* make a life together, come what may. There would be obstacles aplenty in their path – a host of them of her own making, by the looks of it. Nonetheless, they would be cleared. Somehow. They must be.

But why in God's name was she determined to make everything more difficult?

Chapter 6

He was the most aggravating man she had ever had the misfortune to encounter! How dare he insinuate – nay, not insinuate, but say outright and without compunction – that Cheapside was far removed in every sense from his Mayfair townhouse and his uncle's fashionable residence? And that he would prefer to keep her close at hand, in the genteel quarter? In a gilded cage, no doubt, if that could be arranged!

Elizabeth hastened into the elegant bedchamber that had been hers for the night, and resisted the childish impulse to slam the door behind her. She pressed it noiselessly back into its frame as a well-mannered lady should, but neither her reflections nor her brisk movements were particularly ladylike as she began to pack her trunk in a haphazard but very energetic fashion. Only the bare necessities had been taken out, so the task was completed in no time at all – at which point Elizabeth did allow herself the puerile satisfaction of flinging the lid shut, before crouching down to trade satin slippers for her serviceable boots.

Frankly, she was of a mind to make her escape to the maligned Cheapside as soon as might be! But it ill behoved her to disappoint Miss Darcy on account of the young lady's infuriating brother. The gentle and amiable girl deserved better than an abrupt adieu, Elizabeth reminded herself as she straightened up and went to place her discarded shoes into the trunk.

She draped a shawl over her shoulders, and something of a growl escaped her as she wrapped her arms around her waist. Without a doubt, he was the most exasperating man alive! A spiky mass of contradictions with sharp edges and ill-fitting facets, some of them as abrasive as they come. What sort of a man could inspire the whole gamut of human emotions within the space of a mere day – nay, within less than eighteen hours?

She met the mental calculation with a snort. In only eighteen hours he had managed to offer marriage quite out of the blue — trust her with family secrets — show himself as an affectionate brother — be playful and light-hearted, and engagingly flirtatious, and apt to make her foolish senses flutter — disconcert her with unprecedented openness and some remarks on her relations which, upon reflection, should have sparked more censure than they had — then unsettle her all the more with a forceful and insistent demand for an answer to his proposal — belatedly make an effort to calm the waters he had insensitively stirred — show thoughtfulness and astounding generosity to a maid who had destroyed a treasured heirloom that had belonged to his departed mother — and half an hour later flinch and squirm at the very notion of her staying in Gracechurch Street and do his utmost to prevent her. Not bad work for so little time!

A soft knock drew her from the incensed enumeration of Mr Darcy's questionable achievements.

"Come," Elizabeth called, rather brusquely, and then was sorry for it when she saw the door open to admit the man's blameless sister.

With marked hesitation, the young girl stepped into the room.

"I came to ask how you were getting on. Mrs Annesley and I are ready for our walk. She has already made her way downstairs. Are you…?"

"I am also ready," Elizabeth assured her. "We can leave whenever you wish."

But, strangely, Miss Darcy seemed in no haste to do so. She fidgeted in obvious discomfort and needlessly rearranged her shawl, then finally spoke:

"In fact, I also came to ask… That is, I hope that the scene you witnessed in the breakfast room did not make you too uncomfortable. Sometimes our relations can be… exceedingly outspoken."

In other circumstances, Elizabeth might have cheerfully quipped, *'If you think so, you should hear mine.'*

As it was, she merely said, "Oh, pray do not regard it! I thank you, but there is no cause for concern," and offered nothing further. Just as she had thought better of finishing her sentence earlier, during her brief and most dissatisfying exchange with Mr Darcy. It would have served no purpose to tell him that, while she stayed in Cheapside, he might become acquainted with some of her relations for whom she need not blush. He clearly had no desire to meet them.

But Miss Darcy was not quite finished. She glanced up and added, "Regrettably, my aunt Catherine tends to be more outspoken than most. She is... She has always claimed that a union between my brother and my cousin Anne was my mother's favourite wish. I... Of course, I could not possibly comment. I was too young when Mother passed away. But I am quite certain that my brother does not wish it, even though he did not say as much, not to me. Not to anyone, I imagine, except our cousin Richard and perhaps—" She broke off and bit her lip. "Well, in any case, I thought I should mention that, knowing him, he would have been quite... forthright on the subject, had he felt it was the right time to speak."

Elizabeth's eyes widened. This sounded suspiciously as if the sweet girl sought to reassure her as to why Mr Darcy had not openly declared to Lady Catherine and his other relations that he would not marry Miss de Bourgh because his wishes veered in a different direction. But that could only mean that his sister was aware of his intentions!

And then many disregarded pieces belatedly fell into place. In all likelihood, the exact details of the volatile state of affairs between Mr Darcy and herself still eluded his sister, but she *was* aware of his interest. This must have been the reason why Miss Darcy had allowed them a lengthy spell of privacy in her sitting room in the middle of the night – why she had praised him to the skies prior to his arrival – why she had steered the conversation towards Derbyshire and described Pemberley in great detail, as if aiming to acquaint her with its intricacies – why she had urged her to speak of herself, her home in Hertfordshire, her family.

Elizabeth suppressed the urge to roll her eyes. She should have caught all those signs last night. Whatever had become of her powers of perception?

With some effort, she suppressed a scowl as well. Why ask when she already knew the answer? Her powers of perception had been addled by the man himself. She had not ascertained Miss Darcy's motives because she had been far too busily engaged in seeking to make sense of Miss Darcy's brother. For what it was worth. Not a vast deal, seemingly. At this point in time, it was a struggle to believe that the tender-hearted girl and the provoking man were in any way related.

Miss Darcy's generous concern for her feelings was touching. Of course, she could not tell her that it was entirely misplaced. Nor that, of all the girl's relations, there was but one whose self-absorbed remarks had vexed her. A white lie was in order, so Elizabeth brought herself to voice it:

"You are very kind, but pray do not make yourself uneasy. All is well. Come, let us find Mrs Annesley. A long walk is just what we need."

ৎ৽৻ ৶ঌ

"I will not wait for my belongings, but leave now in my brother's carriage," Lady Catherine declared to Darcy at the end of a mutually disagreeable conversation. "Have Burton drive the barouche round, will you, as soon as my trunks are packed. I venture to hope that your maids can be trusted not to break anything else," she sniffed as she swept out of the room ahead of Lord and Lady Malvern – and before long, Darcy had the satisfaction to see his front door closing behind the trio, each of them bothersome in their own inimitable ways.

"I would say that the pair of us deserve a stiff brandy," his cousin observed, patting him heartily on the back, only to concede with some reluctance, "But there are things to be done, and such rewards will have to wait. Are you ready to leave?"

"More or less. Firstly, there is something I should find."

"And that is?"

"The address of the boarding house where Mrs Younge stayed before she took up residence in Edward Street. There is but the smallest chance that she had recommended it to Wickham. Even so, 'tis another avenue which should not be disregarded."

Fitzwilliam gave a grim nod of agreement and, without further ado, they repaired to the study. As always, Darcy's papers were impeccably ordered, so the required information was found in mere minutes. Still, that gave the colonel sufficient time to splash some brandy into a glass and down it in one draught. He gestured towards the decanter, silently inviting Darcy to partake of his own reserve, but the latter shook his head.

"As you said, we should be off. I would have liked to wait for the ladies' return," he owned, "but it cannot be helped."

"I could ride ahead and have Pruett and Banks send someone to enquire at that boarding house as well," Fitzwilliam offered with a nod towards the slip of paper that Darcy had produced from the recesses of his desk. "Then I might give Mrs Younge the pleasure of my society and see if a good night's sleep had restored her memory. Meet me in Edward Street in two hours or, failing that, at the *Cheshire Cheese* in Fleet Street in three. But for heaven's sake, have some sense and bring along a brawny fellow or two. Not the part of town where the likes of you should wander off alone."

"What of you?"

Fitzwilliam shrugged.

"I have seen worse than Fleet Street and Seven Dials. I can look after myself."

"And I cannot?"

Fitzwilliam cast him a droll glance as if the notion was diverting and simply said, "No." He placed the empty glass beside the decanters and raised one hand to silence Darcy's protest. "I would much rather not find you rolled and left in some back alley with a broken skull, if it is all the same to you. I imagine you can find better uses for your time than lying in bed to recover. Speaking of which, have you had the chance to finish what you had to say to Miss Bennet?"

Darcy grimaced. A similar question had come his way the previous evening, on the heels of an apology for the unavoidable interruption, as soon as they had found themselves at a safe distance from Rosings. He could supply a host of unpalatable details now, but he was not of a mind to give them. Thus, his reply was a curt, "After a fashion."

The colonel shook his head in mock despair.

"There is no merit in being so tight-lipped, you know. In fact, it is prodigiously irksome."

"So is your loose tongue," Darcy retorted. "Why did you have to natter about Bingley?"

"Bingley?" the other echoed, nonplussed. "What of him? I did not natter—"

"What would you call it, then?" Darcy cut him off. "Any fool would have grasped that whatever I told you about my efforts to persuade him against an imprudent marriage was disclosed in confidence, yet you could not wait to gossip like a crone."

"Oh, that," Fitzwilliam said, unabashed, then resumed with unwarranted satisfaction, "So it *was* Bingley you spoke of. I thought as much. No other man of your acquaintance would suffer you to lead him like a pup. He is a fine-enough fellow, I grant you, but too biddable for my liking, which makes him a poor choice of friend for you. Too willing to encourage you in the bad habit of directing others."

"That is as may be," Darcy replied sharply, "but you had no business to relate a private conversation to Elizabeth."

"Perhaps not," the colonel conceded. "And I would not have, were it not for your blatant interest in her. I thought it would not hurt to let her know that you look after the ones you care for, little as—"

With a loud snort, Darcy countered, "Perhaps your misguided ploy would have served me better if the lady in question were not her elder sister."

Fitzwilliam gave a colourful oath and sheepishly raised his eyes to meet his cousin's glare.

"Terribly sorry, Darcy," he said with deep contrition. "Landed you right in it, eh?"

"Just so," came the grim confirmation.

"But… what of the strong objections you spoke of?" Fitzwilliam asked, his air puzzled and concerned.

Darcy dismissed the question with a flick of his hand.

"They have little bearing in my case. Pemberley is a long way from Hertfordshire. Besides, Elizabeth is not—"

He broke off and frowned. His main argument against Bingley's marriage was that his friend would have been accepted as a means to an end. It was plain to see that Miss Bennet's heart was not touched. He was about to say that Elizabeth was nothing like her cool, insipid and calculating sister, nor was she indifferent to him as Miss Bennet was to Bingley. But, knowing what he now knew, could he still vouch for her affection? She said she would have refused him. If she cared for him, why would she?

"Is not what?" Fitzwilliam prompted, distracting him from the troubling question.

"No matter," he said tersely, his jaw taut.

Still remorseful, Fitzwilliam resumed with some determination:

"Let me apologise again for speaking out of turn. I hope I did not make things too difficult for you."

"You did," Darcy resentfully disabused his cousin of the comforting notion.

"Oh dear. Awfully sorry, old chap," the colonel muttered, clasping his shoulder. "Still, you did clear the air, did you not? The pair of you and Georgiana seemed quite cosy at breakfast."

"Yes, well, so much for cosiness," Darcy grumbled, and at that Colonel Fitzwilliam rather lost his patience.

"One of these days you will drive me to distraction with your cards to your chest and all that cursed nonsense. 'Tis me you are speaking to, Coz, not my father. So out with it – are you engaged or not?"

Darcy scowled. This was not the first time – nor would it be the last – that his cousin should be nettled by his innate reserve, and he by Fitzwilliam's proverbial forthrightness. He was in no humour to oblige with a straight answer, but he knew of old that the confounded man would accept nothing less. So, after the briefest deliberation, Darcy could only say, "I am not."

Fitzwilliam's eyes widened.

"She *refused* you?" he incredulously spluttered.

Darcy grimaced at the belated notion that he should have said he was not engaged *as yet*. This was hardly a good moment to share Elizabeth's admission that she had considered a refusal. Not that he was inclined to disclose and dissect her comment at any other point, like some diffident youth – or an anxious damsel. So he merely shrugged, "We need more time to speak in peace. Which is precisely what I do not have," he observed with another scowl.

"True," the colonel acknowledged, the corner of his lips quirked in sympathy. "This business with Anne is not helping matters."

"No. It is not, in more ways than one. Nor is Elizabeth's insistence to remove to Gracechurch Street," he irritably added.

His cousin gave a derisive bark of laughter.

"What, you imagined you would court her under Lady Catherine's nose? Or indeed Pater's?"

Fitzwilliam's sardonic air was profoundly irksome, but Darcy was compelled to own that the other might have had a point – and, frankly, he should have already considered that particular aspect. Nevertheless, he jeered, "So, am I to court her in *Cheapside?*"

Fitzwilliam arched a brow.

"I do believe our aunt spoke of the place in the very same tone. Perhaps you ought to bear that in mind, should you be tempted to employ it in Miss Bennet's presence. She might draw the comparison as well – and find it less than flattering."

Lips tightened, Darcy glowered at his cousin. This had been Fitzwilliam's game for many years now: whenever he was inclined to purposely provoke him, he likened him to Lady Catherine. The tactic was successful every time.

"Thank you," he acidly replied. "I shall take note."

"Do," the colonel said, his teasing manner suddenly abandoned. "And while you are at it, pray do yourself a favour and cease bristling at well-meaning advice."

"Have you anything else to propose for my general improvement and future felicity?" Darcy scoffed, but his cousin was undaunted.

"I have, in point of fact. When you bring yourself to court her in Cheapside – as, by the bye, you know damned well you must – you might also wish to consider that you often come across as aloof and supercilious to those who do not know you better."

Darcy shrugged and brushed the irrelevant remark aside.

"That is a matter of opinion. Besides, Elizabeth knows me well enough."

"I was speaking of her relations," Fitzwilliam pointed out. "As to Miss Bennet, for your sake, I hope you are in the right. I can imagine why you could scarce say ten words to her at Rosings, let alone pay her any particular attention or talk about anything of consequence, but I venture to hope you did better while you were staying with Bingley at… whatever his *pied-à-terre* is called."

"Netherfield," Darcy supplied – a laconic answer, nothing more – as he grudgingly marvelled at Fitzwilliam's knack for disconcerting him with views so very different from his own, yet valid all the same.

No, he most certainly had not paid her any particular attention in Hertfordshire, nor spoken to her of anything of consequence. In fact, he had made every effort not to. It would have been an unforgivable unkindness to give rise to expectations while he was not prepared to fulfil them.

He frowned. Fitzwilliam had no way of knowing that the passing comment uncannily complemented Elizabeth's. She had told him that she had seen no sign of his regard and admiration, something which he had found very hard to credit. Yet it must be true.

Well, now she knew — and it still was not enough.

In the restless hours of the night, he had wondered with no little discontent precisely what it was that she wanted — and, for that matter, what more there was for him to give. A great many other ladies of his acquaintance, if not most, would have declared themselves gratified by the prospect of becoming Mrs Darcy.

He gave a quiet snort. Perhaps he would have lost less sleep last night if he had not dwelt quite so much on his resentment, but called to mind a couple of salient facts. Namely, that if he had wanted to offer for any of those other ladies, then he would have. It was Elizabeth he wanted — and however mystifying, frustrating or contrary she chose to be, one thing was certain: since she had not leapt at the opportunity when it was first offered, he would have no cause to wonder if she married him for his name and fortune when she finally agreed to be his wife.

In the meanwhile, Fitzwilliam seemed to draw his own conclusions, however erroneous, for he drawled, "I take it from your self-satisfied smirk that you did do better at Netherfield. Praise be. It will stand you in good stead later. Unless, of course, you choose to do your favourite impersonation of a haughty prig when you call on her in Cheapside."

To save himself another lecture and more unsolicited advice, Darcy sought to prevent his smile from turning sour as he bent down to lock the compartment where he had found Mrs Younge's previous address, then put the key away.

"I will go with you to see Banks and Pruett," he decided, and forbore to correct Fitzwilliam's misapprehension as to the cause of his improved humour. "Come, let us get on with it."

As for his cousin's final jibe, he wisely chose to ignore it. He would get on with that as well. He *would* court Elizabeth in Cheapside, if needs must. But, by Jove, it had better be a whirlwind courtship!

Chapter 7

A peal of laughter gave the cousins pause as they advanced into the hallway, and Darcy could not fail to ask his footman, "Simon, are the ladies back from their walk already?"

"No, sir," the answer came, leaving him none the wiser as to who was in his drawing room, until the younger man made his meaning clearer: "That's to say, they never left. Just as they were readying to go, Mrs Norbert came to call with her daughters. And then Mr Tyndall and his sister."

"I see," Darcy said and changed course. As well he should, Fitzwilliam did not question him, but quietly followed.

They made their way within, and greetings were exchanged with the unexpected visitors. Unwelcome visitors, largely, truth be told. The eldest Miss Norbert and Miss Tyndall could even teach Miss Bingley a thing or two in the art of fawning. Both of them found something to say to him before he had taken many steps, and once he had reached their side of the room, so did Miss Norbert's mother. Not her sister though, who placidly resumed her conversation with Mrs Annesley and Georgiana with commendable indifference to his addition to the party, making him wish that the other three would follow her sterling example – or at least direct some of their attention to Fitzwilliam.

It was not to be. Much to his annoyance, Darcy found that Elizabeth's voice was drowned out by their senseless prattle. She was sitting at the farthest end, on the sofa next to Georgiana's, and seemed to be having a very lively chat with Tyndall.

Her animated features and the smile she flashed at her companion suddenly acquainted Darcy with a possessive streak he never knew he had. The surge of vexation was as groundless as it was contemptible, and well he knew it. He had no intention of becoming one of those overbearing husbands who never left their wives out of their sight and flew into fits of jealousy at the slightest provocation. But with everything still unresolved between them, he craved her attention, her society, and above all, as much of her time as was required in order to secure her acceptance. And the fact that whatever Tyndall had to say was so absorbing that she had barely acknowledged his own entrance gave him an uncomfortably vivid understanding of what people generally meant when they spoke of raised hackles.

He would have liked to believe that he would have been just as put out if Elizabeth's attention were monopolised by Miss Tyndall or one of the Miss Norberts. But it would not do to resort to self-deceit.

"And that was when Goulding renounced punting on the Cam for ever," Darcy could just about hear Tyndall say over Miss Norbert waxing eloquent on some musical evening or another.

The man was rewarded with a chuckle and a cheerful, "A sensible choice, then," at which point Darcy gave Miss Norbert and Miss Tyndall a rigid bow, excused himself and moved on to join the rest of the party.

Since making room for himself between Tyndall and Elizabeth after the manner of some domestic fowl preparing to sit on a nestful of eggs would have been patently ridiculous, he was obliged to make do with the empty seat across from them. It was precious little comfort that Tyndall saw fit to include him in their conversation:

"Ah, Darcy! I was just reminded this morning that 'tis a small world indeed. It appears that Miss Bennet and my friend Goulding hail from the same part of the country. You might remember him."

"I do," Darcy confirmed, while Tyndall leaned back, carelessly crossed his long legs and elaborated:

"Goulding and I were at Trinity together. A fine fellow, although a touch too spirited for his own good, at times," he said with a wide grin towards Elizabeth, as if at a private jest.

Keeping an even countenance was a challenge under the circumstances, but Darcy flattered himself that he could claim a measure of success in that regard, while Tyndall continued:

"Even so, he is excellent company whenever we chance to meet in town. A pity I have not seen him all that often over the past four years, but it would be fair to say that the fault lies with me, and not my friend. Goulding had asked me more than once to come and stay with him, but all manner of other engagements had perversely contrived to get in the way. Now I wish I had made a greater effort to oblige him. It seems that Hertfordshire has many charms to recommend it."

And there it was again, the surge of red-hot possessiveness. A most disagreeable sensation and disproportionate to boot – but what other response was there to one's ill-timed visitor paying shamelessly unsubtle compliments to one's intended?

"So, Miss Bennet, will your stay in town be of some duration?" Tyndall pressed on, as though he had not made enough of a nuisance of himself already.

To Darcy's partial satisfaction, her reply was evasive:

"I fear I cannot say. Not until I have consulted with my sister. But I hope the pair of us might stay for a little while."

"I do not doubt that Mr and Mrs Gardiner will be delighted to have you," Tyndall declared, and his new and equally obvious attempt at gallantry raised Darcy's ire on more than one count. *Must* he keep talking? For that matter, how long had he been sitting there in cosy conversation with Elizabeth? Long enough for him to learn her relations' name and that her sister was in town, apparently. And last but not least, was she determined to mention her Cheapside connections to *everybody?*

"Speaking of which," he quietly addressed her for the first time since their disagreement in the hallway, "is there any particular time for which you would like me to order the carriage? Not that it matters," he added – for, truly, it did not. The entire exercise was nothing but his own, perhaps less than adroit, attempt to let her know that he had endeavoured to make his peace with the sorry business. "It can be ordered for any time, of course."

She looked up and evenly replied, "I thank you. It is of little consequence. Whenever it would be convenient."

"May I observe that ours is at the door?" Tyndall boldly took advantage of the fact that the pair of them were civilly deferring to the other. "My sister and I would be very happy to convey Miss Bennet to her relations when we take our leave."

"Or Mrs Annesley and I could, a little later," Georgiana suggested, and while her wish to spend more time with Elizabeth was nothing but pleasing, Darcy could not honestly say what antagonised him more: the preposterous notion of his sister venturing to Cheapside without his protection – or Tyndall's unparalleled presumption in offering his services.

"There is no call for any of that. In fact, I was about to mention that my cousin and I must head off more or less in the same direction," he said crisply, and worked to soften his tone when he added, "It would be a pleasure to escort you, Miss Bennet, if you are eager to be reunited with your family."

Hands clasped together in her lap, this time she spoke without hesitation, "A very good notion. My trunk is packed, so I am ready at a moment's notice. No doubt, you will wish to leave as soon as possible," she concluded, an edge to her voice.

"Oh? Must you go already?" Tyndall exclaimed, making no secret of his disappointment.

With great determination, Darcy forbore to scowl at him. Instead, he fixed his glare on the Blue John chalice on the mantelpiece behind the brazen fellow and echoed Elizabeth's remark:

"Aye, to be sure. As soon as possible."

⊷⊶ ⊷⊶

Thus, adieus were made, Elizabeth's trunk was fetched, the carriage was brought to the door with all the promptness Darcy generally expected from his well-trained people, and in short order they were on their way.

No sooner had they cantered into Piccadilly than Fitzwilliam casually asked, "Would you mind telling me what the deuce you are doing here?"

Darcy cast him a half-puzzled, half-irritated glance.

"What sort of a question is that?"

The other shook his head and gave a mild chuckle.

"Are you so doltish as to need it spelled out, or are you merely feigning obtuseness? Either way, I shall put it plainly: why are you in the saddle and not in there, with her?" he asked, indicating the light carriage ahead with a tilt of his chin.

"That is a foolish thing to ask, and you know it," Darcy countered, his mien that of one remonstrating with a purposely awkward child. "How would it look if she was riding unattended with me, all the way across town?"

Fitzwilliam shrugged in unconcern.

"You could have brought a maid along."

"Indeed! And how much can be said in a maid's presence?"

"Or you could have asked me to do the office of a chaperone."

Darcy snorted.

"I am not under the delusion that you look like a respectable matron."

"A pity that I have not raided Lady Catherine's trunks, then," his cousin shot back, unabashed. "One of her bonnets and a large cloak might have come in handy for a creditable impersonation. We do share the Fitzwilliam profile, after all."

Despite himself, Darcy chortled.

"That, I would have liked to see."

"Who knows, perhaps one of these days I might oblige you. But to return to the matter in hand, I daresay your laudable scruples will become expendable once we reach the Strand. You are not likely to come across anyone you know beyond Somerset House."

"True," Darcy acknowledged. "But *she* might."

Fitzwilliam rolled his eyes.

"Is that so? Frankly, Coz, if I did not know any better, I would say you do not wish to speak to the girl."

"Leave be, Richard," Darcy muttered. But a few moments later, he was compelled to own, "What I do not wish to do is corner her again."

As was his wont, Fitzwilliam readily picked out the salient word:

"*Again?*" he asked, brow arched. No answer came, but that did not trouble him unduly. He met Darcy's stubborn silence with a grin and a shrug. "Have it your way, then. Methinks I can pester you later to regale me with diverting tales—"

"I have no intention to—" Darcy began, but he was not suffered to continue.

"Oh, hold your fire," the colonel airily cut him off. "You know very well that sooner or later you will tell me what you did. As for making amends, if you think you can have greater success in her aunt's parlour than in your own carriage, then by all means go to it, and good luck to you."

For the third time that day – or was it the fourth? – Darcy was forced to grudgingly allow that a strong understanding was no guarantee of shrewd judgement, and that his cousin had more common sense than he.

The hurly-burly that surrounded the old inn at Charing Cross – quite on the par with the electrifying bustle she had encountered at the *Swan with Two Necks* in Cheapside on the one occasion when she, Jane and Mr Gardiner had travelled post to Meryton – could not fail to distract Elizabeth from her companions. It almost defied belief that there should be quite so many people, vehicles and horses gathered together in one place, which made the spectacle all the more arresting. She turned her head to watch it for as long as she could while the carriage briskly negotiated the corner, and could not help wondering how far these men and women were going, what had enticed them to set off, and what sights they would see before they reached the end of their travels.

The smile of excited speculation vanished when she turned around in her seat to face forward, and found Mr Darcy's eyes fixed on her, his lips curled up at the corners. He had better not imagine that she was beaming for his benefit, or indeed on account of his presence in the carriage!

Elizabeth glanced out again and refused to give any thought to his reasons for approaching her window a short while ago, while the conveyance was rolling along Haymarket, to ask if she would object to him and his cousin riding with her for the remainder of the journey. All she could tell him then, with the right amount of indifference, was, "Why should I? It *is* your carriage, after all."

And that was that. The young footman perched at the back of the vehicle was asked to ride Mr Darcy's horse and lead the colonel's, and the two gentlemen availed themselves of the seat across from hers.

The din around the coaching inn had so far precluded conversation, but as they proceeded apace along the Strand, Colonel Fitzwilliam – the more amiable of the two – smilingly observed:

"I would hazard to guess that you take pleasure in travelling, Miss Bennet."

"Was I so very obvious?" Elizabeth asked with a little chuckle. "Then there is nothing for it, I shall have to confess to a twinge of envy for those about to board the coaches at the *Golden Cross.*"

"Where would you wish to go?" Mr Darcy intervened with his habitual directness.

For her part, Elizabeth chose not to match it. The honest answer would have been *'the north country.'* Mrs Gardiner's accounts of the Lakes and the wild beauty of the Peak had sparked great interest in seeing those wonders for herself. But he could be relied upon to take such an admission as a personal homage. So she gave a vague gesture and casually replied, "Oh, anywhere. I expect most places would have their share of delights to offer."

"But you do favour wide open spaces and variety of ground, do you not?" he continued, giving her the uncomfortable suspicion that he had somehow guessed the substance of her thoughts.

Elizabeth pressed her lips together. It was a ludicrous notion. He could not have. Of course not, how could he? Seemingly, a few hours in his presence were enough to nudge her towards lunacy.

"It would be fair to say so," she conceded and turned away, childishly diverted to note that the evasive answer she had given him was also an uncannily fitting comment in response to her arch reflections.

Silence fell in the fast-moving carriage, until Colonel Fitzwilliam made another attempt at civil conversation:

"Do you often come to stay with your relations in town?"

"Not as often as I should wish," she candidly acknowledged. "Once a year, generally. Twice, on occasion."

"And do they—?" the colonel began, but Elizabeth was not to learn what he was about to ask.

As disinclined to listen to talk of her relations as he had been to allow his sister and Mrs Annesley to convey her to their home, Mr Darcy spoke at almost the same time:

"It is a pity that today was not—"

The cousins glanced at each other and, predictably, it was the well-mannered colonel who indicated that Mr Darcy should continue. He lost no time in doing so:

"…was not as I would have wished."

His eagerness to steer the discussion as it suited him only served to add to Elizabeth's prior reasons for vexation, so she yielded to the sudden urge to put him on the spot:

"And what would *you* have wished to do today?" she asked, rather sharply.

All things considered, she fancied she could guess his thoughts: that, if he had his way, by now he would be riding to Longbourn to secure her father's consent. But nay, even *he* would scruple to say as much – that is, assuming there was a limit to the arrogant directness of an overbearing man.

The affably pensive look that settled on his countenance caught her unawares.

"Hm… let me see," he pondered. "I daresay Hatchard's would have been a good place to start, if this were an untroubled day of leisure. After that, a visit to Georgiana's favourite shop in Jermyn Street would have been a must, and only the prospect of a lengthy walk in the parks would have lured her away from their vast collection of music sheets. Given the appeal of open spaces, on a fine day such as this I expect I would have spoken in favour of a walk in Kew Gardens, all the way to the Pagoda perhaps, and the Moorish Alhambra. A drive to Hampton Court might have also been an option, but that would have left very little time for dinner if we were of a mind to catch the best part of Mrs Siddons' performance. Still, if Hampton Court and Kew were so attractive as to keep us busily engaged for hours, we could have settled for a brief stop at Astley's instead, and left Mrs Siddons' remarkable Lady Macbeth for another day, when we could appreciate it fully. What say you – would that have been acceptable?"

"I… Yes, I believe it would," plain honesty compelled Elizabeth to own.

In truth, Mr Darcy's depiction of his ideal day was exceedingly alluring. So much so that many seconds passed – unpardonably many – until she realised that he had described a day from their envisaged married life. No other circumstances, not even an announced engagement, would have allowed them to openly show themselves everywhere together accompanied only by his sister. Yet the thoughtfully conjured pictures were so pleasing that his speaking of their union as a *fait accompli* had, for once, not struck her as a self-absorbed presumption.

"You forgot to mention ices at Gunter's," Colonel Fitzwilliam chortled from the opposite corner. "Georgiana would have been severely disappointed."

"Oh, we could not have that!" Elizabeth replied in kind, willingly indulging them in their game. "What of another confectioner along the way?"

But Mr Darcy shook his head with mock solemnity.

"I fear my cousin is right. To my sister's way of thinking, only Gunter's will do."

❦

The remainder of the journey to Gracechurch Street was too short for Elizabeth to find the answer to a new question that had sprung to mind long before they had reached Temple Bar Gate: what was it about his sister and his cousin that caused them to bring out his most appealing traits quite so effortlessly?

The night before, in Miss Darcy's sitting room, he had teased her on her supposed ability to weave enchantments but, by the looks of it, the true sorcerers were his nearest relations. His sister and Colonel Fitzwilliam seemed to be the ones endowed with occult powers, since they and they alone could turn the insufferable ogre into a remarkably agreeable companion.

When his ogreish *alter ego* vanished, he could join his cousin in relating anecdotes with spirit. He could point out some inconspicuous landmark and nonchalantly bear the colonel's raillery at his interest in ancient monuments and dusty old tomes. He could chat about this and that, and engage in witty banter. And above all, with as little as a glance or a half-smile, he could easily remind her of the times when she had found him irresistibly attractive.

Thus, when the carriage drew to a halt before Mr and Mrs Gardiner's home and Mr Darcy stepped out to hand her down, Elizabeth impulsively asked, "Will you come in?"

"I think not," he instantly replied, without so much as a courteous pretence of pausing to consider. "Pray convey our regards to your sister and the rest of your family, but given this morning's delays, Fitzwilliam and I had better get on with our business. I will call as soon as possible."

Elizabeth pursed her lips. She was growing prodigiously tired of his maddening propensity to disappoint her. Aye, they had matters of the greatest import to attend to – but an introduction and a civil greeting would have required mere minutes.

Her displeasure was increasing by the second, but by then it was directed largely at herself for expecting any better and failing to see the pattern: each time she had let her guard down, he had invariably made her regret it.

"Very well," Elizabeth retorted crisply as she dipped a slight curtsy, then turned away and hastened up the short flight of steps to knock on her uncle's front door.

Once Simon had fetched her trunk and handed it to Mr Gardiner's footman, she did not linger on the doorstep to watch Mr Darcy and his cousin retrieve their mounts and resume their eastwards journey on horseback, while the carriage made an awkward about-turn to head the other way.

He would call as soon as possible, would he? Hm. That was precisely what Miss Bingley had told Jane – and then had not deigned to show her face in Cheapside for a fortnight. If that was what Mr Darcy had in mind, he would discover that she was nothing like her trusting and all-forgiving sister, who had stayed in morning after morning, making allowances for uncivil tardiness. Such was Jane's way – but certainly not hers. *She* would not make excuses. Nor would she be waiting.

Chapter 8

He came to call the very next morning – and so early, too, that they were still at breakfast.

Elizabeth had given her aunt and uncle only a brief and selective account as to why she had appeared on their doorstep in Mr Darcy's carriage, at least a fortnight sooner than expected. But she had shared everything with Jane once they had retired for the night. Everything, that is, except the little she had learned of Mr Bingley, for she *would not* distress dear Jane with thoughtless talk of her easily-dissuaded suitor. Nothing else was left out, and by now Jane was informed of every particular, however trifling.

Thus, Elizabeth was not surprised to find that her sister's eyes spoke volumes when the upper housemaid came to let her mistress know that a Mr Darcy and a Colonel Fitzwilliam were awaiting her pleasure in the sitting room.

Elizabeth answered Jane's steady gaze with a faint shrug.

"Let us see how he behaves," she murmured for her sister's ears alone a few moments later, as they left their little cousins with the governess and followed their aunt out of the breakfast parlour.

∘৽৹ ৶৹∘

The room was tastefully appointed, and his host about a decade younger than Darcy had expected. Ladylike and softly-spoken, too – a couple of basic accomplishments which Mrs Gardiner's sisters by marriage had never acquired. The master of the house remained shrouded in mystery. Mrs Gardiner had promptly informed them that her husband could not have the pleasure of their acquaintance, for he was from home. An early start to see to his affairs and his warehouses, no doubt. Still, if first impressions were ever to be trusted, Mr Gardiner's choice of life companion fostered a small measure of hope that he might not be a male replica of Mrs Bennet or, perish the thought, the even more vulgar Mrs Phillips. But only time would tell.

Darcy shuffled irritably in his seat while everything around him worked to demonstrate his cousin's all-too-valid point: it was well-nigh impossible to say anything of consequence to Elizabeth in her aunt's parlour. For one thing, the room was nowhere near large enough to allow any private discourse, even if he could find a way to orchestrate it. Moreover, as rotten luck would have it, she was sitting as far away from him as the parlour could divide them.

He released a huff of impatience as his cousin nattered on, indifferent to his plight. Yet, frustrating as that was, he grudgingly allowed that Fitzwilliam's gift of the gab had its advantages. Had he called without his voluble relation, *he* would have been the one obliged to spout civil nothings.

Miss Bennet was likewise disinclined to engage in conversation. As was her wont, she had offered a vapid smile along with a few words of greeting, and now held her peace. Quite out of character, Elizabeth would not say a great deal either. There was every reason to believe she had not revealed his family's troubles to her relations, for she had enquired about Anne in the most general terms. She had merely voiced the hope that the previous day had been productive, and did not pursue the matter once Fitzwilliam had just as cautiously replied, "Sadly not."

She had changed the subject, then lapsed into silence. Her aunt was the only one who matched Fitzwilliam's willingness to speak of the state of the roads and the uncommonly wet weather that had rendered them almost impassable one week prior.

With no little effort, Darcy suppressed the urge to roll his eyes. The weather – Lord above! Granted, the hackneyed topic was the staple of tentative exchanges between strangers, but that only served to render it hopelessly trite. Frankly, he would rather swallow his own tongue than resort to threadbare *clichés* in Elizabeth's hearing.

Yet no sooner had her eldest sister noted – without her personal brand of vacuous smiles this time – that the weather had thankfully improved of late, than Darcy was struck by the irony of his earlier reflections. The monumentally dull subject did offer an opening, and he should avail himself of it. So he raised his head and set to do just that.

"This morning *is* particularly fine. I hope it heralds a stretch of good weather. Then perhaps my sister will have the pleasure of your company on the walk she was proposing yesterday."

Of necessity, his phrasing was ambiguous. He could not explicitly single Elizabeth out, so he endeavoured to do so without words. As he spoke, he kept his eyes on her – and her alone.

Whether or not she understood the message, Elizabeth was quick to look away.

"Miss Darcy is very kind," she said. "Pray convey my regret that our little scheme came to naught. But I should not wish to give her the trouble of making new arrangements. Especially as the weather is notoriously unreliable at this time of year."

"There is no trouble," Darcy assured her. "The carriage could be sent for you on any day that holds promise of good weather."

"I thank you, but that will not be necessary. We can make our own way."

The *'we'* pleased him as little as the vagueness of her answer. Would she come or not? And when? He leaned back in his chair as he tried to think of an acceptable way of pressing her for greater clarity, but his efforts were brought to an abrupt halt when he found himself addressed by Mrs Gardiner:

"Will you travel north any time soon, Mr Darcy? Derbyshire is delightful in the spring. And indeed in every season."

"So it is," he agreed, finding it gratifying that Elizabeth must have spoken of him and, among other things, informed her aunt that his home was in Derbyshire. Yet he was not in the least amused by the suspicion that Mrs Gardiner was sounding him out, seeking to gauge the firmness of his intentions – or worse still, that she was already angling for an invitation to Pemberley. Perhaps he had been too hasty to think her any better than Mrs Bennet. "But no, I have no plans to travel north for the foreseeable future," he said regardless, choosing to oblige with an answer to her query, however forward. The confirmation that he was not going anywhere, if he could help it, was meant for Elizabeth's ears anyway.

"Our aunt is understandably fond of the north country," Miss Bennet observed, suddenly inclined to rejoin the conversation. "She hails from——"

"Shall I see to tea and coffee?" Elizabeth offered and rose to her feet.

Darcy could not but find her eagerness both comforting and endearing. In her haste to cast for ways to extend their call – *his* call – she had gone as far as to speak over her sister, something she had never done before. It went sorely against the grain to disappoint her.

"Pray do not go," he urged her. "We cannot stay for very long."

"Oh. Of course," Elizabeth agreed and resumed her seat with manifest reluctance, which gave him the meagre solace of yet another encouraging sign.

If only they could speak in peace! But the present company precluded everything except a long, meaningful glance, a reassuring smile and an oblique reference to his inescapable duties:

"As you know, it cannot be helped. But I hope we might be allowed to call again."

It came as no surprise that Elizabeth made no answer, but left that to the lady of the house, as was right and proper.

"Pray do," Mrs Gardiner civilly replied. "You are most welcome."

"So, do you have any amusements in mind for the coming weeks?" Fitzwilliam asked, earning Darcy's silent gratitude with his endeavour to ascertain when the ladies might be found at home.

"Our plans are not firmly fixed," Mrs Gardiner said, "but I know that my nieces would like to see the great exhibition at Somerset House if they are still with us in May. Also, my husband and I are eager to arrange an evening at Covent Garden as soon as he can reclaim the full use of his time. We were in awe of Mrs Siddons' unique interpretation of her role, so we would dearly like them to experience that particular delight," she added with a fond smile towards Miss Bennet and Elizabeth, which they were quick to return.

"An excellent notion," Fitzwilliam exclaimed, while Darcy sought to catch Elizabeth's glance. Mrs Gardiner's unexpected reference to the much-acclaimed performance could not fail to evoke their conversation in the carriage, and he ventured to hope that the recollection was as pleasing to her as it was to him.

But she would not look his way, so his attempt at a wordless exchange remained singularly unsuccessful.

He started when Fitzwilliam laid a hand on his arm with a puzzling, "Were you not, Darcy?"

He blinked and tore his eyes away from her.

"Pardon? I was not attending."

"I was asking if you and Georgiana were of a mind to see *Macbeth* again," Fitzwilliam said with an infuriating little quirk at the corner of his lips.

"No, not for a while yet," Darcy retorted, vexed with himself for being caught staring like a mooncalf, and no less with his cousin for blatantly emphasising his distraction.

"Why not?" the confounded man queried, as if unaware of the most notable demand upon their time.

Darcy skewered him with a swift glare and tersely reminded him, "Sadly, our evenings are not our own as yet."

It was Elizabeth, and not his cousin, who indicated that she understood his meaning.

"Nor are your mornings, I imagine. So we should not detain you."

Darcy cast her a warm look of appreciation and reluctantly rose from his seat.

"I thank you. Yes, we had better go," he said as he collected his hat and gloves. "We are bound to ride this way again on the morrow," he added, although he was quite certain that Elizabeth already knew as much. "Perhaps something might be arranged for another time. A visit to Montague House, for instance? At least such plans will not be at the mercy of the weather," he observed with a little smile.

As had been the case earlier, the sole reply came from Mrs Gardiner.

"Indeed," she said and stood.

Her nieces followed her example. It would have been foolish to hope for a private adieu, and it was just as well that he had not. Elizabeth merely flashed him a parting glance and dropped a demure curtsy.

⁕⁕⁕

"Do *not* start," Darcy grimly warned, once he and his cousin had swung into their saddles and ridden away from the Gardiners' trim house.

"Start what?" the other asked.

Yet the show of innocence was not fooling anybody, least of all Darcy, which was why he spoke in no uncertain terms:

"I am in no humour to be told how I might have done better. I did as best I could under the circumstances."

Fitzwilliam urged his mount along with a click of his tongue and airily observed, "That, I can believe, knowing your tenuous grip on the fine art of conversation. And now bluster if you must, but I will still upbraid you for missing such a sterling opportunity."

"Balderdash," Darcy snorted. "I saw not one shade of opportunity."

The colonel gave a forceful nod.

"You can say that again. You did not see it. Not even when I handed it to you on a plate. Why in heaven's name did you not offer them your box at the Theatre Royal?" he promptly elaborated, without waiting for Darcy to finish his spluttering request for clarifications. "To say nothing of your company," he drawled with a tilt of his head and a telling smirk.

Darcy rolled his eyes.

"Why not indeed?" he scoffed. "After all, there is nothing else I should be doing at the moment."

"Just so," Fitzwilliam retorted, his air suddenly devoid of all trace of levity. "We have already established that the pair of us have no business blundering about and drawing Wickham's notice. So what do you propose to do until he is rooted out? Stay cooped up with Pruett or Banks in their garrets, driving yourself to distraction in the process – and them too, for that matter? Go and keep Lady Catherine company or brood in your study over brandy? For I do not think so ill of you as to imagine you would expose Georgiana to your foul temper."

Darcy did not oblige with an answer – not that his cousin was expecting any.

"Frankly," Fitzwilliam continued, "showing up at a theatrical performance as though nothing had happened would be the best thing you could do just now. It would work to everyone's advantage, over and above the benefits you stand to gain."

To that, Darcy felt compelled to reply with a grimace, "I will concede that a show of unconcern would not go amiss. But I dispute the benefits you speak of. There is nothing to be gained from parading her relations in trade before all and sundry."

"And here comes the supercilious old prig I have been waiting for with bated breath," Fitzwilliam shot back. "How is anyone to know that they hail from Cheapside? Mrs Gardiner looks no different from the average lady of fashion."

"Perhaps," Darcy grudgingly allowed. "But there is more to it than that."

"Such as?"

"It serves no purpose to create a precedent. Nor do I wish to bring Miss Bennet to Bingley's notice, if we happen upon him."

Fitzwilliam snorted.

"That is the feeblest excuse you could possibly offer. It is the so-called precedent that rankles, and more fool you. Let Bingley fend for himself. 'Tis high time he learned to do so. By the bye, I am not surprised he lost his head over the lady. Miss Bennet is exquisite."

"Aye, to those who favour marble statues," Darcy muttered.

"Let me refer you to the story of Pygmalion," Fitzwilliam grinned. "Even the coldest marble can be brought to life with the right touch."

"Must you be so coarse?" Darcy protested, his lips curled in distaste.

Fitzwilliam shook his head in mock reproach.

"The coarseness you speak of is in your mind, not mine. There I was, adding a dash of sophistication with a well-placed allusion to Ovid, and you fling this at me. What, pray tell, is indelicate about his poems? In fact, no, do not answer that. Any moment now you will start to quote from his *Ars Amatoria*, and that is bound to tax your equanimity."

"You had better have a care for yours. You never used to favour marble statues."

"People change," Fitzwilliam observed with a shrug.

The glance Darcy fixed on him grew steady and solemn.

"I hope this is one of your questionable jests. Or must I remind you that you need to marry money?"

"And ungenerously point out that you do not? Charming. No, save your breath and do not remind me. But if it comes to that, you can always employ me as your steward once we muzzle Boney. Your ladylove might be pleased to have her eldest sister settled at Pemberley as well."

"You are *not* in earnest!" Darcy spluttered, both at the notion of such a union for his cousin and the awkwardness that would insidiously creep and swell between them, should his best friend be in his employ.

"You shall have to wait and see, then, will you not?" the colonel replied. "But to return to your own matrimonial intentions and the furthering thereof, if you will not show yourself at the Theatre Royal alongside the Gardiners, why not ask them and their nieces for dinner?"

"Have you lost your mind?" Darcy snapped. "This is not the time for me to be hosting entertainments."

"I was speaking of a small family dinner, not some lavish affair," Fitzwilliam countered. "Only the four of them, you, Georgiana and myself, if you will have me."

Darcy's eyes narrowed in suspicion.

"Is that a ploy to spend more time with Miss Bennet?"

The other cast him a quelling glance.

"No. It is not. And on that note, pray do not mistake me for Bingley. The day when you can govern me as you do him has not dawned yet. And if it ever does, you may take me out and shoot me."

"I am not seeking to govern anybody—"

"No. Merely to lecture one and all on what is good for them."

"That is rich! What of you lecturing me whenever you are given half a chance?" Darcy was quick to point out. "How is that any different?"

His cousin shrugged.

"There is a world of difference. I am older and wiser."

"That reasoning applies to me and Bingley. But you and your two years' worth of added wisdom?" He snorted. "You flatter yourself."

"Not at all. I am speaking of the wisdom garnered at the school of life. By that reckoning, I am your senior by at least a decade. But let us not quibble over the exact figure. Now, that small dinner I mentioned: if you were to ask them on—"

"What of Georgiana?" Darcy soberly intervened.

The colonel arched a brow.

"What of her?"

"You are urging me to bring the Gardiners into her circle. Does that not trouble you at all?"

Fitzwilliam stared at him as if he had just sprouted two more heads.

"You aim to marry their niece," he said slowly and distinctly, as if spelling out a glaringly obvious matter to one with the aggravating habit of never paying much attention. "How is that not bringing them into Georgiana's circle?"

Darcy shrugged.

"It does not necessarily follow that one should keep company with all of one's relations. How often do you dine with our aunt Beatrice, by way of example?"

But Fitzwilliam dismissed the argument with a wave of his hand.

"That is specious nonsense," he said matter-of-factly. "You are proposing to avoid relations who live in the City, not twelve miles east of King's Lynn. How do you imagine you can achieve that?"

Darcy made no answer. For Georgiana's sake and not least Elizabeth's, they most certainly could not afford to flaunt connections in trade. Surely Elizabeth could not fail to understand that. For now, however, he was in no humour to discuss the matter.

"If you are aiming to distract me from your sudden fascination with Miss Bennet," he said instead, "and moreover the preposterous notion of acting as my steward—"

"Oh, for goodness' sake!" the other exclaimed. "It was a jest, Coz. In poor taste perhaps, but a jest nonetheless." He shook his head in wry amusement as the mild exasperation in his countenance gave way to a wide grin. "I value my sanity – and so should you. If that ever comes to pass, we will be sure to drive each other barmy."

Darcy exhaled in no small measure of relief and silently hoped that Fitzwilliam was likewise teasing him by feigning interest in Jane Bennet. The same argument applied in Richard's case as much as in Bingley's, if not more: his cousin deserved better than a placid union of convenience. Still, he sensibly chose not to labour that point. Fitzwilliam had rightly observed that Bingley welcomed guidance, but he most certainly did not. If, perish the thought, there came a time when Richard must be protected from himself, a far more careful approach would be in order. Keeping to banter would serve better at the moment.

So Darcy returned his cousin's grin and matched his tone:

"So much for your hollow boast of wisdom and a decade's seniority. Your penchant for immature jests tends to demonstrate the opposite."

"Now who is aiming to distract the other, eh?" the colonel retorted. "Never mind my maturity, or lack of it. What do you propose to do about the Gardiners?"

Darcy frowned. This was as unappealing as discussing Jane Bennet.

It was not in his nature to dissemble, but even one who abhorred disguise would keep his own counsel in order to preserve the peace. Thus, he tapped his mount's flank with his crop and merely said, "I shall think about it."

৵৹ ৹৵

Just then, in a small and very neat bedchamber on the second floor of a certain house in Gracechurch Street, Elizabeth *was* genuinely disposed to think of Mrs Gardiner and bring her name up in conversation. As soon as the door closed behind her and her sister, she spun round and began:

"See, Jane? What did I tell you? It makes no difference that he came today. He might as well have called in three weeks' time or never, if he would not open his lips to say a civil word to our aunt Gardiner."

"They did speak," Jane said, but Elizabeth was quick to counter that generous observation.

"Thanks to our aunt's good manners, not his. She asked him a question. He was obliged to answer. But he seemed almost angry at being spoken to, and gave the curtest of replies. Which, by the bye, was my reason for stopping you from mentioning our aunt's ties to Lambton. I would not see her connections disparaged to her face as beneath his notice, just as—"

"Oh, Lizzy, I am quite certain that he would not have—" Jane intervened, only to be interrupted in her turn when Elizabeth decisively resumed.

"Just as he had disparaged Cheapside. I told you what he had to say of this part of town, and how he turned up his nose at the very mention of Gracechurch Street." She scowled. "I expect a month's ablutions shan't be deemed enough to cleanse him from its impurities."

Her elder sister chuckled, then cast her an apologetic glance.

"I beg your pardon, Lizzy. I should not laugh. You are upset. But you do contrive to be diverting all the same. A month's ablutions!" she echoed with a smile. "He did not give me the impression that he disapproved of his surroundings, nor that he purposely ignored our aunt—"

"And you," Elizabeth pointed out.

"…merely that there was only one person in the room with whom he wished to talk," Jane went on to speak her mind, despite the interruption. "They say that incivility to all but the object of one's affections is the very essence of love. If I do not think any less of him as a result, why should you?"

"Jane, you never think ill of anyone," Elizabeth tenderly exclaimed. "Not even those who merit the severest censure. You are the most generous soul I know. If you—"

But then she caught herself and said no more. Not even when Jane mildly prompted, "Yes, Lizzy?"

Elizabeth shook her head.

"Nothing, dearest. Nothing."

She closed the small distance between them and put her arms around her sister in a warm embrace. She would not distress Jane with a full account as to why Mr Darcy did not deserve her kindness, nor the benefit of the doubt. She would not list his sins and Mr Bingley's just for the paltry satisfaction of proving her point. When Mr Darcy called again, he would eventually prove it for her – even to Jane. And only her sister, in her angelic goodness, would find any surprise in that.

Chapter 9

Pruett and his army of informants had discovered nothing. Nor had Banks and his people. No tidings on Saturday, the second day after the elopement, when Darcy and his cousin had gone to speak with one, then the other, after their brief call in Gracechurch Street. To their vast disappointment and frustration, Banks and Pruett had nothing to tell them on Sunday, either.

As was often the case, Darcy was compelled to own that Fitzwilliam had judged the situation rightly: they could not spend their time waiting for news in those men's garrets. Even their daily calls were met with a measure of guarded impatience and the repetition of the firm assurances that both Banks and Pruett had already given: there was no need at all for them to come – word would be sent with the utmost haste to Berkeley Square if there was anything to report – something was bound to come up over the next few days, for surely the fugitives could not conceal themselves for ever. Should not the gentlemen direct their energies towards the polite quarter and seek to discover if a licence had been issued?

But there was nothing that the pair of them could do in the polite quarter either. The matter was in the hands of Lord Malvern's connections. So far, there was no evidence that a marriage licence had been issued for George Wickham – which was good news to an extent, but it gave no certainties and brought the rogue no closer to retribution.

Likewise, nothing was gained from sending scouts to investigate Mrs Younge's previous residence, nor from revisiting her current abode a second and a third time. All that Darcy could take with him upon leaving Edward Street was the renewed conviction that the woman would have dearly loved to sell the information they required, if only she had it.

The lack of success on so many fronts could not fail to tax Darcy's patience. Thus, curbing his temper required no little effort while he and his cousin cantered along Cornhill towards Gracechurch Street. But it would not do to call in manifest ill humour.

On this occasion, the visit was left for last, after the lengthy enquiries in the unsavoury part of town – not only because both he and Fitzwilliam were eager to learn of any possible developments as soon as might be, but also to allow Elizabeth and her relations to return from church and whatever else they might be doing on a Sunday. There was ample reason to believe that by now they would be found at home. If nothing else, the steady rain that had begun to fall some two hours prior was bound to discourage them from outdoor amusements.

It was to be deplored that, as a result, he would have to make an appearance on the Gardiners' doorstep in comprehensively drenched apparel. But it could not be helped. He could not bring the carriage. It was enough of a challenge for him and Fitzwilliam to avoid attracting notice even on horseback. Riding in an emblazoned coach to Edward Street and the back alleys where Banks and Pruett had their lodgings would have been completely irresponsible. A hired chaise was the sensible option, Darcy belatedly thought and frowned. More fools them for not making provisions for the changeable weather.

The dripping greatcoats left trails on the wooden floor when the Gardiners' footman carried them away to be dried somewhere out of sight and, as Darcy rearranged the folds of his dampened neckcloth, a murmur of voices drifted towards him from the end of the corridor. The intermingled baritone gave him a brief pause. Ah. So the time had come to make the tradesman's acquaintance. It was not an attractive prospect, but needs must. And it would be good to have his curiosity appeased.

He instinctively straightened his shoulders and nodded towards the maid who was waiting to escort them, in silent indication that he was ready to proceed. The girl led the way and announced them, but as soon as he was ushered into the parlour, Darcy discovered the error of his suppositions: the masculine tones had not been Mr Gardiner's. There was but one man in the room – and that man was Tyndall.

Darcy suppressed a grimace and bowed. He would have vastly preferred the merchant's society.

⊱❦❦⊰

What the devil was Tyndall doing here?

The same words came to plague him again and again with the insistence of an irritating insect, and having them circling in his head was all the more annoying for knowing full well that the question was rhetorical and the answer blindingly obvious. To one accustomed to the stale tedium of the *beau monde*, Elizabeth was a breath of fresh air – and Tyndall, damn him, had not failed to recognise that. Fitzwilliam had casually remarked upon it too a few days ago, in Kent, once she and the rest of the Hunsford party had returned to the parsonage, leaving them both to suffocate in the dreariness that pervaded Rosings.

She was far less expansive now than on that particular occasion, but her every feature radiated a vibrant, irresistible vitality even when she was silent. She would stand out among the conventional embodiments of perfection that were generally found in the grand salons – all trained to look just so, smile just so, deport themselves just so; all tiresomely alike – just as a living, breathing woman would stand out among a host of lifeless faces painted on canvas. No wonder she drew him more than any of them ever had. If anything, he should be astonished that his defences had not crumbled sooner.

Was Tyndall also drawn to her like a moth to a flame?

Darcy frowned. He could derive but small satisfaction from finding that the intruder received no encouragement. Of course Elizabeth would not encourage another man's attentions – in his presence or otherwise. There was not an ounce of coquetry in her, nor was she a shameless flirt like her two youngest sisters. Thus, it came as no surprise that Tyndall was left to converse with their host, Miss Bennet and Fitzwilliam, while Elizabeth frequently turned away to assist Miss Gardiner with her sampler. He could not fault either of them for their perseverance. For all Tyndall's efforts, Elizabeth would not be drawn into conversation. As for her cousin, the child kept at her cross-stitch with great determination, although her thread often became so frightfully tangled that she was forced to ask for help in unravelling the mass of loops and snarls. Her steadiness of purpose, rarely found in one so young, might well be called a stubborn refusal to give in. Darcy smiled despite himself. Perhaps little Miss Gardiner and Elizabeth had that trait in common.

When the only marginally older Master Gardiner shuffled in the seat beside him, Darcy tore his gaze away from Elizabeth and fixed it upon the papers spread before him on the small square table. He picked up the uppermost for a closer look at the diagrams and symbols that currently were as hard to follow as if they were written in a barely comprehensible code. Whatever had possessed him to consent to tackle them?

His lips tightened. Tyndall was to blame – again. Tyndall, and his own foolish impulse to prove himself. Prove what, for goodness' sake? That he could succeed where the other had failed? That Tyndall was not the only one willing to give assistance?

Darcy fought to suppress a scowl that would have portrayed the very opposite of amiable helpfulness as he was forced to own that all he had achieved so far had been to permit Tyndall to tether him to this spot, and thus regain the freedom to saunter away and join the others.

The scowl won – so, in an endeavour to conceal it, Darcy lowered his head over the irksome sheet of paper. It was maddening to discover all-too-late that he had been used to Tyndall's advantage – nay, worse still, that he had foolishly played right into the other's hands. Upon reflection, the man must have been eager to extricate himself from the rashly undertaken task – for no sooner had Darcy and his cousin walked into the parlour and greeted Mrs Gardiner, her nieces and her children than Tyndall had drawled from across the room:

"Ah, just in time. How is your trigonometry, eh, Darcy? Colonel? I offered to rescue Master Gardiner here from the clutches of a difficult conundrum, but seemingly I spoke too soon. I daresay I would have had better success with some epic poem or a translation from Latin, but I never was one for advanced mathematics. I could find no use for it," Tyndall had shrugged with the instinctive disdain most gentlemen and their educators harboured for any discipline that was remotely practical.

Aye, a smattering of Latin, Ancient Greek and the classics was all that young scions were expected to acquire, Darcy had inwardly scoffed in response. Nothing so plebeian as an understanding of the principles that governed the natural world.

Despite Mrs Gardiner's civil insistence that he ought not trouble himself, he had agreed to take Tyndall's place beside the boy, at the table by the window, to demonstrate that he was not so narrow-minded – and could do better.

He was no less goaded by the other man's nonchalant ease among Elizabeth's relations. Unjustifiably claiming the privileges of an old acquaintance, Tyndall had carelessly ruffled Master Gardiner's hair, then wandered off, leaving Darcy and the boy in the airily disparaged realms of mathematics to do battle with calculations of distances and angles. Complex calculations, too, for a child of twelve – or however old Master Gardiner was.

"Are you not rather too young to contend with trigonometry?" Darcy observed, half-heartedly following that thought, as he dropped the sheet of paper on the table.

"I hope not, sir," the child murmured, his tone somewhat defensive, but his thin voice gathered strength as he continued, "My father thinks that the sooner I have a good grasp of it, the better."

Did he? Whatever for?

Navigation was the first use that sprang to mind, so Darcy asked, "Are you aiming to enlist as a midshipman?"

The boy shook his head.

"The sea makes me ill. I would much rather stay on land and build canals and bridges. Papa said that if I am dedicated and cons— conscientious," he added, faltering on the unfamiliar word, "then he would ensure that I learn from the best, such as Mr Telford."

Darcy arched a brow, surprised in no small measure. Unless Mr Gardiner was pacifying his son with empty promises after the manner of self-absorbed or overindulgent parents, then he might be a reasonably influential fellow, if he hoped to have the ear of Telford, who had been instrumental in the building of countless bridges, hundreds of miles of new roads and the longest aqueduct in the country. The speculations could not fail to pique his interest. It was encouraging to think that Mr Gardiner might be a cut above the average shopkeeper.

"I see. Well, let us return to this," Darcy said, gesturing towards the papers on the table. He had already spent far too long at the wrong end of the room, and since he was not prepared to appear as ineffectual and ready to give up as Tyndall, he had better address the task in hand, and be done with it.

He was pleased to find that, once he could resolutely keep his eyes and thoughts from wandering in Elizabeth's direction, the answer to the trigonometrical conundrum became evident in mere moments.

He dipped the pen in the inkwell and boldly wrote down the five necessary equations, then pushed the piece of paper towards Master Gardiner.

"There," he said with the satisfaction of a mission well-accomplished. "This should clarify matters."

But, having studied the offering for a little while, the boy shuffled in his seat again and self-consciously mumbled, "I fear it does not, sir. But no matter. I…"

The child's voice trailed off and he made to collect the papers, while Darcy was at pains to suppress another scowl. Confound it! Was he supposed to fritter away even more precious time and explain everything in exhaustive detail, as though he had been employed as this boy's tutor?

The flare of irritation vanished without trace when Elizabeth left her seat and came to join them.

"You might as well leave this for now, Edward. You can always ask your tutor to explain it on the morrow," she said, as if she had guessed his thoughts.

She ran her fingers through her cousin's wavy locks, then brought her hands to rest on the boy's shoulders, her stance both reassuring and protective. Darcy flashed a puzzled glance towards her. Whatever was she seeking to protect the youngster from? Not *him* and his vexation, surely! Perish the thought that he had made himself quite as obvious as that. Nay, like as not, it was something else entirely that she aimed to avert – such as the lad spending most of his Sunday in the frustrating maze of trigonometry. An understanding smile fluttered on his lips. Of course. She had no brothers, so she could not know that the chore paled into insignificance against the full breadth of hardships a young boy must learn to face, particularly when he was sent to school.

"Why leave it for the morrow?" Darcy replied with a faint shrug and reached for a fresh sheet of paper.

Suddenly, the prospect of playing tutor was infinitely more appealing, and being consigned to the furthest reaches of the parlour became an advantage rather than an imposition. Should she stay, he would be in no haste to quit this spot.

Encouraging one's daughters towards mathematics would have been a singular choice, even for a gentleman as eccentric as Mr Bennet, so she must be a stranger to the subject. But with an agile and inquisitive mind such as hers, Elizabeth might find some interest in the solution to Master Gardiner's conundrum, if it was properly presented.

The corners of his lips quirked in vague amusement as Darcy inwardly acknowledged that his patience for the task – now in limitless supply – was shamefully self-serving. Even so, it would be to the boy's benefit as well if he were to describe the process step by step, from the very beginning.

He dipped his pen again and began to draw the diagram in careful detail: the towers, whose relative height was yet to be determined; the rounded arch that spanned the distance between them; the observation point at the uppermost window of a distant folly; the lines connecting it to the keystone of the arch and the tops of the towers.

It was highly gratifying to find that his efforts did not go to waste. When Elizabeth released her cousin's shoulders, it was only so that she could pull the spare chair and take a seat – and not just because she had suddenly become fascinated with trigonometry. More often than not, her gaze was fixed on the pair of them, and not the paper.

Her scrutiny was distracting – delectably so – yet Darcy flattered himself that he was still able to make sufficient sense as he proceeded to write down the calculations, explaining all the while what it was that he was doing. Seemingly, it was not a hollow boast. He was only halfway through when Master Gardiner gave a triumphant little cry of satisfaction and his countenance brightened.

"Ah! Now I see where I was going wrong." The child cast him a wide smile. "Much obliged, sir. I think I can carry on from here."

The boy availed himself of a pen and crossed out his earlier scribbles with great energy, then thought better of trying to salvage something from his previous attempts. He drew a fresh sheet and eagerly began to reproduce Darcy's drawings, the tip of his tongue sticking out at the corner of his mouth in concentration.

The sight was pleasing in itself, but Darcy's true reward was not long in coming.

"Thank you," Elizabeth said quietly. "That was… most helpful."

"My pleasure," he replied – and meant it.

She busied herself briefly with repositioning the inkwell, then glanced his way again.

"Have you and your cousin discovered anything this morning?"

Darcy's mien sobered.

"No. Nothing so far."

"Nothing at all?" She sighed. "I am sorry to hear it."

She absent-mindedly smoothed the narrow band of lace around her cuff, then rose to her feet, much to Darcy's disappointment.

"We should leave you to your task," she said to her cousin, reaching out to stroke his shoulder.

Intent upon his work, the child gave a vague murmur and kept writing. As Elizabeth made her way back to the others, there was nothing that Darcy could do but follow. It was indeed a pity that young Master Gardiner had been quite so prompt in grasping the essence of the problem. At this point, he wished the boy were slow-witted and in need of having it explained half-a-dozen times.

◦◦◦

Not coming across as a miserable curmudgeon was becoming more challenging by the minute, and Darcy feared he was losing that battle – for Tyndall would not budge. He had extended his call well beyond the limits generally accepted in polite society – and, of necessity, so had the pair of them – yet the accursed man was still there, chattering away and laughing at his own jests in the most provoking manner.

Despite his best efforts, Darcy could not forbear a frown. The day had been thoroughly wasted. Even if he were finally spared Tyndall's presence, civility demanded that he and his cousin also bid their farewells before long. That was bad enough. But he would be damned if they were the first to do so!

When Fitzwilliam straightened in his seat with an incongruously cheery, "Well, we should be going," Darcy would have dearly loved to throttle him.

Yet a moment later he was compelled to own that he should have given his cousin more credit. There was something to be said for his relation's tactical skills, Darcy grudgingly allowed when the colonel turned towards Tyndall and casually added, "If you are leaving soon, might we be so bold as to petition for a couple of seats in your carriage?

I assume you did not come on horseback. We did, for our sins – and I shall not speak for Darcy here but, for my part, I have had one wet ride too many this morning."

Pretending to shy away from riding in the rain like some vain fops excessively concerned for the state of their apparel sat ill with Darcy, and the prospect of bidding their adieus at the same time as Tyndall pleased him no better. Even so, his annoyance was somewhat mitigated by the satisfying spectacle of Tyndall struggling to think of a good reason to refuse Fitzwilliam's request – and finding none.

There *was* none to be found. Tyndall had already tarried overlong in Gracechurch Street – and well he knew it. Thus, in due course, the three of them descended the front steps of the Gardiners' residence together.

Perhaps it was a trifle unwise of Fitzwilliam to abandon the false excuse so soon and carelessly observe as he tugged his gloves on, "Ah. I should have had a better look out of the window. The rain is but a mere drizzle now. So I shan't trouble you after all, Tyndall, if it is all the same to you. I should not subject Samson to the ignominy of being tethered to your carriage, if I can help it. What say you, Cousin? Will you ride with me, or would you prefer to keep your powder dry?"

"I had better ride with you," Darcy replied without hesitation. It was an easy choice. He was not in the least inclined to expose himself further to Tyndall's society.

He would have thought that the other was just as eager for them to part company, especially if he had come to see Fitzwilliam's tactical manoeuvre for what it was. Yet as he ambled towards his waiting carriage, Tyndall unexpectedly pressed him:

"Are you quite certain? I should be pleased to drive you home. For one thing, I have not had the chance to ask what brings you to this part of town. Not your habitual scene, by all accounts."

The smirk that accompanied the remark provoked Darcy into retorting without thinking, "Nor is it yours. So I could ask the same."

No sooner had the words passed his lips than he cursed the folly of letting himself be drawn into such an exchange. He should have known better. This could so easily slide into the undignified posturing of a pair of cockerels ruffling their feathers and disputing territory. He had not lost his senses as far as to engage in something so ridiculous – least of all on the Gardiners' doorstep!

Guarding his tongue and keeping himself under good regulation became even more difficult when Tyndall replied with perfect nonchalance, "The appeal of novelty, what else? The charming Miss Elizabeth is a most refreshing change from the *ton*'s simpering misses. As for her elder sister, damn me if she is not one of the handsomest women I have ever beheld. A shame about their low connections," he muttered, indicating the surroundings with a slight gesture, then he grinned and shrugged. "I daresay this goes to show that among us bipeds, 'tis the thoroughbreds who lack vigour and lustre when compared to unfettered specimens born and raised in the wild. By the bye, they come from small country gentry, I take it?"

"Yes," Darcy confirmed tersely, not trusting himself with a longer reply.

Tyndall nodded in response.

"I gathered as much from the young ladies' accounts of their home, and from Goulding's letters. I leafed through them the other day and came across the odd reference to the Miss Bennets, their family and their father's estate. I was hoping you might tell me more on the way to Berkeley Square, but no matter. 'Tis Goulding I should ask for pertinent details. He is better placed to give them."

"What details?" Fitzwilliam intervened and, for once, Darcy was almost glad of it.

"Oh, this and that," Tyndall said with a casual flick of his fingers. "Who are their people, what is their standing, that sort of thing."

"What is this, some juvenile *coup de foudre?* I thought you were past the trying age," Darcy scoffed, unable and unwilling to contain himself.

But Tyndall seemed to be of the same ilk as Bingley: not quick to take offence. He laughed.

"Age is irrelevant. No one is safe from the thunderbolt. But no, I would not say it is a *coup de foudre* – and, in any case, I am not one for impulsive action. Let us just call it a healthy interest in an attractive possibility." He readjusted his collar, then glanced up to settle an assessing look on Darcy. "Frankly, if I did not know better, I would have suspected you of the same. But you do not have the air of one who has gone a-courting, and besides you are bound to set your sights a great deal higher than the cousin of your aunt's parson," he evenly said, thus giving Darcy more than one reason for resentment.

Firstly, he found it impossible to tell if the other was voicing genuine opinions or was provoking him on purpose, in a sly quest for information. Secondly, he was vexed to find that Tyndall seemed to have learned everything there was to know about Elizabeth and her connections. And thirdly – a point of contention which, truth be told, was clamouring for the uppermost place on the list – it was beyond galling that the man should have the effrontery to comment on his air, his courtship and his aspirations. The barefaced impudence was intolerable.

"Now, me," Tyndall continued, unperturbed, "I can afford to consider a modest squire's daughter if she takes my fancy, irrespective of her relations in trade. I daresay that, once plucked from their midst, she would make for a creditable addition to anyone's table."

"She would," Darcy said curtly, and with a brief touch to the brim of his hat, he stalked towards his tethered mount.

❦

"Let me commend you for your restraint. Much as I tease you about it, there are times when it comes in handy," Fitzwilliam remarked while they were making their way back at a far more leisurely pace than Darcy would have chosen, had he not felt the need to allow a growing distance between them and Tyndall's fast-moving carriage.

He gave a quiet mutter of agreement. Aye. Thank goodness for restraint, such as it was. A reckless and hot-headed man would have sent Tyndall on his way with a flea in his ear. Which would have been both unwise and inconsiderate. His prospective betrothal should not be sprung upon the world using Tyndall as a mouthpiece. Not just because he abhorred being the subject of gossip. His engagement *would* give rise to tittle-tattle – that was unavoidable. But setting fire to tinder now with a premature announcement would be tantamount to forcing Elizabeth's hand. And she would not appreciate that.

The corner of his mouth quirked into a dark smile of satisfaction. She would not appreciate Tyndall's brand of courtship either, nor the man's presumption. Certainly not now, when she was aware of his own feelings. Tyndall might be a giddy sort of fellow, given to laughter and chatter, but she would not be swayed by his facile good-humour.

And let him expound his views to her face, Darcy thought with wicked relish. Let Tyndall liken her to a wild, country-born filly with more vigour and lustre than a thoroughbred, for all the good it would do him.

Darcy's grim smile widened. Elizabeth would deliver an impeccable set-down on the occasion – and that would make for splendid entertainment. But since it was impossible for him to be an invisible witness to that conversation, he would content himself with not finding the wretched man underfoot in Gracechurch Street again. Next time his proverbial restraint might fail him. And he might well give Tyndall a piece of his mind – and the devil take the hindmost!

Chapter 10

Today more than ever, the jesting comment that Bingley had once made about him was uncannily close to the mark: he *was* in a pretty awful temper on this dull and wet Sunday, while restlessly moving about his house with nothing to do.

Georgiana was from home. When he had returned from Cheapside, Darcy had learned from his butler that Lady Malvern and her daughters had called earlier – in order to evade Lady Catherine, he not unreasonably suspected – and, upon their departure, had asked Georgiana to come with them and spend the rest of the day with some acquaintance or another.

Fitzwilliam had taken himself to Malvern House to notify his father and their aunt of the developments, or rather lack thereof, and then aimed to escape to his club.

Darcy had refused the invitation to join him in that questionable amusement. The company of rowdy officers held precious little appeal at the best of times, and he was highly unlikely to derive any enjoyment from it today.

He had busied himself for a while with some neglected correspondence, and was now spending his time in the least profitable manner: brandy in hand, he was brooding over the recent past and the immediate future. Three days had elapsed since his aborted proposal at Hunsford – a mere three days, but unnecessarily eventful. If he had his way…

The useless reflection made him slam the half-empty glass on the nearest table with an oath. He had always scoffed at those who would waste time dwelling on *'if only'*. It was for fools and weaklings to sit about bemoaning their misfortunes and lost opportunities. A man worth his salt made his own luck.

He strode to his desk and availed himself of pen and paper.

If he did not wish to have his time with Elizabeth spoiled by Tyndall, the answer was simple: they should meet on his own terms – at his own house. Fitzwilliam was in the right: an invitation to a small family dinner was in order.

He began to write, addressing himself to Mrs Gardiner, of course. Yet once he had penned the straightforward opening, the arrival to specifics gave him pause. What day should he choose? The morrow was too soon. Civility demanded that he give more notice. Were they likely to be free on Tuesday? Wednesday? He frowned at the prospect of notes going back and forth between his house and the Gardiners', in a protracted endeavour to agree upon a convenient date.

Darcy set his pen down and leaned back in his seat. There was an easier way. It would be irregular – and moreover would make him look like an impatient schoolboy – but so be it.

He flicked the lid of the inkwell down, crumpled the unfinished letter and disposed of it in the basket, then crossed the room to tug the bell pull.

"I need the carriage," he told the footman, when young Simon promptly came in to attend him.

⚬⚬

'Of all the idiotic notions,' Darcy inwardly cursed his impetuous decision as he followed Mrs Gardiner out of the parlour.

His interview had been with her alone. Her nieces were out for a brief stroll with the children, the lady had informed him when she had received him for a second time that day – and while doing so, her lips had twitched in the most suspicious manner. Not an apologetic smile, but one of mild amusement. As though she had seen him for the besotted fool that he was. Which was little wonder. Coming to call twice within the space of mere hours *was* awfully conspicuous. But he had reconciled himself to that, even before he had left his home. He was a lovestruck fool, and frankly he would not have it any other way. Elizabeth and her relations might as well know it.

The purpose of his call had been explained to Mrs Gardiner without delay – but the result was wholly unexpected.

"I am sorry to say that my husband and I are unable to accept your invitation," she had murmured, to Darcy's sharp disappointment. "He must leave for Bristol at first light, and will be absent for at least a se'nnight."

The obvious solution could not fail to present itself: the lady and her nieces could come without Mr Gardiner. They could safely be fetched in his own carriage – or, better still, he would come to escort them. But before Darcy could say as much, Mrs Gardiner had proposed other arrangements:

"This is rather unorthodox, I fear, but might I persuade you to join us for dinner tonight instead? We are to sit down to it shortly, given my husband's early departure. Would that be convenient?"

Before he knew it, Darcy had accepted. And it was only now, while the lady was escorting him towards Mr Gardiner's study, that he began to reflect on the consequences with something very much like panic. He had foolishly agreed to meet the challenge on their ground, not his – and, above all, alone. Fitzwilliam would not be there to lend assistance with his habitual ease in conversation. This time he *would* be the one obliged to spout civil nothings and present himself in a favourable light without any of the comfortable trappings of familiarity.

'A damned foolish notion,' he thought once more, as Mrs Gardiner opened the door at the end of the corridor and preceded him within.

"May we join you, my dear? I am come to introduce our guest. This is Mr Darcy."

৵৹ᠻ ᠻৡৎ৽

"No, Lizzy, let me rearrange it," Jane insisted and hastened to unpin the troublesome lock, which earned her a wry look from her sister when their eyes met in the looking-glass.

"Do not fuss so," Elizabeth countered. "'Tis but dinner at home. What matters—?"

"Oh, I am only doing this for my own amusement. I am convinced he will not even notice, either way. Humour me for a moment longer and hold still. Let me fix it… just… so! There. That is much better," Jane beamed, tilting her head sideways for a long, assessing look. She puffed up her younger sister's sleeves, and smilingly observed, "Now, Mamma would point out that keenness is a most attractive quality in a gentleman. But fear not, I shan't wax eloquent on that subject. I will only say that the ablutions you spoke of have not delayed his return. And it would be fair to own that Mr Darcy does improve on closer acquaintance."

Elizabeth made a face and did not oblige with any such acknowledgement. But she voiced no protest either. And her loving sister could not fail to note that this time she did not retort, "Let us see how he behaves."

⚜

Darcy's first surprise of the evening – or the second, if he counted the impromptu invitation – was that Mr Gardiner was an intelligent man. Not in the sense of having the shrewdness of a man of business – although, for all he knew, Elizabeth's uncle must have possessed that too, if he could run a successful enterprise. The remarkably pleasant surprise lay in finding him nothing like his sisters. Mr Gardiner spoke like a man of sense and education who was no stranger to good taste and good breeding. Moreover, he was a genial host.

More surprises were in store for Darcy, and they surfaced one after the other, once a maid had made an appearance to let them know that the ladies had come down and were waiting for them in the parlour.

Darcy learned that Mr and Mrs Gardiner had four children, not two, and the little ones were all allowed to dine in company instead of the nursery – a well-deserved concession, by the looks of it, for none of them could be faulted for their manners. Not even the youngest, a round-faced girl who seemed to be but four or five years of age.

The children had a governess – another surprise – and the young lady was permitted to dine with the family. The fare was excellent and the dining room pleasantly appointed, but Darcy could scarce register such details, too caught up in the seemingly endless succession of fresh discoveries. Namely, that Mrs Gardiner hailed from Lambton – she had revealed as much during the first course. That the sedate Jane Bennet could speak at length and with as much animation as the others, and it was only a passing reference to autumn walks in Hertfordshire that brought a shadow to her visage. It was no less surprising to find that the conversation flowed with ease around the dinner table – and that he was not averse to contributing, as his earlier tension gradually released him from its tight coils, and his discomfort abated. It was not long before he found himself able to converse with Mrs Gardiner about familiar places and mutual acquaintances, and chuckle at the recollection of boisterous harvest *fêtes*.

And throughout all this ran the vibrant red thread of Elizabeth's manifest good spirits. She verily glowed as she laughed and chatted more freely than ever. Gone was the subdued air that had clouded her countenance over the last couple of days. He could almost say that he had never seen her thus at any other time. Certainly not in Kent. Perhaps not even in her home, nor in her other familiar surroundings. He could not say what had effected this transformation, but it was wondrous to behold.

She sat across from him, and it was only with the greatest effort that Darcy could tear his eyes away from the enchanting picture she presented.

It would be a vast deal harder to tear himself away from her at the end of the evening – and well he knew it. There was nothing he could possibly want more than to hasten the day when he would be allowed to take her with him.

The epiphany that followed was long in coming – unforgivably so, as he would eventually berate himself with horrified harshness. Yet it did come at last. It was forced upon him about an hour later, when they had repaired to the music room and he sat with a cup of tea in his folded hands, a smile tugging at the corner of his lips and his enthralled gaze fixed upon her with impunity, for there was nothing untoward or conspicuous in giving his full attention to a musical performance. One that had been often rehearsed, apparently, for there was nary a flaw in the execution. Elizabeth sat on the long bench before the pianoforte with the eldest Miss Gardiner on one side and Miss Emily, the youngest, on the other. Miss Gardiner was the chief performer, while Elizabeth turned the pages and added the odd set of harmonious chords in the right places. The final notes of the rondo were entrusted to Miss Emily, who played them with chubby little fingers, then spun round to gleefully beam at her cousin.

"That was just right, Lizzy, don't you think?" the girl chirped, and was scooped up into a warm embrace.

"Of course I do! Both of you played your parts to perfection. No wonder your Mamma and Papa are so very proud of you," Elizabeth replied as she exchanged affectionate glances with her aunt and uncle, then dropped a kiss on Miss Emily's cheek and another into Miss Gardiner's flaxen ringlets.

And that was when realisation hit, leaving Darcy aghast at his former blindness. He was no better than Tyndall! Just as dismissive. Just as self-absorbed. He had not been quite so crass as to liken her to a lustrous filly – neither in his thoughts nor, Heaven forbid, in casual conversation with others – but he, too, had been of the firm opinion that the only way forward was to pluck her from her relations' midst. To separate her from all these people whom she loved so dearly. How in God's name had he not seen until this very moment what anguish the separation would have caused her?

The tug at his heartstrings was as sharp as a physical pain, and Darcy's heart lurched at the thought of ever seeing her suffer – and, worse still, being the one to blame for her distress. She verily glowed tonight because she was happy. What sort of a selfish beast would take this away from her, and expect her to find ample compensation in what he had to offer?

The violent surge of self-recriminations was stemmed by a sole comforting notion: praise be, he had held his tongue and had not made that unconscionably cruel request in form! He squirmed as he remembered his response to Elizabeth's declared intention to remove to Cheapside, at the time when he had judged Mr and Mrs Gardiner and found them wanting without having even met them. She had doubtlessly detected his disdain for her connections in trade, but at least he had not betrayed the full breadth of his shortcomings.

'Thank goodness for small mercies,' Darcy inwardly scoffed and promptly sought to smooth his countenance, lest the self-directed scorn be misconstrued as dissatisfaction with the present company.

There was good reason to hope that he had wiped the scowl off his face by the time Elizabeth glanced towards him, for there was no censure in her eyes. Nor was she in any haste to look away as her lips curled up into a smile.

⁖⁖⁖

Jane Bennet and the Gardiners were already ranking quite high in Darcy's estimation, even before they went and endeared themselves to him even more – the first by offering to assist the governess in taking the little ones to their chambers, and the older couple by choosing to sit together on the furthermost sofa, and quietly discuss something or other.

Thus, for the first time in two days – two very long days – he was allowed a few moments of quasi-private conversation with Elizabeth, and he was grateful to all three for the kindness, regardless of whether it had been extended inadvertently or on purpose.

Either way, it gave him the opportunity to claim a seat beside her – the one Miss Bennet had vacated – and softly say, "I would like to thank you and your relations for this evening. It was… remarkably pleasant."

An engagingly impish smile came to tug at the corner of her lips.

"I am glad to hear it. Sudden arrangements have such a way of going awry. 'Tis more through luck than judgement that they meet one's expectations."

And there it was again, the delectable admixture of sweetness and archness that had bewitched him from the earliest days of their acquaintance. Its return easily made up for two whole days of awkward silences and all-too-brief exchanges. He had always delighted in her teasing, even when he was not altogether certain of her meaning. As was the case now. Was she only referring to his sudden addition to the family party, or did she also have in mind something else entirely? Such as his sudden proposal, for instance?

This was not the time for him to earnestly declare that he would bend both luck and judgement in order to ensure that nothing would go awry in *that* regard. As for his expectations for this evening, he had better not reveal that they had been exceeded in every way. It would have been tantamount to owning that he had thought little and had therefore expected little of her relations – and, given his recent epiphany, he was not about to remind her of past sins.

"I had no notion what I should expect," Darcy said instead – which was not that wise either, on reflection, but the honest answer was out before he could check it. Nor could he help adding with a faint smile, his voice lowered to a near-whisper, "I hope you will agree that we are well into uncharted waters, you and I."

"Are we? That is rather ominous," Elizabeth airily countered. "Now, if we are to trade old dictums, I might say that there is nothing new under the sun."

"In general, perhaps. But this is very new to me. And I am not at my best in unfamiliar circumstances," Darcy brought himself to own by way of justification, for what it was worth.

He had no reason to rue his frankness – quite the opposite – when her lips twitched in the most adorable manner in response.

"So I have noticed. But today it came to me that you are not alone in this: I know at least one other gentleman who makes for an agreeable companion only when he is at ease."

The imperative to ascertain of whom she was speaking detracted from the surge of pleasure at learning that she had read him rightly and that tonight she had found him an agreeable companion. Ill-judged as it might have been, Darcy could not forbear asking, "And that gentleman would be…?"

"My father."

"Ah." That was a relief, and before he knew it, the lightness of heart was evinced in a wide grin and a jocular, "I see. 'Tis good to know that Mr Bennet and I have some traits in common."

"More than you imagine," she cheerfully retorted, but said nothing else, so Darcy was compelled to prompt her.

"Such as?"

Elizabeth gave a flourish of her hand.

"I could present you with an exhaustive list, but that would deprive you of the satisfaction of seeing for yourself. Besides, delineating character is long and thirsty work. Would you care for another cup of tea?"

"I thank you, no. In fact, I should take my leave," he acknowledged with profound reluctance. "I should not detain your uncle any further from his preparations for the journey, and Georgiana must be wondering what has become of me."

"Oh, yes, of course," Elizabeth concurred, shuffling back into the seat she was about to quit. "Pray give my regards to Miss Darcy. And I hope you and your cousin have better success on the morrow."

He nodded in appreciation and pensively replied, "Yes, I expect Fitzwilliam and I will go back to enquire into his men's progress, much as they would rather we did not."

"Oh? How so?"

Darcy shrugged.

"Having the pair of us underfoot is of no use to anybody, so I cannot fault them for asking us to stay away and wait for tidings. Nonetheless, I will be hard-pressed to oblige."

"That, I can well imagine," Elizabeth said with feeling, and there was great solace to be found in the sympathetic look she cast him.

But the tame sense of comfort burst into flames when she reached out and pressed his hand.

The touch was light and brief, a fleeting caress. Her slender fingers were instantly withdrawn, and she curled them in a tight clasp around her other hand as though she already regretted her intrepidity – so, with no little effort, Darcy restrained himself from reclaiming the exquisite indulgence, much as he was tempted. And temptation soared as he sat motionless beside her, the back of his hand still tingling, his gaze sweeping searchingly over her face.

He could not meet her eyes – they were studiously averted.

He only caught a swift glance filtered through lowered lashes, and then she looked away, leaving him to the sweet agony of drinking in every detail of her appearance, and yearning for so much more than this. Yearning for privacy. For her lithe form in his arms – her lips on his. For the long-awaited day when they would begin to build a life together.

A stab of fierce desire pierced through him and set him on fire when she self-consciously bit the corner of her lip, her bosom rising and falling with shallow breaths – and Darcy had to clench his hand into a fist until his knuckles whitened to stop himself from reaching across the narrow space between them to at least wrap his fingers around hers. He could not trust himself, not even with so small a liberty. Certainly not here, in the Gardiners' parlour, and moreover their presence. His boldness could scarce hope to escape either their notice or their censure – for, unlike her, he would not have drawn back in a hurry.

And that was when a heady notion cut through the haze of intoxication: the all-too-brief caress had been the first tender gesture she had initiated of her own accord!

Darcy swallowed hard as wispy shreds of reason fought for ascendancy and sensibly suggested that, God willing, there would be others – *if* he had the good sense not to rush her.

So he leaned back, and forced himself to breathe. He would not open his lips till he believed himself to have attained some semblance of composure. But when he finally spoke, the words still came out in a ragged whisper:

"I hope this will be—" He broke off, cleared his throat and began afresh. "I hope this wretched business will be resolved over the coming week, before Mr Gardiner's return. Then perhaps you and your relations might find the time to come for dinner in Berkeley Square and join me and Georgiana for a performance at the Theatre Royal. *Macbeth*, if we are in luck. I remember your aunt mentioning plans of that nature yesterday, and I was thinking…"

Darcy let his voice trail away and gave a vague gesture only to find, to his great pleasure, that there was no need to elaborate. Elizabeth looked up and said with a soft smile, "I would like that very much. And so would they, I am quite sure, if that could be arranged."

"Excellent!" Darcy beamed. "I shall look forward to it, and so will my sister. By the bye," he tentatively resumed, "I meant to ask: may I bring her along next time I call?"

Elizabeth's brows arched and the second glance she flashed him held a distinct measure of surprise, the cause of which Darcy was quick to fathom. But before he could roundly chastise himself for his previous reluctance to foster any degree of closeness between his sister and Elizabeth's Cheapside relations, she smoothed her skirts and evenly replied, "By all means, pray do. I should be very glad to see her."

"Would…? Hm. Would tomorrow morning be convenient?" The hesitant look he settled on her gave way to self-deprecating amusement when he added, "Although I might be well on my way to taxing your aunt's patience. Much like Fitzwilliam's men, Mrs Gardiner might prefer she did not have us underfoot so often. She will be right in thinking that calling four times in three days is…excessive."

Elizabeth chuckled.

"Fortunately, my aunt is fond of society." Her teasing air sobered a little when she continued, "She will be honoured to make your sister's acquaintance. And I daresay that, between us, we could keep Miss Darcy entertained while you and the colonel make your enquiries."

"You are very kind to offer," he said softly. "Yes, I think Georgiana will be delighted to spend the morning here with you. She is not at ease in unfamiliar surroundings either," Darcy explained, a rueful quirk tugging at his lips when he mentioned that family trait, "but I have no doubt that, as others before her, she will find her reserve melting in no time at all. This is a most welcoming home, and the family atmosphere is… very pleasing," he finished, striving to keep his tone matter-of-fact – no mean feat, for, in truth, it was a vast deal more than that.

It was exceedingly appealing, and no less heart-warming. A safe haven from the trials and vexations that abounded without. And he wanted the same for himself. With every fibre of his being, he wanted to come home to her, and bask in the soothing comfort that only a true communion of hearts and minds could bring. The comfort that had evaded him year after year, ever since he had learned to turn mature and discerning eyes upon the world.

It was the oddest time to consider age-old poems, but the Homeric lines sprang to mind all the same – and struck the deepest chord, for they were fitting. Very much so, in every way.

There is nothing more potent, nor more admirable than this: when a man and a woman who share the same ideas about life keep house together. It pains their enemies and delights their friends, but only they themselves know what it truly means.'

It would mean everything – he knew as much already.

And he could scarce bear to go through yet another day without it.

"My sentiments exactly," Darcy heard her say and, however quiet, the faraway whisper jolted him from his musings as, for one staggering moment, it seemed as though she had answered his innermost thoughts and his best hopes.

But once he had gathered his wits about him and dismissed the wild notion, the return to sanity did not come as the starkest disappointment, for she eyed him squarely and cast him a bright smile.

"I am glad to hear you were left with the same impression. This *is* a very happy home. Perhaps more so than many. I have heard it said that happiness in marriage is entirely a matter of chance, but—"

"Not so," Darcy intervened, with a firm shake of his head. "Pure chance may make a beginning and bring kindred spirits into each other's path. But it is for unwavering devotion to build the rest. That, and some unfathomable quality which, from what I understand, is very highly prized – and all the more for being so elusive a virtue."

"And that would be?" Elizabeth asked, her eyes crinkling at the corners.

So he matched her impish little grin with a wry one of his own and airily replied, "I hear it goes by the name of patience. If we are still trading old dictums, some say that all good things come to those who wait."

Chapter 11

Had he been at leisure to dwell on such things, on the following morning Darcy might have reflected on other words of wisdom: those pertaining to the best-laid schemes of mice and men. The messenger arrived just before half past ten to let him know that someone bearing a strong resemblance to Wickham had been spotted less than two hours prior in a coffee house in Carter Lane, chatting with an older man as though he did not have a care in the world.

The fidgety urchin who would have never gained admittance into Darcy's study under normal circumstances was still panting with exertion when he was ushered in, which was little wonder, since he had made his way thither at a run, all the way from Pruett's lodgings. Between sharp intakes of breath, he said that his master had been informed, and by now so must Banks be. Three inconspicuous but able-bodied and fast-footed fellows had already been dispatched to Carter Lane as reinforcements, with firm instructions to keep a close eye on their quarry, discreetly tail him and be sure not to lose him, on pain of being skinned alive.

The boy's dirt-smeared countenance split into a fleeting grin as he said so – a sure sign that he and the others were spurred not so much by the empty threat as by the expectation of a handsome recompense for their efforts. A half-crown should be the lad's immediate reward, alongside a hearty breakfast while word was sent to Malvern House to summon Fitzwilliam, Darcy determined. But firstly, nothing should be left to chance.

"Is your master quite certain it was the right man?" he asked. "Did he show you the miniature?"

The boy cast him a wary glance.

"The what, sorr?"

"The man's likeness. The little painting, this wide," Darcy explained, spreading out his thumb and forefinger to show a good approximation of the artefact's size.

On the day when he and his cousin had sought out Pruett and Banks after conveying Elizabeth to her relations, he had entrusted the miniature to Fitzwilliam's people, so that they could show their informants precisely whom they were meant to be seeking. Thus, for the first time in eight months, Darcy had reason to be glad he had not destroyed the reprobate's likeness but, in deference to his departed father, he had suffered it to remain displayed in the master's study in town, just like its twin had been left in place, above the mantelpiece in his sire's favourite sitting room at Pemberley.

"Oh, that," the boy replied, his eyes brightening in comprehension. "Aye, sorr, the guv'nor gave us a butcher's. Gave us a look, that's ter say. 'Tis yer man an' no mistake. Juss that 'e ain't that dapper an' 'is nose's crooked."

It would be, Darcy thought with a grim smile, pleasantly reminded of his own role in reshaping Wickham's features last summer, in Ramsgate. A pity he had contented himself with as little as that on the occasion. But the time had come for the blackguard to receive his just deserts in full.

"Very well," he said to the boy, then glanced at his footman. "Have a maid take him below-stairs and feed him, and send Joseph to Malvern House to fetch Colonel Fitzwilliam at once," he instructed.

Then, as soon as he was left alone, he reached for pen and paper to write to Mrs Gardiner and indirectly let Elizabeth know that their plans for the day had to be cancelled. It was a severe disappointment, but it could not be helped. Elizabeth would understand the urgency. With any luck, he and Georgiana might be able to call on the morrow and let her know that Anne was safe and the unhappy business was finally reaching its conclusion.

Less than half an hour later, the Darcy carriage was hastening towards the East End. Of necessity, Georgiana was left at home to listlessly employ herself in the usual manner. And little did she know, once she had repaired to the music room with her companion, that she could have spared herself the trouble of leafing through her collection of music sheets in search of a sufficiently attractive piece — for, in a few short minutes, a distraction would arrive from just around the corner.

ꙥꙥ ꙥꙥ

"Look, Charles! There – look! It *is* Mr Darcy's carriage. The arms are unmistakable. Can you see, is he within? I am almost certain I caught a glimpse of him. In any case, it was a gentleman not a young lady, so it must have been him. No one but he or his sister would be making use of his conveyance. Hm... I had no notion that he had returned from Kent. I wonder where he is going in such haste. And did you see that scrawny urchin perched up alongside the coachman? How very singular. Well, I daresay Miss Darcy will be able to give us an inkling into the meaning of all this. Tell Rossiter to drive us to Berkeley Square. I wish to call upon her."

"And *I* wish you would not make yourself so damnably conspicuous, Caroline! He would have offered for you by now, if he was of a mind to do so," Bingley snapped, short-tempered as he had been since the end of November, and wholly out of patience with his sister and her matrimonial ambitions.

Not surprisingly, Miss Bingley's retort was just as sharp:

"That is a horrid thing to say! Ask Rossiter to turn about, will you? Or must I see to that myself?"

"No one in their right mind would attempt to turn about on Piccadilly," her brother countered, his eyes narrowed in vexation. "Oh, very well. Have it your way and make a fool of yourself if it pleases you," he muttered, then called out to their coachman, "Drive round, Rossiter, and take us to Berkeley Square."

⁂

"I beg your pardon? Miss Elizabeth stayed *here?*" Miss Bingley gasped when, after a fair number of carefully worded questions, her most notable achievement had been to extract from Miss Darcy the one piece of news which could neither pain nor shock anyone more than herself.

"She did," the young girl replied, supremely unconcerned about the enormity of such a revelation. "Sadly, it was only for one night. She was most eager to repair to Gracechurch Street and be reunited with her elder sister."

In its own way, the second shock was as bad as the first, and Miss Bingley flinched when her foolish brother lurched forward in his seat with a breathless, "*Miss Bennet* is in town?"

⋄⊙⊙⋄

"Charles, have you lost your mind?" Miss Bingley spluttered as she vainly struggled to keep pace with her brother, in great danger of losing her footing and gracelessly stumbling down the front steps of the Darcy residence. "It was monumentally discourteous of you to take your leave so soon, and in so abrupt a fashion. Why, you were positively brusque! Not to mention the gross incivility of quizzing our friend and pestering her for the tradesman's address. Miss Darcy was appalled and disconcerted," she reproached him, her eyes shooting daggers.

Miss Bingley was all the more incensed when her inconsiderate relation rolled his eyes and carelessly retorted, "You exaggerate, as always. But be that as it may. I shall call upon her later and apologise. I do not doubt that she will understand. For now, I have a more pressing matter to attend to."

"More pressing than not giving offence to my dearest friend?" Miss Bingley scowled.

"Your dearest friend, is she? You would not value her society half as much if she were not Darcy's sister," Bingley remorselessly scoffed. "But she is too kind to take umbrage, else by now she would have been vastly offended by your shameless and self-serving fawning. Enough of this!" he commanded with unprecedented firmness and raised his hand to silence his sister's protests. He left it to the footman to assist Miss Bingley into the carriage and stepped forth to instruct his coachman: "Drive us to Grosvenor Square at once. My sister wishes to be conveyed home," he unblinkingly delivered the manifest untruth. "Then take me with the utmost haste to Gracechurch Street. Once you reach St Benet's, you are to look across the road for a red brick house with a large, front-facing gable and stone ornaments around the windows."

Rossiter tugged at the brim of his hat and nodded.

"Very well, sir. Fear not, I'll find the place with ease, now that I know where I'm meant to be going. It's been a while since I drove Miss Bingley to pay a call there, but—"

"*What?* " his master hissed, eyes widened in outrage.

⋄⊙⊙⋄

Four miles east as the crow flies, Messrs Banks and Pruett were faced with troubles of their own. They were cooped up in the cramped lodgings of the latter, along with a pair of wildly impatient gentlemen who were utterly unable to sit still. In all fairness, their agitation was excusable, but even so, their pacing to and fro after the manner of caged beasts made the low-ceilinged room seem even smaller, and the wait all the more unbearable for it.

Their equanimity severely taxed, the four were counting the minutes until the scouts' return. But, to their disadvantage and mounting discomfort, nigh on five hours would elapse until one of the informants would finally burst in to impart between ragged breaths that their quarry had been tailed to a house on the outskirts of Greenwich.

•❧ ❧•

While Mr Pruett and his increasingly volatile companions were struggling to withstand the rigours of enforced proximity in a tight space, Mr Bingley's sanity was just as grievously threatened – although for very different reasons.

Violent anger, the likes of which he had never experienced before, had gripped him from the moment when he had discovered that his sister – *his own sister!* – had schemed against him and left him to pine for weeks on end within three miles of the woman he loved.

He had scarce restrained himself so as not to make a scene in his people's hearing when Caroline had added insult to deep injury by claiming that she had done so for his own good, since he was so patently unable to see his best interest and act accordingly.

Her cold-hearted impudence deserved the harshest treatment, so he had lost no time in telling her that she would rue the day when she had chosen to deceive him.

It was a modest mercy that the distance to Grosvenor Square had been covered swiftly and he was spared her reviled society, even though he had been forced to stoop to ungentlemanly conduct and threaten to bodily remove her from the conveyance, as well as unreservedly declare that she was a fool if she imagined that such paltry tactics would prevent him from calling in Gracechurch Street.

Yet the blind rage had not abated while his carriage had driven him apace to his destination. It had relentlessly swirled in the maelstrom of emotions that consumed him – anger; dark resentment; anxiety; barely contained anticipation. He could not govern any of them, nor had he tried to do so. Thus, the maelstrom had lost nothing of its power by the time the chaise had drawn to a halt and he had burst out, flinging the door open.

And now he sat on pins and needles in Mrs Gardiner's parlour, still reeling from the shock of Jane's turn of countenance when, for the first time in twenty weeks almost to the day, he had been once more admitted to her presence. Under his very eyes, she had turned frightfully pale and had verily swayed when she had stood to greet him.

The other ladies – her aunt and her sister – had slowly risen to their feet as well, but he could not spare more than a glance towards them. Likewise, it was for Jane's benefit and hers alone that he had haltingly begun to speak… to explain himself – and severely doubted that he had made much sense in the process.

He had tried to account for his sudden appearance in her aunt's parlour and, above all, for not calling a vast deal sooner. Yet, by the looks of it, very little was achieved by telling her that he had been kept wholly in the dark about his sister's call in Gracechurch Street, and even less by his stuttering return to the same topic – twice. If anything, he feared that he had only made himself ridiculous or, worse still, contemptible. As contemptible as one who strenuously sought to excuse himself by casting all the blame on others.

Whether or not Jane's eyes did hold contempt, Bingley could not tell, for she would not glance towards him when she finally spoke. Her reply came in a dull, flat voice, its lack of expression chilling:

"You need not concern yourself, sir. There was no expectation that you should call. Your choice to quit Netherfield without notice had already indicated that ours was but a passing acquaintance."

"Not so!" he fervently burst out. "I mean— I—" He drew a sharp intake of breath, and the sudden request was out of its own volition: "Miss Bennet, may I have a private word?"

For one hideous instant, he was convinced she would refuse.

But no, she nodded, hesitantly at first, and then once more with firm determination. Not towards him, though. Her wordless signs of acceptance were in response to wary looks from her relations.

Mrs Gardiner accepted the silent dismissal with good grace, civilly offering a transparent excuse as she rose from the sofa:

"In fact, I had to see to the children, in any case. Pray excuse me. I shall only be gone ten minutes," she said, smoothly turning the manufactured reason into a clear message for the visitor to heed: that there was a time limit to the privilege.

Jane's sister was substantially less amenable. Miss Elizabeth remained seated and had no qualms about openly questioning Jane's choice:

"Are you quite certain that this is what you wish?"

"Yes. It is. I... I will see you shortly," Jane said and, lips pursed, Miss Elizabeth stood. But the glance she cast him was overtly hostile as she followed her aunt out of the door.

Having scrambled to his feet to bow them out, Bingley slowly lowered himself to perch on the edge of his chair, his gaze fixed on the one who owned his heart.

She would not look his way. Her eyes had flicked towards him once, then moved to stare at something or other on the left side of the room, and Bingley shuffled in his seat, acutely aware that the few minutes of privacy were slipping away, so he had better make use of them and *speak*. Yet his throat closed up, and panic swelled at the terrifying thought that this was his one and only chance to do so, and his every hope of happiness hung on his ability to choose the right words – *now*. In less than ten minutes!

The strangest sort of dizziness – crippling and horribly inopportune – crept upon him, rendering him tongue-tied and lightheaded, and with every fibre of his being he fought through it. He fought to clear his head and speak at last.

"It was not a passing acquaintance," he choked out. "Not for me. Nor was I aiming to quit Netherfield – least of all without notice. My plan was to return in mere days!" Once he had made a beginning, it was a vague relief to find that the following words tumbled out with ease. "I would have returned by the week's end. As for this place, I would have called here as soon as I heard... *had* I heard—"

He broke off with a flinch. This would not do. There he was again, seeking to absolve himself by blaming his sister. Bingley bit his lip and frowned. His confounded sister did have a vast deal to answer for, but that was not the salient point. He must address the crux of the matter.

So he cleared his throat and began afresh:

"I stayed away from Hertfordshire – from *you* – because I felt I had to," he said with the utmost urgency, and her shoulders tensed at that, but she still kept her eyes averted.

He could only see one side of her face, most of it concealed by trailing ringlets. He wished he could search her countenance for some indication of her thoughts, but he was vouchsafed none. The only faint sign of emotion was a rosy tint that stole upon her cheek as he continued:

"It was made plain to me— No, *I* eventually understood that if I stayed, I would have imposed upon you. And you might have obliged me out of… kindness. I could not – would not have that," he declared, his voice growing almost fierce. But the aberrant inflection was instantly conquered by the earlier tones of painful hesitation. "Yet here I am today, come to appeal to it – to your kindness," he clarified with great diffidence, "and beg to be allowed some time to persuade you that my prime concern is *your* happiness, not mine."

His heart lurched when he heard her gasp, but it was too late to hold his peace. So he threw all caution to the wind, and went on to say the words that should have been spoken last November, and had burned in his soul ever since:

"A month is all I ask," Bingley said swiftly, his voice gathering strength as he repeated, "One month – that is all. I hope you do not think I ask too much. I can only assure you that I will respect your wishes. I would do anything to gain your affections – there is nothing I want more. But if, one month from now, you still want to have nothing to do with me, I shall obey. And I give you my word that I shall never trouble you again."

Unbearable anxiety welled up in him even before he had finished speaking, now that his deepest truth was brought into the open and the die was cast. He did not even dare speculate what her response might be; and when it came mere seconds later, it filled him with despair, for Jane hid her face in her hands and burst into loud, racking sobs, her shoulders heaving with shuddering breaths.

Before he knew it, Bingley was on one knee beside her.

"Forgive me," he brokenly pleaded, and stammered yet again, "I beg you to forgive me… I should not have— I… I spoke without thinking. Rash. Thoughtless. I was—"

He did not have the time to find adequate words of apology and self-reproach, nor could he regain his senses and keep his word, scramble to his feet and spare her his unwanted presence.

All of a sudden, Jane let her hands fall into her lap and stunned him with the brightest smile.

"No, not at all," she exclaimed with a forceful shake of her head. "Pray forgive *me*. That was… quite foolish. 'Tis just that I had lost every hope of… this. Of you. Of us. I am so happy. So very, very happy!" she avowed, and her shining eyes set his heart aglow.

"You… care for me? Already?" Bingley asked in a low, disbelieving whisper.

A strangled sound tore from his chest when Jane nodded, fresh tears welling in her eyes.

Bewildered joy and harrowing guilt washed over him, leaving him struggling to comprehend just how he had been favoured with his inconceivable good-fortune. Nor could he fathom how he could possibly atone for misreading her so completely – for failing her and leaving her for such a length of time. He could not speak – beg her pardon – enquire – strive to understand. Not yet. But worship and awed gratitude were above enquiry. So he abandoned himself to both. When Jane's hand came up to stroke his temple, he bowed his head till his brow touched her knee. And healing seconds ticked away, unheeded, while he remained thus – a blest penitent before his angel of mercy.

Neither one noticed the door opening by the smallest fraction. Nor were they brought down from their seventh heaven by an ill-timed creak when the door was discreetly closed again.

Chapter 12

"There, guv," the sentinel said in a whisper, even though the house he indicated was the best part of thirty yards away. "He went in there some two hours gone, an' didn't come out again."

Darcy nodded as he took a long, assessing look. The two-storeyed house – a smallish villa – stood back from the lane, half-concealed behind a screen of tall beeches and evergreen shrubs, which would greatly increase the chances of a stealthy advance towards it.

Without a word, he motioned the sentries towards the carriage, which had been left at a safe distance along the Greenwich road. The young lads – the oldest but fifteen or thereabouts – were asked to sit back and wait with the coachman, but Darcy had an assignment in mind for the two sturdy footmen he had brought along. The instructions were concise and swiftly delivered: the men were to locate the servants' entrance and restrain anyone who might attempt to sneak out once he and his cousin had made their presence known at the front door. Thus, there was nothing left to settle, so in short order the four of them were surreptitiously making their way towards the secluded house.

The screen of shrubs gave them an undeniable advantage in their endeavour to keep out of sight for as long as possible, but creeping through the dense undergrowth was no mean feat, and it would have been infinitely preferable if the evergreens were something other than spiny barberry and holly. Scaling the sharp-pointed railings that marked the boundary between the woodland and the overgrown garden was another challenge, but having overcome that final obstacle, it was child's play to dart across the last remaining yards and reach the pedimented entrance.

With the sparse and decisive gestures of a military commander, Fitzwilliam signalled the footmen to hasten around the corner and see to their appointed task, then cast a questioning glance at his relation, his head meaningfully tilted towards the door.

A nod served as sufficient confirmation that Darcy was ready, so Fitzwilliam lost no time in rapping forcefully upon the wood. He must have thought that he had knocked too briefly, or his temper got the better of him, for mere seconds later he rapped again with renewed vigour – and when that brought no joy either, he took to pounding the weather-worn oak with the side of his fist, until at long last his efforts were rewarded with the sound of a key rattling in the lock.

A proponent of self-restraint only on certain regimental duties – and not many of those, either – the colonel did not wait for the door to swing fully back. A glimpse of his reviled quarry was enough to spur him into action. He thrust his arm through the narrow opening and lunged at Wickham's throat.

The squeak of terror that came from somewhere to his right did nothing to temper his bloodlust. In fact, the colonel scarce heard it over the crash of the door slamming into the wall, once he had violently shoved it aside with his shoulder.

It was something else entirely that gave him pause, and also drew Darcy's notice as the latter made his own way into the entrance hall, rather less tempestuously than his cousin, but with as much thirst for vengeance. And what stopped them in their tracks was a youthful and very clear voice that rose with the full ring of authority:

"Now – now! Enough of that, if you please. I will not have you frightening poor Mrs Jenkinson. Look, you have already scared her out of her wits!"

Miss de Bourgh's commanding tone was more effective than the command itself. Darcy turned to stare at his younger cousin, as did Fitzwilliam, his right hand still gripping his foe's lapel. Quick to take advantage of the colonel's temporary distraction, Wickham tugged himself free, then proceeded to rearrange his coat and neckcloth with studied motions, a smug little smirk at the corner of his lips. But neither one of the newcomers could take note of the infuriating turn of his countenance, and thus become even more incensed. Both the colonel and Darcy stood verily gaping at their cousin, whom they had not heard raising her voice since her girlhood – if then.

If pressed to describe her habitual manner, considerate relations would have settled for *'subdued'*. A more fitting description would have been *'mousy'*.

Yet there was nothing mousy about Anne now, as she stood fixing them both with the sort of a quelling stare that a stern governess reserved for her charges when they were especially unruly.

She finally spared them the censorious look when she found herself obeyed, whereupon she spun round to face her companion, who had sought refuge behind her and still cowered in terror, darting anxious glances from one intruder to the other.

"There, Mrs Jenkinson. 'Tis just as I told you," Anne said with a touch of condescending impatience. "You have nothing to fear. My cousins have not come to drag you to the stocks. Their quarrel is with me and my factotum."

"Your factotum?" the men asked more or less at the same time, but while the visitors' exclamations were ones of surprise, Wickham's came with a chortle of amusement.

Anne shrugged as she replied to him first:

"I thought you would object to being regarded as my footman."

"What?" Darcy spluttered, which earned him a derisive little snort from Miss de Bourgh.

"What, indeed? Surely you did not think I meant to marry *him!*" She rolled her eyes and scoffed, "You might have given me credit for more taste than that. No offence, Wickham," Miss de Bourgh said in passing to the latter, very much as an afterthought.

"Some taken, but I shall not grumble," Wickham said with a thin smile and nonchalantly took a step back when Fitzwilliam darted a vicious glare his way, looking very much like he was of a mind to return to the business of throttling.

Perhaps the colonel might have given in to that impulse, had Darcy's retort not captured his attention:

"Anne, would you mind telling us what the deuce is going on?" he growled. "Whom *do* you mean to marry?"

Anne settled a level gaze on him and said simply, "Not you. But you must have gathered that already. I can only hope it did not come as a surprise. Nor as a disappointment."

Darcy saw no reason why he should be anything but honest.

"Unlike Lady Catherine, I had no expectations in that regard. But you are evading my question."

Anne pursed her lips and grudgingly nodded in acknowledgement, then said, "Well, you might as well come in, now that you are here. Close that door, Wickham," she instructed. "And Mrs Jenkinson, you may retire, if you prefer. Tell the maid to bring you a cup of tea in your chamber. And she might as well ask those two footmen into the kitchen for a glass of small beer. I expect they will appreciate the kindness, after their foray through the undergrowth. 'Tis the least I can do to thank them for their diverting antics. As for yours, how do you wish to find them rewarded?" she matter-of-factly asked her cousins. "I would suggest coffee, but I imagine you would prefer brandy or port."

The fact that Miss de Bourgh was offering refreshments as though her improvised living arrangements were on the par with any gentlewoman's lasting abode and well-run household made little impression on her impromptu visitors. Predictably, the colonel reacted to the mordant reference to their *'antics'*:

"You saw us coming?"

"Naturally," Anne shrugged. "The shrubs on the left side of the drive were swaying in the most suspicious manner on a windless day such as this. By the bye, Cousin, I pity you and your regiment if, as a rule, your advance upon the enemy is no stealthier than that. But I must confess, the best entertainment came from espying you and Darcy climbing over the railings. You are remarkably agile. And I must also commend you for your intrepidity."

"Hear-hear," Wickham chortled. "Most laudable indeed, seeing as the spiky ends are devilishly sharp. I venture to hope neither one of you suffered any mishaps," he said, but the impudent grin he cast them suggested he wished to hear the very opposite.

The man's crass hint to the potential damage to their *derrières* and breeches paled into insignificance beside his manifold sins, past and present, but that was no reason why Darcy and the colonel should refrain from glowering at him.

"Guard your tongue," Fitzwilliam spat through gritted teeth. "There is a lady present."

"Just so," Anne said. "But what I would most like to know just now is how you found me. And so soon, too. I imagined you would make an appearance eventually, but…"

Her voice trailed off, and her questioning glance darted from one of her cousins to the other. It was Darcy who took it upon himself to reply:

"You led us on a merry chase, I will tell you that," he reproached her. "Now pray be so good as to explain yourself."

Anne arched her brows and cast him a look of marked displeasure.

"Let me disabuse you of the notion that I must explain myself to *you*, if you still labour under that misconception in spite of what you have just said about your lack of expectations," she retorted. And then she turned around, half-heartedly motioning them to follow her into the sunlit parlour she must have quitted when they had been admitted into the house.

Silent and sullen, her cousins obeyed and strode into the room to watch her take a seat with the resigned and condescending air of a queen in exile. Anne gestured towards the empty chairs and the half-full decanters, but Darcy and the colonel declined – one of them with a shake of his head, the other with an ill-tempered mutter.

"As you wish. But pray refrain from pacing," Anne requested, just as the pair of them began to do precisely that. So they spun round, arms folded over their chests – two matching embodiments of barely restrained impatience, their severe gazes fixed on her.

It was only when Wickham sauntered in and casually leaned against the wall that Darcy and the colonel darted their eyes away from Miss de Bourgh to scowl at him. His impertinence in intruding upon a private conversation between cousins was infinitely galling – but, with no little effort, Darcy held his peace and forbore to demand that the rogue leave them and stay away from affairs that did not concern him. Unfortunately, Anne had made this *his* affair too, whatever had possessed her to involve him. So instead of barking orders to Wickham, he sternly addressed his younger cousin:

"Come now, Anne, out with it! 'Tis high time you told us what game it is that you are playing."

"'Tis not a game," she shot back. "I made plans to marry. And I will thank you both not to interfere."

"Marry *whom?*" Darcy asked again, just as irritably as the first time.

Supremely indifferent to his display of temper, Anne smoothed her skirts with slow deliberation, then glanced back up towards him.

"Nathaniel Maynard, if you must know."

The name meant little to Darcy. Seemingly, the same could be said of Fitzwilliam, for the colonel was quick to splutter, "Who?"

"My neighbour. Former neighbour, I should say. Lord Metcalfe's younger brother. His lordship's family name is Maynard," she informed them. And both of them deemed her explanation insufficient.

"Is that so? Lord Metcalfe never speaks of him," Fitzwilliam observed with manifest suspicion – a sentiment which Darcy shared.

He lost no time in expressing it.

"What are the boy's prospects?" he asked. "For all we know, he may be after your fortune."

Across the room, Wickham gave a loud snort at that, but Anne's derisive reply served to distract her cousins from the man's impertinent reaction.

"I take objection to the implication that I would not have attracted his notice otherwise," she testily said to Darcy, then emphasised with blatant sarcasm, "The *boy* is eleven months your senior. You may not have seen him since he left his home to enlist as a midshipman, but that was a long time ago. As for his prospects, they are strongly related to Lord Metcalfe's disinclination to speak of him in company these days." She did not wait for her cousins to press her for details and airily continued, "He had offended his brother's sensibilities by exchanging a distinguished career in the Navy for the captaincy of a merchantman. One might say that he jumped ship," she chuckled, visibly pleased with her pun, then sobered. "I expect I had something to do with that contentious decision. The relatively less dangerous profession must have had its merits once we became attached. But as to the appeal of my material possessions, you may be assured that he is no pauper. A first lieutenant's share of prize money for many a year has made quite a difference to his coffers. So I am as convinced as I can be that he is not marrying me for my fortune. Not to mention that his current choice of employment serves him just as well, if not better. Although everything would have been a vast deal easier if he were a first mate rather than a captain."

"How so?" Fitzwilliam asked.

Anne rolled her eyes and peevishly elaborated, "Because he could have asked his captain to marry us! All I would have had to do was gain permission to board his ship and wait until we sailed into open waters."

"The marriage would not have been valid," Fitzwilliam snapped in response, and Darcy inwardly agreed.

Anne's brow creased in a measure of doubt.

"Would it not?"

"No," Fitzwilliam declared. "And if your Mr Maynard claimed otherwise, then he was aiming to deceive you."

"*My Mr Maynard,*" Anne mimicked, "claimed nothing of the sort. And since he is *Captain* Maynard and thus patently unable to perform the rites of his own marriage at sea, your point is moot. Besides, it goes against Darcy's. He suspects Nathaniel of marrying me for my dowry and possessions. You are warning me against an invalid marriage. So I suggest the pair of you reconcile your views. Captain Maynard cannot be both a fortune hunter *and* a scheming seducer. So what is he to be?" she challenged them, glancing from one to the other.

"You may choose to amuse yourself at our expense, but this is no laughing matter," Darcy sensibly observed as he chose to abandon his belligerent pose behind the sofa.

He let his arms drop and finally advanced to take a seat across from her. A few seconds later, their intemperate cousin grumbled under his breath and followed suit. It was a good choice, for their change of posture diffused some of the almost palpable tension in the room. Miss de Bourgh crossed her hands on her lap and quietly conceded, "I daresay you are not wrong there…"

"Then will you not see sense and return to Rosings?" Darcy urged.

He should have known better. The question turned out to be both ill-chosen and ill-timed. Anne's incipiently compliant air vanished.

"I most certainly *shall not!*"

"Then we find ourselves at loggerheads," Darcy retorted, still very far from tactful. "I trust you do not expect me and Fitzwilliam to sit back and let you elope with some stranger!"

"And *I* trust that the pair of you will not conspire to spirit me to Rosings gagged and bound!" Anne shot back, then drew a deep breath, as though to calm herself. She must have had some success in that regard, for her voice was even when she spoke again. "Nathaniel is no stranger to *me*. We grew up together," she pointed out, but her cousins would have no truck with it.

Fitzwilliam gave a gesture of impatience. As for Darcy, he voiced the thoughts of both:

"That is as may be, but you have not seen him in an age!"

"He has written to me nearly every month for the past five years, ever since his last long stay in the country, when we became attached," Anne countered. "Oh, yes – he has written, and so have I," she revealed with unconcealed defiance. "Through his old nanny. Whom I could visit with impunity in her little cottage on Lord Metcalfe's estate – and Mamma none the wiser," Anne added with great satisfaction, then chortled. "Even though Mrs Jenkinson dutifully informed her each time I chose to stop there on our outings, Mamma retained the impression that my calls on Nanny Gilbert were paid out of the goodness of my heart. The censure I attracted from her on that score was merely for exerting myself overmuch on account of other people's former servants," she finished with a little grin.

Despite himself, Fitzwilliam returned it.

"I am staggered to hear that Mrs Jenkinson was able to keep your secret," he remarked. "I would have thought that deceit was utterly beyond her."

"Heavens, Cousin!" Anne exclaimed. "Of course she was not in the know. She was left to wait for me in the phaeton while I spoke to Nanny Gilbert and exchanged letters. I did not disclose anything to Mrs Jenkinson. Have you not seen her quivering like a jelly before the pair of you? Mamma would have had everything out of her in a matter of moments, were I foolish enough to trust my companion with my secrets. I did not even trust my lady's maid with anything but the delivery of a few other letters. Certainly not the correspondence between myself and Captain Maynard!" she said with a grimace, as if the notion was preposterous, then shrugged. "Teague is loyal enough, but I wanted her to be able to deny any knowledge of my plans with the full conviction of the innocent when questioned – which I imagined she would be, sooner or later. I gather from Richard's far-from-inscrutable countenance that she *had* been questioned. Or, to put it plainly, that Mamma had got to her. So I will not scruple to observe that my choice to conceal most of my schemes from Teague shows some greatness of mind, even if I say so myself," Anne added, as disposed as Lady Catherine to crow about her own achievements, which was no wonder – she must have learned all there was to know about self-gratulatory smugness at her mother's knee. "So there we have it," Anne resumed. "My secrets were well-guarded – but, to my way of thinking, they were guarded for long enough. Captain Maynard and I had planned to wed at the end of next year, when he is to settle back in England, but I do not wish to wait another eighteen months. Not if I can help it. And I must say, in that respect Mr Collins' encounter with Wickham was a godsend. All of a sudden there was someone I could commission to make arrangements for Nathaniel and I to marry in the short time between one voyage and the next. Not to mention the appeal of simply going off to wed, instead of enduring Mamma's displeasure at the match. As it turned out, it was easy work to involve Wickham and have him lease this house in my name, then join forces with Nathaniel's attorney to set the wheels in motion—"

"Why on earth would you trust *Wickham*, of all people?" Darcy intervened, casting a baleful glare towards the man he loathed. "You could have taken me or Richard into your confidence, instead of one who was likely to betray you!"

"Now, see here, Darcy, you have always thought the very worst of me," Wickham said, shaking his head in a show of injured dignity. "Must you constantly suspect me of nefarious intentions? That is precisely why it never crossed your mind that I might genuinely care for your sister."

Anne's brow creased into a puzzled frown.

"What has Georgiana to do with this?"

"Nothing whatsoever," Darcy told her with firm emphasis, then scoffed over his shoulder: "Parade your sheep's clothing to others. I was not born yesterday. Genuine! You make me laugh. There is nothing genuine about you. Defrauding and deceit form your life's purpose. And the only one you care for is yourself."

Wickham tutted.

"That is quite an indictment. Defrauding and deceit, eh? May I point out that I did not go tattling to your aunt for personal gain, nor made away with Miss de Bourgh's... er... shall we say, tactical reserves?"

"How very noble of you to hold back from betrayal and thievery for once," Darcy sneered. "A true model of decency and honour."

Wickham made a face and shrugged.

It was Miss de Bourgh who spoke:

"I was not born yesterday either, Cousin," she said to Darcy in mild reproof. "I had no intention to present Wickham with an irresistible temptation. The necessary funds were made available to him in dribs and drabs, and he is yet to be fully recompensed for his assistance. And, to be fair, he did serve me well. Better than others might have. Unlike Wickham, my mother's footmen look to *her*, not me, for their monetary comforts. As for Captain Maynard's attorney, he is too old for so much excitement. Mr Sutcliffe could apply for the marriage licence on Nathaniel's behalf, see to the bond and arrange all the legal minutiae, but he is in no fit state to undertake nerve-racking journeys, nor stand guard and keep me and Mrs Jenkinson safe until Nathaniel can supplant him. Well, not long now," she said with a sigh of satisfaction. "He put into port last—" But then she caught herself and amended, "He made good time and his ship docked when it was expected. He received my note informing him of what has been arranged, and sent word to say that he would join me hither as soon as possible. And when he arrives, we shall marry. One of you may give me away, if you wish – but have the goodness to not seek to thwart me. I shall not suffer you to do so," she declared, her tone and manner uncannily like her mother's. "This is my choice, and I am of age. There is nothing else to be said about it."

The last half-hour should have given her cousins sufficient indication of the assertive side of her, much as it had been concealed from them until that day. Even so, it caught them by surprise and rendered them speechless. It was Darcy who gathered his wits first:

"And then what?" he challenged his headstrong cousin. "What purpose does it serve, your haste? Just to style yourself as Mrs Maynard and wait for his return here or in some other questionable location, instead of the safety and comfort of Rosings? Or are you aiming to go home and present your mother with the *fait accompli?*"

"I have no intention whatsoever to return to Rosings. Heavens, no!" Anne forcefully declared with a shudder. "I will board Nathaniel's ship and join him on his final voyage."

"You are *not* in earnest!" the colonel exclaimed, just as Darcy gave a less articulate expression of disbelief and horror. "You cannot expose yourself in this fashion!" Fitzwilliam insisted. "What of your precarious health?"

Anne chuckled.

"A ruse, Cousin. Nothing but a ruse. I am in excellent health, I thank you."

"A *ruse?*" Darcy found his voice at last, then spluttered, "For what purpose?"

"To delay Mamma in her foolish endeavour to forge our union, of course," Anne retorted with the air of one stating the obvious, then reproachfully added, "You might have noticed I was not quite so lethargic until Mamma became increasingly vocal on that subject."

"That is—" Darcy burst out, then stopped short. With a touch of guilt, he grudgingly allowed that he *should* have noticed the timing of the alteration. Besides, the words that had just sprung to mind were in no way suited for polite society and definitely not fit for Anne's ears, so he forced himself to rephrase: "Of all the convoluted notions! Why did you not tell her that you had no taste for such an arrangement? Or at least tell *me?*"

"Why did *you* not tell her? Nor speak to me about putting it to rest?" Anne shot back. "You humoured Mamma in this treasured scheme of hers for years. What reason had I to take you into my confidence? For all I knew, you might have been pleased to add Rosings to your holdings and my dowry to Pemberley's coffers."

Before Darcy could even begin to defend himself against the accusation, Anne cast him a saucy look and slyly said, "Admittedly, I was more than a little reassured of late, once I noticed that your interest veered in a different direction. But by then Wickham and I had everything settled. Speaking of which, what is your success with Miss Bennet?"

Across the room, Wickham gave a bark of laughter.

"How riveting," he drawled. "That would be Miss *Elizabeth* Bennet, I take it?" A knowing grin accompanied his speculation, and the grin grew wider as he answered his own question. "Indeed, who else? Last I checked, the other Bennet girls were safely tucked away at home, not visiting at Hunsford. And if I am not mistaken, you have had an eye for her as far back as our interesting encounter on the main street in Meryton," he went on to push his luck.

Darcy lost no time in curbing his impertinence.

"You would do well to hold your tongue," he growled, "unless you are uncommonly keen to lose some teeth."

Anne darted her eyes heavenward.

"Really, Darcy! What sort of talk is that? You had much better tell me, have you got off your high horse and proposed to the girl or not?"

"That is no one's concern but mine," Darcy sternly retorted, then scowled. He would be damned before he regaled Wickham with any hint that the rogue had been instrumental in interrupting his proposal and spoiling his plans! Although, on reflection, thank goodness for dodged bullets. Elizabeth did say that she would have refused him then…

"Very well," Anne sniffed, rather offended. "In that case, I shall be quick to point out that the same can be said of my own matrimonial intentions. And on that note, pray oblige me and pretend you have not found me. To put it plainly, I would much rather you did not tell Mamma."

"What, you would sail away into the sunset and leave the poor old battleaxe in the dark?" Fitzwilliam exclaimed, which earned him a look of severe reproach from Darcy on account of his unguarded use of the irreverent sobriquet in Wickham's presence.

It was especially infuriating to hear the latter chuckle. Yet that might have been in response to the scoundrel's own reflections, for Wickham observed, "I daresay her ladyship would be pleasantly surprised – and doubtlessly relieved – to learn that the groom is Captain Maynard, not me. The lesser of two evils, and all that," he chortled.

A diverted little smile tugged at Anne's lips.

"I always knew you had your uses," she airily retorted.

The colonel tutted in vexation and Darcy gave an irritable huff, then hastened to ask, "When is the wedding? Have you and Maynard agreed upon a date?"

Anne eyed him with profound suspicion.

"Why should you wish to know?"

"I never thought I would say this, but Wickham has just made a valid point," he replied with no little reluctance, but his air grew earnest as he proceeded to elaborate. "The captain *is* the lesser of two evils. Perhaps you should give your mother the chance to reconcile herself to that and attend the wedding. I do believe that, in the end, both you and she would be happier for it."

Anne made to speak, and the turn of her countenance clearly showed she was about to protest, so Darcy added, "Fear not, I was not aiming to bring a blazing row upon your doorstep on your wedding day. Nor too long in advance, for that matter. Fitzwilliam and I could claim we found you on the day before, and bring her here then. Hopefully, by that time Maynard will be at hand to support you. There, will that do?"

Anne made no answer, so her other cousin felt compelled to press her:

"You and your mother should not part in anger," he said in a tone of gentle persuasion. "And Darcy's suggestion seems to be just the thing. Come, Anne, what say you?"

For some time, Miss de Bourgh persisted in her sullen silence. "The wedding is on Wednesday," she finally said.

⁓⊛⊚⊛⁓

Half an hour later, Colonel Fitzwilliam and Darcy were returning to the carriage — sauntering along the drive this time, rather than fighting their way through the undergrowth — but not before ensuring that Wickham's role as Miss de Bourgh's factotum was at an end, and insisting that she send him packing.

Neither one of her cousins would countenance anything else. Anne might not wish to come and stay with family, but there was no reason why she should still rely on Wickham, when Darcy's own footmen could serve and protect her.

It went sorely against the grain to see Anne sign a note to her banker, whereby a princely sum was to be paid to the bearer on demand. It was just as galling to see Wickham take it with a bow, a simpering smile and a suave, "I thank you, Ma'am. I am most exceedingly obliged."

They could have prevented that, of course. Between them, the colonel, Darcy and his footmen could have easily ensured that Wickham left the house empty-handed and with a flea in his ear. But it was Anne's affair, not theirs, and it had been her choice to strike that particular bargain. Moreover, such an interference would do more harm than good. Deprived of his payment for services rendered, Wickham was sure to become vindictive and cause all manner of mischief.

Ironically, he — who had severely alarmed three households — had already received his payment, but those enlisted to obstruct him had not. So while Pruett's people were conveyed to the East End, they were told to go and inform their master — and Banks as well — that the quest had been successful, and the colonel would personally ensure that loyalty, stealth and diligence would be promptly rewarded.

Once the young fellows vanished, Darcy leaned back in his seat with a quiet sigh of satisfaction. It was over, thank goodness. Anne was found, she was safe, her current circumstances and future plans caused far less concern, and their previous fears were shown to be unfounded. So the worrisome affair would be resolved in two days' time — and, more to the point, it no longer was so worrisome. Which, as far as he was concerned, could only mean one thing: after many a troubled hour, he had every right to seek the antidote.

So he called out to his coachman:

"Drive on to Gracechurch Street."

✦

"Sorry, sir, the family's from home," the young maid said, nervously tugging at the sides of her apron, and Darcy drew a deep breath in frustration at finding his best hope of the day dashed by malicious gods and one fidgeting domestic.

"I see," he muttered, hard-pressed to conceal his disappointment. "Will Mrs Gardiner and her nieces return soon from their outing?"

But the girl shook her head and carelessly delivered yet another blow:

"Oh, no, sir, they ain't gone on an outing. The Mistress, the Miss Bennets and the little'uns set off for Longbourn. They shan't be back for days."

"Longbourn!" Darcy exclaimed. "They had not received bad tidings, I hope?" he asked swiftly, far too perturbed by the intelligence to give much thought to the impropriety of pressing the maidservant for private information about the family she served.

He could not know that the girl would have never been allowed to answer the door under normal circumstances. Not just because that was the footman's prerogative, had he been at home, but because she was young and green, a very recent addition to the household, and had yet to learn the ways of a good servant – not least, to hold her tongue.

That commendable ability still eluded her.

So the young maid beamed, "Nay, sir. They are the ones with tidings to impart. Grand ones, too. The very best: an upcoming wedding!"

Chapter 13

An upcoming wedding!

For one stunning moment, Darcy thought that the girl spoke of his – and he could not tell if the overriding sentiment was delight at Elizabeth's choice to finally bring everything into the open, or mild alarm at Mr Bennet learning of his intentions in his absence rather than from him, as both custom and common civility dictated.

But then, the uncommonly talkative maidservant went on to clarify the matter: the expected wedding was Miss Bennet's, not Elizabeth's. A mightily agitated gentleman had come to call earlier that morning and proposed.

'Bingley? Naturally, who else?' Darcy inwardly chided himself.

It must have been Bingley.

How that had come to pass, he could not fathom, but if he harboured any doubts whatever as to the identity of Miss Bennet's impetuous suitor, all were put to rest once he had conveyed Fitzwilliam to Malvern House and returned home.

He had barely had the chance to read Mrs Gardiner's note – delivered in his absence to announce, but not explain, their sudden departure – then speak to Georgiana, share his tidings and hear the account of her own eventful day, when Miss Bingley was announced, which rather made him suspect that she kept his house under surveillance.

"Oh, Mr Darcy! You are here at last," she cried, thus reinforcing his suspicion. "I hope you will not take it amiss if I came as soon as I could. I had to come. And I bring the worst tidings. This morning, my misguided brother proposed to that— Ahem! To Jane Bennet. And was accepted! I am at my wits' end, sir, and in dire need of your assistance."

'And what, pray tell, am I to do on the occasion?' was Darcy's first thought, but that would have been an ungentlemanly question.

The gentlemanly thing to do was urge the uninvited visitor to sit, rest, and have a care for herself. A cup of tea, perhaps? A cup of tea might make her feel a little better.

"I thank you, sir, but no amount of tea can fix this," Miss Bingley whined. "He cannot take back his proposal now. Not even if he were of a mind to do so – and it pains me dreadfully to say that he is not. He is beside himself with joy, the foolish, *foolish* man! Oh, how I wish he were not told that the simpering creature was in town!" she cried, wringing her hands, but the distraught gesture was very far from eliciting Darcy's compassion, for she coupled it with a sidelong glance towards his sister – and that covert look was blatantly reproachful.

Darcy's eyes narrowed. The infernal woman had the audacity to blame Georgiana? His fingers curled in a tight grip around the back of the chair he had pulled for the unwelcome caller. Perhaps Miss Bingley's troubles might have been avoided, had she kept to Hurst's house and her own sister's drawing room instead of tracking him like a bloodhound and forcing herself upon his notice at every opportunity. Had Bingley called alone in search of him, the visit would have lasted a mere quarter of an hour, and nothing but a few civilities would have been exchanged with Georgiana.

He cast his sister a reassuring glance and saw her fidgeting in discomfort, which gave him all the more reason to settle a stern look upon the other.

"You have said quite enough, madam. I perfectly comprehend your feelings. But this is out of your hands now. Your brother has made his choice and—"

"Made his choice!" Miss Bingley echoed his words in a tone of outraged disagreement. "He has not made his choice, sir. He has been lured into it! By that minx, who went so far as to claim she had been attached to him from the earliest days of their acquaintance and had long wished for his addresses!"

To put it mildly, *that* was unexpected.

"She said so?" Darcy asked, dumbfounded.

"Of course she did!" Miss Bingley snapped. "And only one as upright as you would find it surprising. The artful girl would say anything to ensnare him. After all, he is the most advantageous connection that family of hers could hope for!"

"Oh, I believe they could do a little better," Darcy retorted, his ill humour vaguely tempered by the diverted little twitch of Georgiana's lips and the approving glance she cast him. But even that could not do away with the unease brought by Miss Bingley's revelations. So, Jane Bennet had long held Bingley in her affections?

"They could? What do you mean, sir? Pray be so kind as to explain your meaning," the irksome visitor pressed him, and Darcy gave a swift, impatient gesture, as if he were flicking at some buzzing fly.

"No matter," he said tersely.

Miss Bingley had some reply to make, of course – the woman was inordinately keen to demonstrate that she could not hold her tongue if her life depended on it – but Darcy would not heed her, too caught up in his own reflections.

If Miss Bennet had disclosed that she had long been attached to his friend, then it must be true. Whatever she might be, she was not artful. An artful woman would have shown *more* interest and affection than she felt. It was the decorous and reserved young lady who guarded herself from the impertinent curiosity of busybodies by not parading her innermost feelings. Seemingly, Jane Bennet did not perform to strangers either...

Darcy released a forceful huff. It had become increasingly obvious of late that his claim to a strong understanding was woefully unfounded. An intelligent and astute man would not have missed so many salient points, nor so many telling signs!

This was a minor epiphany in comparison to the one experienced the previous evening – but an epiphany nevertheless: Jane Bennet was as reserved as he, and as unwilling to expose her private concerns to the scrutiny of others. What he had regarded as her placid indifference to Bingley's attentions had only been a means of protecting her good name and her heart!

He flinched as a most unwelcome realisation struck: it was no wonder that Elizabeth should regard him with a mistrustful – nay, jaundiced – eye, if she held him responsible for ruining the happiness of her most beloved sister. Frankly, he should count it a miracle that she still gave him the time of day!

And yet he had been enough of an arrogant fool as to take offence at her reluctance to accept his hand in marriage, when in fact he should have admired her all the more for her principled way of thinking –

for her lack of guile and her disdain for self-aggrandisement at any cost – long before learning that she had ample reason to hold back.

As for Jane Bennet, she truly must be as angelic as Bingley thought her, if she was willing to welcome him to Gracechurch Street and talk to him as though nothing had happened, instead of persuading her sister to shun him and her aunt to show him the door.

But goodness knows what Elizabeth had made of the day's events. Worse still, he could easily imagine what her response would be, should his friend give a full account of their lengthy debates last autumn.

'The deuce!'

Were it not for Anne's wedding, which he really should attend, and the awkward affair of effecting a reconciliation between her and her mother, he would leave town in a trice and be at Netherfield by nightfall.

Ah, but would he be welcome?

He grimaced. That was decidedly unlikely. If he were in Bingley's shoes, he would not be quick to forgive. Perhaps an express was in order – a letter of congratulations and sincere apologies. Bingley was a kindly, good-natured fellow, and might be willing to pardon presumption and misjudgement. The heartache caused to his beloved was another matter. Whether or not he would find it in him to forgive that weightier transgression remained to be seen. Once more, Darcy was compelled to own that he would not have – and it was unnerving to be so heavily reliant on the hope that, unlike him, Bingley was not resentful.

Darcy squared his shoulders. Aye, he must write to his friend at once. It was most unfortunate that he could not write to Elizabeth as well, nor convey anything of consequence to her by means of a reply to Mrs Gardiner's note. The matter would have to be addressed face to face – and soon! Right after Anne's wedding.

The current priority was a well-crafted letter to his friend – as soon as he succeeded in ridding himself of Bingley's sister, who had been rambling on about her misfortunes for some time, pressed him thrice to speak, and now clung to the edge of her seat, the very picture of unconcealed impatience.

"There is nothing I can say," Darcy finally addressed her, "or rather, nothing that you would like to hear. As you have just pointed out, your brother does not wish to be released from his engagement. And even if he did, there is no honourable way to bring it to an end."

"Then you must help me find a dishonourable one!" Miss Bingley shot back.

"I *beg* your pardon?"

To Darcy's surprise, his reprimand was almost instantly followed by his sister's:

"Miss Bingley, you cannot possibly suggest that my brother would involve himself in anything dishonourable! What would you have him do? Arrange to have your brother kidnapped – or Miss Bennet – or both? And then keep them apart, one in Pemberley's dungeons and the other imprisoned in some ruined tower, after the manner of a Gothic novel?"

For all the vexations of the day, a chuckle threatened to burst free, and Darcy barely managed to suppress it. It was greatly reassuring to see that Georgiana's newly found aplomb had not vanished once she had learned that Anne had not, in fact, been deceived by Wickham. But who would have thought that his shy sister would go as far as to chide their brash acquaintance, and bring veiled sarcasm into play as she did so?

Not Miss Bingley, by the sound of it. The lady answered as though Georgiana's question had been in earnest:

"Goodness, no, nothing quite so drastic. Dungeons indeed! I did not even know that Pemberley *had* dungeons. You must tell me more about them later," she carelessly dismissed both the subject and the speaker, then turned towards Darcy. "But as to my brother, sir, perhaps you could persuade him of the merits of a long engagement. A very long engagement. And then, once we have gained time, I hope we can settle upon acceptable ways to fulfil our purpose."

"That purpose is not mine—" Darcy declared, only to be forcefully interrupted.

"How can you say so? Why, last November you were adamant—"

"That is immaterial. I was unaware of Miss Bennet's sentiments at the time," Darcy cut her off, lest she shame him before his sister with a full disclosure of how he had failed his friend or, worse still, with a recitation of his haughty pronouncements on Elizabeth's family.

"Her sentiments!" the other scoffed. "Her avowals are nothing but a cunning ploy in order to secure him!"

"Oh, come now, Miss Bingley," Darcy exclaimed, no longer able to refrain from checking her. "You know as well as I do that Miss Bennet has not a cunning bone in her body. I will own that, to my discredit,

I mistook her reserve for indifference. But no one who is acquainted with the lady can accuse her of duplicity."

"I never thought I would see the day when you would champion a Bennet," Miss Bingley acidly replied, and it took Darcy all the restraint he still possessed not to retort that, God willing, before long she would also see the day when he married one.

The momentary satisfaction notwithstanding, it would have been exceedingly unwise. Having her disclose his wishes to their mutual acquaintances would have been even worse than giving Tyndall the opportunity to do so. At least he would have spread the news without the vitriol. Miss Bingley would have certainly added a thorough disparagement of Elizabeth and her connections – so Darcy was grimly glad of his forbearance.

Yet there was every reason to believe that it would not last long. The woman was insupportable. And since he was not of a mind to quit the room and leave Georgiana to contend with her, any moment now he would resort to the ultimate incivility of suggesting to Miss Bingley that it was time she took her leave.

He did not have the opportunity to find out whether or not he would have given in to that compelling impulse. A fraction of a second later, Simon came in to announce Lady Catherine.

❦

"Darcy, I hope you can tell me more than—" her ladyship began as she swept into the room, but she broke off and thinned her lips into a grimace when she laid eyes on Miss Bingley. "Oh. You have visitors. I see," she observed, without taking the trouble to conceal her displeasure.

For his part, Darcy was just as disinclined to obey the dictates of civil intercourse, but obey them he did. He stood, drew a chair for his aunt and spoke, his voice brittle:

"Lady Catherine, you may remember Miss Bingley."

As she lowered herself into the seat, his aunt deigned to acknowledge the prior acquaintance with the lady by means of a condescending nod, but said nothing further. It was the considerably younger interloper who offered a vocal greeting – and an unctuous one at that – along with the hope that her ladyship was well.

"No, I am not," came Lady Catherine's brusque reply. "On that note, Georgiana, oblige me and escort your guest to the music room. I wish to speak to Darcy," she demanded with no effort at civility.

The desire to shield his sister from the unpleasant *tête-à-tête* in nowise abated, Darcy hastened to speak up:

"There is no cause for that," he said, which earned him a wide smile from Miss Bingley – a sure sign that she had mistaken his intervention for reluctance to relinquish her society. He suppressed a snort and resumed, safe in the knowledge that the agreement with Anne had already been explained to Georgiana, so his sister would not judge him for dispensing falsehoods. "I have no tidings to impart, Ma'am. I imagine Fitzwilliam already said so."

"He did," Lady Catherine tersely conceded. "But I was hoping you would tell me more. Your cousin had merely muttered something about a false trail, then dashed out again. To his club, I expect, or goodness knows where else. And there was I thinking that, at a time like this, one would make an effort to be with family," her ladyship scoffed, casting a venomous glance towards Miss Bingley, who flinched at the glare.

Yet, true to form, she was quick to rally:

"What false trail? May I know what it is that you are seeking?" she asked, her questioning look eagerly darting between Darcy and his aunt.

Predictably, it was Lady Catherine who answered.

"You *may not!*" she enunciated. "'Tis none of your affair. This is a family matter. And so it should remain," Lady Catherine viciously concluded, glowering at her nephew as though wordlessly demanding confirmation that he had not shared their troubles with Miss Bingley.

Darcy stared meaningfully back and retorted firmly, "Indeed, Ma'am. I would not have it otherwise."

"Hmph!" was Lady Catherine's sole reply as she leaned away, barely mollified.

This time, Miss Bingley had some difficulty in regaining her composure.

"I beg your pardon, Ma'am. I was not seeking to intrude," she faltered. "Merely to offer my assistance."

"You?" Lady Catherine sniffed. "And how do you propose to assist me, Miss Bickley?"

"Bingley, Ma'am," the other pointed out with a rather offended sniff of her own.

"Pardon?"

"My name. It is Bingley, not Bickley," she crisply clarified.

"I stand corrected," Lady Catherine replied with careless impatience, and made no attempt at an apology. "But while on the subject of assistance, Nephew, I need one of your footmen to go and remind Miss Elizabeth Bennet that I brought her to town to attend *me*, not visit her family. Your uncle's people would not know where she is staying. As you are well aware, I am not one for complaining, nor for making unreasonable requests," she continued, and her preposterous assertion served to briefly temper Darcy's indignation at his aunt's demand and the supercilious tone of voice she uniformly employed when speaking of Elizabeth. "So I suffered her to go and do as she pleased, since it did not affect me. But now I find it does," her ladyship morosely declared. "I have a desire for invigorating company, yet your cousins seem to have an inordinate number of engagements that take them all over town. So pray oblige me and have Miss Bennet know that I request her society at Malvern House. Outspoken as that girl might be, at least she is not dull."

Before Darcy could have his say, Miss Bingley rushed to speak, her satisfaction barely concealed under a coy smile:

"From what I hear, Miss Eliza Bennet left town this morning. I am horrified to learn that she had not even troubled herself to notify you." She shook her head. "Such lack of manners! Deplorable, but not in the least surprising. Still," she resumed brightly, "I would be honoured to keep you company in her stead, Ma'am. My friends do say that I am far from dull – and I assure you, I am never outspoken."

"Are you not? What of brash? Or forward? Do your friends have anything to say of that?" Lady Catherine snapped, and for once, her short temper and objectionable conduct served to endear her to Darcy more than he would have thought possible mere moments prior. "Some words of advice, young lady: wait to be asked. Besides, you will do well to remember that the boastful are highly aggravating."

So they were, Darcy inwardly agreed, diverted and mystified in equal measure by his aunt's inability to see that the pot was calling the kettle black. Nevertheless, it was his duty as a host not to allow a visitor to be taken to task under his roof – even if that visitor was Miss Bingley.

So he intervened:

"Aunt, that is beyond the pale. Kindly refrain from—"

He was not allowed to finish. And it was not Lady Catherine's second "Hmph!" – much louder than the first – that made him hold his peace, but Miss Bingley's voice, which somehow contrived to evince the most uncommon admixture of gratification and resentment:

"I thank you, Mr Darcy. You are exceedingly thoughtful, as always. But rest easy, I am well. Just saddened that my offer was misconstrued. Anyway, I should go now, and return at a more auspicious time. But until we meet again, pray give some thought to my request. Anything you could do to help would be vastly appreciated."

And with that, she rose to her feet, bid her adieus and left them. Yet, as far as Lady Catherine was concerned, that was not the end of the matter. No sooner had Darcy and Georgiana returned from seeing Miss Bingley out than her ladyship had something to say to her nephew:

"I trust she is not the reason why you have been so reluctant to do your duty by my daughter," she said, her face pinched, and her manner leaving him in no misapprehension of her sentiments. "Pray tell me you have not set Anne aside for the sake of a tradesman's granddaughter. Her fortune, such as it is, was made in the cotton mills of the north!" Lady Catherine spat, as though she could not possibly imagine anything more reprehensible. "I have long thought that your friendship with her brother was ill-judged. But it does not bear thinking that the likes of her should walk in my sister's footsteps."

"That was never my intention," Darcy said crisply, but it was not enough.

"What does she want of you, then? What was that request she spoke of?" Lady Catherine demanded to know, her eyes narrowed in suspicion.

Darcy shrugged.

"Nothing of consequence. A favour for her brother."

"Hmph!" Lady Catherine said, for the third time.

Then she grudgingly accepted Georgiana's offer of a cup of tea, while Darcy took a seat and steeled himself for counting the minutes until their aunt would take her leave, and he would finally be able to retire to his study and pen the most difficult letter he had ever had to write.

Chapter 14

'If this is how you feel, then you are welcome, and I should be glad to once more call you my friend,' Bingley had generously written in response to the letter in which Darcy had endeavoured to convey his congratulations and a solemn apology for his misjudgement, along with the wish to express the same face to face.

With the greatest care, he had also worded the request that his friend keep his errors from the future Mrs Bingley and her family, so that he would not forfeit their goodwill and the chance to earn their good opinion. But he had not mentioned his other, ardent wishes, and had written nothing of Elizabeth. He could not bring himself to reveal such private matters in a letter – and besides, any hint to ulterior motives would have detracted from his apology and made it sound less sincere than it was.

Thus, Darcy could not nurture any real hope of discovering Elizabeth's name ensconced among Bingley's scribbles, but he had eagerly scanned the barely legible lines for tidings of her all the same, and had been severely disappointed to find none. He had folded the letter and set it aside, only to pick it up again for a second perusal, which had of course brought no joy either. It had merely left him wishing he had penned an innocuous enquiry – *'How are Miss Bennet's relations keeping?'* or something in that vein – which might have prompted Bingley into offering some details. Not that he would have been satisfied with trifling commonplaces. What he needed most was to see his obligations come to an end, setting him free to avail himself of his friend's undeservedly kind invitation.

And that was tantalisingly in sight. Bingley's prompt reply had arrived while he had been on his way to Greenwich along with his cousin and their aunt, on the appointed mission to effect a reconciliation between Anne and her mother.

Being party to their conversation – or, by far the better option, an invisible witness to it – would have doubtlessly been illuminating. But no, the mother and daughter had been left to speak in private. Mrs Jenkinson had not shown herself at all. The very notion of facing a wrathful Lady Catherine must have filled her with unconquerable terror. Out of discretion, and not sheer cowardice, Darcy and the colonel had made themselves scarce as well. They had stepped out through the French windows to stroll in the shrubbery on the left side of the house, and a few moments later Captain Maynard had followed suit with manifest reluctance.

Predictably, the morning had turned out to be one of the least propitious times for making the man's acquaintance. During their long spell in the garden – nigh on three quarters of an hour – it had belatedly occurred to Darcy that they would have stood a better chance of taking the measure of the man if one of them had come to speak to him earlier in the morning, leaving it to the other to escort Lady Catherine thither. But they had not – and under the far less favourable circumstances, the captain had given but the briefest answers to their queries, often losing track of what he was saying, or had made no response at all, too caught up in keeping an eye on the developments in the parlour, little as could be ascertained through the uneven glass.

Thus, Captain Maynard's utter lack of interest in making a good impression had worked to procure him precisely that, albeit in a roundabout manner. It had been encouraging to find that he could not spare them much of his attention, nor draw an easy breath until the three of them had been summoned back into the house.

It had been impossible to tell if the ladies had achieved a true reconciliation. If they had, it could not have been a heartfelt, tearful one, knowing Lady Catherine – and had Darcy and the colonel been foolish enough to expect anything of the sort, a mere glimpse of her ladyship's visage would have soon disabused them of that notion. At the end of the interview, her eyes were dry and her countenance stern, and had remained so for the duration of the journey back to Malvern House. Also, she had remained ominously quiet, which was decidedly unnatural for one given to airing her views at every opportunity.

Cautious questions had not drawn her out. They had only served to elicit a few terse replies, and then a forceful demand for silence.

Even the attempt to offer wordless comfort had been rebuffed. When Darcy had reached out to clasp his aunt's fingers, restlessly tapping against the cushioned seat, Lady Catherine had pushed his hand aside and snarled, "Oh, leave me be!"

Oddly enough, she had not added the old refrain – *'This is all your fault!'* – so Darcy could not help wondering if she had begun to see how her own failings had caused the rift between her and her daughter. Or perhaps that was too fanciful, and a great deal too much to hope for.

Either way, on the following morning, Lady Catherine did choose to attend Anne's wedding, and brought Lord and Lady Malvern with her. Unlike their elders, Anne's cousins did not require any efforts of persuasion. They all came – Darcy, Georgiana, the colonel, his brothers and sisters – and it was thanks to the young Fitzwilliam contingent that the occasion was just as a wedding ought to be: heart-warming and festive.

With such evidence before him, it did not take long for Darcy to conclude that they would continue in that vein at Malvern House, over a light repast that was meant to serve as a wedding breakfast, so he had every reason to believe that Georgiana would thoroughly enjoy the rest of the day in their cousins' cheerful company.

As for himself, the newly married couple would have to excuse him. For Anne's sake, he was glad that her scheme had reached a happy conclusion, but the material point was that her wilfulness had kept him busily engaged for long enough. He could not find it in him to give her any more time than he already had. It was still early in the day – just coming up to eleven. If he left soon enough…

He drew a deep breath. Aye, he *would* leave soon. As soon as possible. He had his own happiness to pursue. And he could scarce wait another minute.

ౚఴ �

The last ten miles were covered on horseback. He could not possibly countenance cooling his heels and waiting for his horses to be baited when he knew full well that, with a fresh mount from the ostler's stables, he would be halfway to Longbourn in that time – if not further.

Riding was a good choice in more ways than one. The unrestrained gallop, as fast as the hired beast could carry him, answered his impatience a great deal better than the ride in his own carriage might have done. It was less than ideal that he should arrive on her doorstep dishevelled and covered in the dust of the road, but with any luck, Elizabeth might read the right message in his haste to reach her.

Darcy made a brief attempt to pat some of the dust off his apparel, once he had dismounted before the pillared entrance to Longbourn – but, as it happened, he was not to learn whether or not his eagerness would have made a favourable impression. The housekeeper – Hill, if memory served – answered the door herself, and gave him less than welcome tidings:

"They're all at Netherfield, sir," she imparted. "Mr Bingley was prodigiously disappointed that a ball could not be arranged at such short notice, so he settled for a picnic instead, to celebrate his betrothal to our dear Miss Jane. You'll find them there, along with half the parish, I expect. You remember the way to Netherfield, don't you, sir? For if not, I'll be sure to find a lad to guide you."

"I thank you, but there is no need. I remember it quite well."

Of course he did. He remembered everything. The early-morning rides along that very bridleway, telling himself that he had chosen it for the pleasure of a canter down a quiet road that led away from Meryton, and not because it was the lane to Longbourn. The day when he had spotted her from a distance atop a knoll crowned by a couple of auburn-leafed chestnuts, only to be treated to the enchanting picture of her snatching her bonnet off and running down the slope with all the gleeful abandon of a wood nymph – nimble and graceful, and more desirable than any other woman on God's green earth. That other day – that other red-hot stab of fierce desire – when she had appeared out of nowhere in the shrubbery at Netherfield, and pertly told him she had come to enquire after her ailing sister. The restless nights, four in a row, when he had tossed and turned in his bed at Netherfield, just as he had in his own home a week ago, and for the same reason: because she was but a few doors down, tantalising him from impossibly close quarters. The nights when sleep would not come because she was many miles away, and it was past bearing that she should never cross his path again. The daytime hours too, when he had forced himself to be rational about it and make every imaginable effort to forget her – such a foolish waste of time and energy!

He would not waste a moment more. The picnic was a complication – and so very like Bingley to rejoice in his newfound happiness by surrounding himself with crowds of near-strangers. But to each his own. Hopefully, Mrs Hill's speculations were off the mark, and his friend had not gone quite so far as to ask half the parish to join him in the celebrations.

ஃ

'*So much for false hope. I should have known better,*' Darcy reflected grimly when he was shown onto Netherfield's southern terrace. From his vantage point, he could see the marquee erected on the lawn and the guests sauntering about. By the looks of it, Bingley *had* invited half the parish. Or, if he had failed to do so, then he had not fallen short by much.

The large gathering presumably included most of the four-and-twenty families of whose acquaintance Mrs Bennet had boasted five months ago. Of their members, he could recognise a few, even from a distance. Lady Lucas and Mrs Purvis. Mrs Long. Mrs Long's youngest niece, whose name eluded him. The Miss Clarkes. Mr Robinson and Miss Goulding.

He descended the stone steps, then headed across the lawn in long strides, nodding towards the odd acquaintance on his way. Yet no one stopped him, and Darcy was more than a little glad of it. A time would come when, in deference to Elizabeth's wishes, he might have to engage her friends and neighbours in conversation – or at least take the trouble of practising that art now and then, as she had archly advised him. Needless to say, now he could not even contemplate it.

So Darcy kept his course, his disappointment at the lengthy search somewhat mitigated by the recollection of their exchange in the drawing room at Rosings. By then, he had already learned from experience that her left cheek would dimple a little more than usual, and her eyes would sparkle with mischief when she was just about to tease him. Those delectable warning signs had served him well many a time, he thought – and instead of finding it exasperating that he was so foolishly besotted as to distinguish between various degrees of dimpling, the musings sent a bright smile flashing across his face.

The uncommon turn of his countenance, in present company at least, made the second Miss Harrington stare in astonishment, then swiftly reciprocate with a wide smile of her own and a flirtatious flutter of lashes. But the double-barrelled approach was entirely lost on him. Darcy did not even recognise her – which was little wonder, seeing as his thoughts were more agreeably engaged. Besides, he had never spent much time in Miss Penelope Harrington's society, and that was not surprising either. After all, she was a close friend of Miss Lydia Bennet's.

As to Miss Lydia's relations, his searching gaze could not alight upon a single one of them. At least not until he looked more closely in the deeper recesses of the marquee, and finally came across what might have been termed the readers' corner, as the clustered chairs were occupied by three people intent upon their books: Miss Long, Miss Mary Bennet and Miss Mary's father.

Secluding themselves there with their reading matter was not the most sociable way to amuse themselves at a picnic, and if they were thus minded, they could have chosen to sit in Bingley's library, sparse as it was. But, of all the foibles that might have drawn his notice, an unsociable quest for peace and quiet was the least likely to make him raise a brow. A faint smile tugged at the corner of his lips at the thought that this reluctance to pander to the tediously chatty could very well be one of the many similarities between him and her father that Elizabeth had hinted at.

He was not eager to discover all the other ones. With his eccentric ways and sardonic humour, Mr Bennet had always wrong-footed him to some extent. A while ago, he had been at liberty to shrug and keep his distance. Not any longer. And it was decidedly unnerving to know that the older gentleman's good opinion must be gained, and soon, for his was the power to grant consent – or withhold it.

Having come across Mr Bennet first and not Elizabeth was unnerving too. Still, there was nothing for it now but to gather his wits and meet the challenge. So Darcy squared his shoulders, and set forth to do precisely that.

◦◦◦

"Ah. Good day to you, sir," came Mr Bennet's response to Darcy's subdued greeting, whereas Miss Long and Miss Mary merely curtsied, then resumed their seats and laid their books aside. The older gentleman likewise abandoned his volume on a nearby table and, making himself comfortable in his chair yet again, he folded his hands on his knee and drawled, "What a remarkable surprise. It has been a long time since we had the pleasure. Pray take a seat, sir, and tell me, how is it that you have decided to honour us with your company?"

The *soupçon* of sarcasm was unmistakable, and it could not fail to nettle him, but Darcy valiantly clung to the determination to be civil.

"My friend's betrothal to your daughter was a strong inducement, sir. Pray allow me to offer my congratulations. By the bye, would you happen to know where I might find Bingley and the rest of your family? I would like to offer them my best wishes too."

"Oh, they went this way and that," Mr Bennet unhelpfully replied with a careless gesture. "But, to my way of thinking, you had better sit in the shade until their return and refresh yourself with a glass of spruce beer. You seem a trifle hot under the collar, if you do not mind my saying so."

In fact, Darcy minded very much indeed. It was galling to learn that he was so obvious. How much did Mr Bennet know, anyway?

"I thank you, no," he demurred as he pondered on what he might do next.

Perhaps one of Bingley's footmen could give some indication of his master's whereabouts, if not Elizabeth's, seeing as Mr Bennet was unable or unwilling to assist him. It was indeed a pity that he had come upon Elizabeth's father, not her mother, Darcy caught himself thinking, and very nearly chuckled at the extraordinary notion that he should be actively wishing for the vociferous matron's company. But she would have been a great deal more accommodating. The merest hint that he was looking for Elizabeth would have sufficed for her to mount the search herself and lead him by the hand.

There might have been truth in that, but this was not the time for pert reflections.

"If you would—" Darcy began, bowing to Mr Bennet and the young ladies. But before he could finish his sentence, excuse himself and leave them, a hearty baritone boomed very close behind him:

"Mr Darcy! Capital, sir! Capital!"

With a grimace he could not fully suppress, Darcy straightened his back and turned around. Much as he had promised Elizabeth three nights ago that he would be patient, he was a great deal more likely to rise to that challenge if she was beside him. Not so much now, when he was eager to find her, and had already had more hindrances and interruptions than he could stomach on any given day.

"Sir William," he said with a perfunctory, stiff bow, but the terseness of the greeting did nothing to dampen the portly man's effusions.

"Delighted to see you, sir! So very good of you to come! I am thrilled for Mr Bingley, and indeed for us all, to have another one of his nearest and dearest joining us for the celebrations."

"Another one? Who else is here?" Darcy asked, rather hoping that the answer would not be *'Mr Bingley's sisters and Mr Hurst, of course.'* But no, that was unlikely. Not because he was certain that they would not come. Quite the reverse. He would not put it past Miss Bingley to mar her brother's happiness in any way she could. But not even Sir William would be so dense as to mistake her manner for a wish to partake in joyous celebrations.

When the gentleman's reply came, it only served to make everything worse:

"Only Mr Tyndall. In truth, I was hoping—"

Whatever Sir William might have been hoping for was of no interest to Darcy. His countenance darkening at the intelligence, he cut the older man off with a startled, "Tyndall is here?"

Once more, Sir William showed himself utterly unable to gauge his listener's frame of mind, and thus tailor his own discourse accordingly. His tone of voice remained maddeningly gleeful, and just as enthusiastic:

"He is, he is! He said he could not resist the allure of a festive occasion – and indeed who can? I have it all from the gentleman himself. He told me, but half an hour gone, that he had happened upon Mr Bingley the other day, at Mrs Gardiner's house, and found him positively giddy with joy. No wonder, says I," Sir William elaborated with a wink, "for dear Jane Bennet is the sweetest girl, and a gem of the first water. Well, anyway, Mr Tyndall said he had always meant to accept Henry Goulding's invitation to come and stay with him for a while, and what better time than this, when the entire neighbourhood is cheered by the prospect of a wedding? From what I gathered, he is aiming to stay at least until the happy event takes place. He said something of that nature to Miss Elizabeth just before they set off on a tour of Mr Bingley's garden follies along with our host, his lady and quite a few others, not least my own frolicsome brood," he chortled with fatherly affection, a sentiment which Darcy would have found commendable in other circumstances.

At this point, he was in no fit state to even register it. His insides roiled and his head spun with disjointed thoughts and dozens of questions. Of the latter, only one was for his babbling companion's ears, and Darcy lost no time in asking it:

"Which way round did they go?"

Sir William's eyes widened and his mouth fell open, which served to give him a ludicrous resemblance to a corpulent and grey-whiskered frog.

"Beg pardon?"

Not in the least amused by Sir William's droll turn of countenance, nor by his inability to understand a simple question, Darcy forced himself to make his meaning clearer:

"The walk you spoke of – the tour of the garden follies: which one did they start with, do you know?"

With a rueful grin, Sir William shook his head.

"Not one for long rambles, me, so I really could not say what follies there might be in Mr Bingley's garden," he disappointingly replied – only to redeem himself a fraction of a second later by adding, "All I can say is that I saw them going up that slope yonder, and then into the woods. Would that help?"

It did. Had they planned to visit the follies in the opposite order, they would have gone towards the lake. So Darcy nodded.

"Yes, I believe it would. I thank you," he civilly offered, and promptly excused himself.

"Not at all, sir, not at all! Enjoy your walk, and I hope you catch up with them," Sir William amicably said, and – oblivious to most things, as ever – he failed to notice that his lifelong neighbour and longstanding friend was fixing him with a hostile glare.

⁂

Unlike the paterfamilias of Lucas Lodge, Darcy generally had a good grasp of what was happening around him, so he did not miss the dark look Mr Bennet had shot towards Sir William. But the reasons behind it remained a mystery. All that Darcy could grasp was that Mr Bennet would have greatly preferred he did not follow the walking party.

Why was that?

As for Tyndall, was the fellow becoming a more serious threat than he had anticipated?

Plain reason could not supply the answers. Nor could pure speculation. And mounting agitation was the least helpful of all. So the questions were still looming when the first folly came into view. It was disappointingly deserted.

So was the second. And the third. How many were there altogether? Darcy could not remember, and wished he had paid more heed to the design of his friend's ornamental gardens as he followed the path that wound among old trees, cut across meadows, dipped down to the lake, then sloped gently upwards to meet the edge of the woods once more.

A faint murmur of voices followed by a peal of laughter hastened his steps, until Darcy could catch a glimpse of the fourth folly, up on a hill, beyond the flowering mass of rhododendrons. A few long strides, and he espied the silhouette that stood under the dome of the rotunda – a shapely figure outlined against the clear sky. She reached out to hold on to one of the columns and playfully circled round it once, then poised herself at the edge of the platform and leapt down, into the waiting arms of her companion.

There might have been a stolen kiss as well. Or several. It was hard to tell from such a distance and with the columns in the way – and besides, Darcy was not of a mind to pry, nor count some courting couple's kisses. He had slowed his steps once he had spotted them, so as not to intrude upon their tryst, but thankfully he was not obliged to lurk, nor cut through the woods to give them a wide berth. The pair did not linger overlong. A few moments later, they sauntered away holding hands, then broke into a run and vanished out of sight when the path curved around a clump of hollies.

Allowing a few minutes more was the wisest course of action. He had no wish whatever to stumble upon them yet again and endure the mortification of finding them kissing under the boughs, another hundred yards or so along the way. With any luck, they might have had the common sense – or rather the discretion – to strike into one of the less-trodden paths that led down to the lake. After all, he did not have all day, and he would much rather not be delayed a great deal longer.

Garden follies were of no interest to him now but, for want of a better occupation, Darcy walked around the slim rotunda and busied himself with the odd glance at the detailed stonework, until he deemed it reasonably safe to proceed.

It was only then that the patch of colour caught his eye. Darcy made a face as he stepped closer. If the young lady in question somehow managed to shield her indiscretions from other passers-by, then she might preserve her reputation, but she had certainly lost her bonnet. He had better take it back with him, he determined, and perhaps leave it discreetly in the marquee, for its rash owner to reclaim with impunity. So he stooped, reached for it – and froze.

The carelessly abandoned item was a honey-coloured affair with a narrow brim and a crown of pleated satin. And he had seen it often enough before. Elizabeth's bonnet.

Chapter 15

Darcy withdrew his hand and stood back, as though the cursed thing were a coiled viper. The world crashed around him and began to spin. So, that... that woman... was *Elizabeth?*

The shock emptied his lungs of air and filled his veins with ice. Motionless and numb, he kept staring at the patch of amber – until the pain came; sharp pain that slashed through the numbness. He looked away and flinched, then his eyes narrowed. Who was she with? Tyndall? Some Hertfordshire beau or another?

Fists clenched at his sides, his head still spinning, Darcy found himself releasing a harsh sound that was half snort, half bark of bitter laughter. Did it even matter who the man was? Hardly! Just some other man whom she had chosen over him!

Gall rose in a vile rush, poisoning everything. With an oath, Darcy spun round and stalked down the incline, heading for the woods. He did not know where he was going and could not care less, as long as it was not back to Netherfield – to Bingley's guests – to Mr Bennet and his contemptible neglect of his duties as a father. Did the man know that his second daughter was on an assignation? Did he not care where she was, and with whom? Or was he perfectly aware, and disposed to allow it?

Another oath followed when the matter became clear as day, and Mr Bennet's grim scowl for Sir William was explained. Oh, he knew! Mr Bennet knew full well what his second daughter was about, and very likely knew the rest as well – his own wishes, his intentions. She must have told her father everything. After all, they were very close. No wonder, then, that Mr Bennet did not want him to go and spoil her walk with the man she favoured!

Fresh bile surged, and pain exploded into anger. Could she not have given him the chance to defend himself? If Bingley had blurted everything out – if she had taken such offence at his old suspicion that her sister would have married his friend for reasons that had naught to do with love – could she not have waited to hear his side of the story?

With her happiness in mind, within a mere se'nnight he had challenged his preconceptions and set aside all manner of precepts that had been instilled into him from his boyhood and, rightly or wrongly, had guided him for upwards of two decades. Could she not have waited *two days* for him to have his say, rather than condemn him without a hearing? Two days and a modicum of trust – or at least a little fairness! Was that so very much to ask for?

ↄﻬ♋ﻬↄ

The loud voice that came from somewhere to his left made him start, and Darcy's head whipped round in its direction. Mrs Bennet's voice – the woman's plaintive tones were unmistakable.

'*Well, she turned up too late, did she not?*', he bitterly scoffed.

Another voice rose in reply to Mrs Bennet's, and then another. He could not recognise them, and refused to even make the effort. Damn them, whoever they were. Damn them all! He was in no humour for company!

He muttered an oath, and would have hastened out of sight, but as rotten luck would have it, he found himself in a clearing, the treeline some fifteen yards away. Other than that, he had no notion where he was. He must have walked around in a daze – and now he had stumbled upon Mrs Bennet, of all the aggravating people!

His shoulders stiffened, and he tossed his head back as he resolved to stand his ground. He would be damned if he was willing to be caught scurrying away like some miscreant. *He* had done nothing to be ashamed of!

A flash of light-coloured muslin through the foliage came as a second warning of the imminent encounter, and before long Miss Kitty Bennet emerged, arm in arm with Miss Lucas, their heads bent close together in conversation. But it was still Mrs Bennet's whine that Darcy heard, easily carrying over the young ladies' voices, even though she had yet to show herself.

"Good gracious! Had I known that a mere half of the garden tour would take so long, I would have stayed behind and sent Mr Bennet to watch over the girls. This is monstrously unfair! I daresay he is having a jolly good time sitting quietly with his book, while I am traipsing up hill and down dale, and suffering a vast deal too. My feet are in agony. I shan't be surprised to find my heels covered in blisters. These shoes are not suited for lengthy walks. Not suited for any sort of outdoor walk, really. Goodness knows what I was thinking when I agreed to such a scheme. Oh, how I wish that dear Mr Bingley had thought of dotting more benches along these paths! I need a rest. A mother's lot is a sorry one, I tell you! I hope you give daily praise that you were spared that trial, Sister. I would not wish it on anyone. I can scarce draw breath, and my nerves are torn to shreds. If I could only be assured that Lydia has not come to some mishap! I entreated her to come along, but she was adamant that she wished to see the waterfall. I do hope she treads with care. Heaven forbid that she should lose her footing and fall into the lake! Jane offered to go and keep an eye on her, bless her heart, but I said to her, I said, 'Nay, my pet, you had much better leave her be and stroll with Mr Bingley.' The dear man! Just now, he is my only comfort. He and sweet Jane, of course. What a great match, Sister! Oh, I knew how it would be! I *knew* that my dearest girl could not be so beautiful for nothing. What a triumph for her, and such a wonderful thing for our other girls! I only wish they would heed me now and then. Time and time again I told them that they would be the death of me, but do they listen? And, for that matter, do they care one jot about me and the hardships I endure for their sake? No, of course not! Those who do not complain are never pitied!"

The ludicrously unfounded claim would have provoked Darcy into laughter, had he not lost his sense of humour. Thus, he could not even offer a thin smile of greeting, once Miss Kitty and Miss Maria had come close enough for civilities. He could only bow in response to their curtsies.

By then, the grumbling matron who was under the impression that she never complained had come into view as well, with Mrs Phillips puffing and panting two steps behind her. Miss Gardiner was the next to step into the clearing, and promptly left the path to run in a flurry of skirts and add more wildflowers to the posy she was carrying. Her two sisters followed, hand in hand, whereas their brother stuck to the path and kept chatting to the two youngest Lucas boys about something or other. A few seconds later, Mrs Gardiner made an appearance too, flanked by a sister of Miss Maria's and one of the Miss Gouldings. Mrs Gardiner darted a glance his way and, having recognised him, she greeted him from afar with a raised hand and a little nod. As for Mrs Bennet, she drew herself up when she noticed him, and – far less civil than her sister by marriage – she said by way of greeting, "Well, I do declare! Mr Darcy! Fancy coming upon *you* here, sir."

Yet again, he only responded with a bow and made no answer. Even if he wished to – which he most certainly did not – Darcy severely doubted that he could speak just then. His throat had gone dry from the moment when Elizabeth had appeared at the back of the procession, behind two scampering ladies and Henry Goulding, who was loudly guffawing with a couple of young bucks. And her attentive escort was Tyndall. Naturally. Somehow, he had expected that.

Darcy forced himself to look away and struggled to form logical, coherent thoughts: he must have been roaming through the woods for longer than he had imagined, if they had had the time to rejoin the walking party.

But the surge and roil of other thoughts – ones not at all amenable to reason – were bringing on something akin to nausea. And he had no power to suppress it, any more than one afflicted with seasickness could hope to quell the storm that caused it.

His jaw tightened. If he had imagined until a few moments ago that he had managed to calm himself somewhat as he had stalked through Bingley's woodland, one glance at her – at the pair of them – had been enough to prove him wrong. Even so, his eyes darted towards her yet again, and he saw her approaching, her lips curled up into a bright smile. It was the warmest welcome she had ever bestowed, and once it would have sent his heart soaring. Now it brought nothing but horror at her duplicity – and no less at his own abysmal folly of choosing to blind himself for such a length of time into thinking her incapable of guile.

He knew beyond a shadow of a doubt that his restraint would be severely tested even before Tyndall called out, "Darcy! Now that is a surprise!" – and Elizabeth seconded him with a swift, "Indeed. I was not expecting you so soon."

'*Clearly,*' Darcy seethed, but did not say the word aloud, and was surprised and grimly satisfied in equal measure to find that he still retained *some* control over his temper and his tongue.

The self-gratulation was premature. The control slipped when Elizabeth added, "I am glad you came today, and in good time for our picnic."

He answered that with a terse, "Are you?"

She opened her lips to speak, but Tyndall was quick to leap in and have his say. He took his life into his hands and had the effrontery to mutter, "This is quite extraordinary. Of late, we keep running into each other in the most unlikely places."

"Aye. Don't we just!" Darcy shot back, his ability to keep himself in check tried beyond endurance.

"Well, I daresay you can discuss your extraordinary encounters on the way to the house," Mrs Bennet spoke up, shuffling on the spot with a wince. "We had better go. We have been on our feet for long enough."

"Too true. We should be going," Mrs Gardiner agreed. "Come, girls, I think you have gathered more than enough flowers. Come along now," she called after her daughters, then turned towards Tyndall. "Would you be so kind as to give me the support of your arm, sir? My sister is in the right: it has been a very long walk, and I am prodigiously tired."

It was a thoughtful gesture, Darcy could not fail to own, particularly as it was unlikely that the younger lady was even less of a walker than Mrs Bennet, and genuinely found herself in need of support. So he cast her a glance in silent reassurance that he was not about to make a scene, nor brawl with Tyndall like a common ploughboy. What good would that do, anyway? A violent release of pent-up frustration – a momentary satisfaction – and then what?

He flinched as he refused to stare into the awaiting darkness. If Elizabeth had chosen Tyndall...

Another roiling wave swelled, choking him. What *was it* about the man that had made him succeed where he himself had failed? What did the other say or do to win her trust and her heart in mere days, when he had laboured for months on end to—

Darcy frowned as he was forced to acknowledge that he had laboured for months to forget her, rather than strive to win her heart. Would it help in any way if he endeavoured to make his case again – ask her to reconsider? Or was everything decided between her and Tyndall?

He flinched again. It must be. She was not the sort to engage in meaningless flirtation. Was she?

It was an abhorrent thought – nay, it was utterly repugnant – but did he know that for a fact? What did he know of her, *truly* know of her, that was not coloured by his deepest wishes? He knew it for an incontestable truth that she had always drawn him; that he wanted her more than he had ever wanted any woman. Had he been too sure of himself – too damnably sure of his abilities to read people rightly – to see that he was making the same pitiful mistake that men have made since the dawn of time, and turned the object of their desire into a picture of perfection, a figment of their imagination that bore but a scant resemblance to the real woman whom their fancy was stubbornly determined to adorn? Only to curse fate or any number of by-standers when the veils of their own making fell away – as though others were at fault, and not themselves and their self-inflicted blindness?

"You seem to have misplaced your bonnet," Darcy blurted out as he trailed behind the walking party alongside Elizabeth, without having even noticed when he had shifted from his spot and fallen into step beside her.

The remark was nothing short of idiotic, he acknowledged with a scowl towards the blameless wildflowers that bordered the path, but the words were out before he could check them.

Disbelief rang in her voice when she asked, "Is that all you have to say?"

Darcy bit his lip and tiredly answered with another question:

"What would you have me say?" His countenance darkened. "I thought I had already said enough by now. Apparently not."

Elizabeth's reply was crisp and prompt:

"Whereas I thought you came with tidings of Miss de Bourgh, and not to censure me for misplacing my bonnet."

Her obvious irritation could not fail to fuel Darcy's. His lips quirked into a sardonic twist.

"Indeed, what right have *I* to censure you for anything?"

"Quite," she icily retorted. "In fact, I am of a mind to question both your right and your inclination. Perhaps you should seek sustenance in the marquee or raise your spirits in some other manner, and return to talk to me when you are in a more agreeable frame of mind."

"That is unlikely," Darcy shot back, his indignation mounting at finding her subscribing to the reprehensible opinion that attack was the best form of defence.

"*What* is unlikely, sir? That you will work to improve your humour – and your manners, I might add, " she persisted in the doomed tactic, "or that you will return to talk to me?"

"Both!" Darcy snapped – a patent untruth spoken in anger.

His humour might be beyond redemption, but they *had* to talk!

He was in no fit state to take himself to task for the alarming new tendency to lose his head as well as his temper under provocation, and retaliate with words he did not mean. Nor did he have time to reflect on that, and count it among the unfortunate effects of his infatuation. The look she cast him froze into ice. With a clipped, "As you wish," and nary a warning, she lengthened her strides and left him behind.

It was the work of a moment for Darcy to catch up with her and stop her with a hand on her elbow.

"Wait!"

Lips pursed, Elizabeth made to draw her arm away, so he reluctantly released it, even as he forcefully said, "We must talk!"

A dark glare was Elizabeth's first answer, and then a scathing, "Must we, now? You will have me giddy. A moment ago you said it was unlikely. Pray, do not exert yourself on my account. Our charming exchange has whetted my appetite for more of the same, as you would imagine, but I daresay I shall be able to endure the deprivation."

"For God's sake, desist!" Darcy burst out. "Elizabeth, what is the cause of this? I thought all was going well, or at least that everything seemed... hopeful between us before Bingley reappeared on the scene. What exactly did he say to make such a difference?"

Elizabeth's eyes widened.

"Do you mean to tell me that this... *this*..." she heatedly repeated, her right hand giving an all-encompassing gesture in his direction, "is to do with your friend offering for my sister? After everything you said?"

"If Bingley told you that last autumn I was convinced she did not return his affections and would have married him for whatever other reasons, then you could have waited until I was at hand to tell you that now I know I was mistaken—"

"No, he did not say anything of the sort," Elizabeth cut him off. "Mr Bingley has the good manners not to meddle in other people's courtship, nor indulge in tittle-tattle."

"Is that so! Then what the blazes did he do to drive you into Tyndall's arms?"

A moment ago, he would have thought it was physically impossible for Elizabeth's eyes to grow any wider. She proved him wrong.

"I beg your pardon?"

"I was there," Darcy rasped, every red-hot feeling erupting into searing incandescence. And everything he had withheld with agonising effort finally poured out. "I happened upon you a while ago. At the rotunda. Once the pair of you had left, I came across your bonnet, forgotten in the grass. I can only assume that your companion was Tyndall, seeing as he is at your side at every opportunity, and would not be dislodged if he could help it. He was allowed to—" Darcy broke off and flinched, then resumed with extreme difficulty, "I cannot do you the injustice of believing that you make a habit of midday assignations, so there must be another... another reason," he choked out. "Is there? Would you at least tell me this: are you...?" His voice trailed off again. For all his efforts, he could not form the words and ask outright if she and Tyndall were as good as engaged, any more than he had been able to speak of stolen kisses at the folly. All that came out in a tortured whisper was, "Am I to wish you joy, and urge him to endeavour to deserve you?"

A host of emotions played across Elizabeth's countenance while he was speaking – disbelief; vexation; outrage – but by the time he had finished, they had all given way to something that looked shockingly akin to exasperation and a touch of amusement. Darcy stared, caught between bewilderment and horror. This... all this... his heartbreak... she found it *diverting*?

Horror prevailed and spilled over into yet another flash of anger when he saw a faint smile tugging at the corners of her lips.

"No. That will not be necessary. I have no interest in Mr Tyndall," Elizabeth replied, then her brows rose and her smile flattened into a reproving grimace. "What I do have," she resumed, "is a younger sister who is hardly ever satisfied with her own bonnets and insists on borrowing mine. Or Kitty's. And in case you are still wondering, last I saw Lydia and Tom Lucas, they were headed for the rotunda, on their way to the ornamental waterfall on the north side of the hill."

In Darcy's experience, explosive joy and the deepest mortification never went together. Yet they did so now and washed over him, rendering him light-headed and scarce able to speak.

"Oh, Lord! Elizabeth, I am…"

"Suitably ashamed of your penchant for leaping to conclusions, I should dearly like to hope," she archly said, before he could think of sufficiently harsh words for himself that could safely be voiced in a lady's hearing.

He drew breath to give her her due and form a profuse apology, but Elizabeth's raised hand made him hold his peace.

"I would also like to believe that you will find ways to rid yourself of that unhappy tendency," she solemnly added, her tone and manner devoid of any hint of teasing. "And on that note, if you happen to be fond of the *Moor of Venice*, I suggest you do not make a habit of playing that role. It is decidedly unflattering, and the performance is likely to bring severe disappointment. Regardless of whether it revolves around embroidered handkerchiefs, bonnets, gloves, or what have you."

Darcy's penitent gaze sought hers.

"I deserved that. And worse," he whispered with profound contrition.

"Oh, I am fairly confident I can oblige with a great deal worse. But I would much prefer I was not given another opportunity."

He shook his head.

"You will not be," he earnestly said – a solemn vow – and his voice grew pleading as he asked, "Can you forgive me?"

His heart leapt in his chest when her left cheek dimpled just so, and a mischievous glint shone in her eyes – the sure signs of imminent raillery, which sparked the exhilarating hope that, undeserving as he was, he might eventually be forgiven for the most appalling blunder of his life. The glance she cast him and the twitch of her lips also gave fair warning that she was about to extract her pound of flesh, and he braced himself for it. She did not keep him waiting long:

"Oh, not so hasty, sir, if you please. Firstly, I must decide if I should be mortally offended by your estimation of my character, or marginally flattered that you seem to remember my articles of clothing quite so well. I expect I shall require no small amount of persuasion to settle upon the latter. Of course, a more generous soul than I would have conceded you have had a trying se'nnight and left it at that, but generosity of spirit has been unequally apportioned within my family.

My sister Jane has been endowed with a vast deal, whereas I –
not so much. But in order to compensate for that deficiency, I shall
allow you a one-time opportunity to enquire into the whereabouts of
all my bonnets. Let us cover that subject now: I currently boast of six,
which are serving in rotation – an extravagance, I am told. Two
of them are safely stored away in my closet; one is on my worktable,
halfway through a substantial alteration; another one was loaned
to my sister Kitty, and I have not seen hide nor hair of it since January;
one was left in Mr Bingley's marquee when the Miss Clarkes and I
decided to indulge in a game of quoits; and the sixth is— Well, we both
know where the sixth is. And as I happen to be very fond of it, Lydia
will have to do penance if it is lost or damaged. For I imagine it would
be too much to hope that you had the goodness to retrieve it."

Darcy's mien grew self-conscious.

"I fear so," he was obliged to own.

"I see. For my part, I fear that my sister has a great deal more
to answer for than losing my bonnet, if one is to judge by your… rather
strong reaction to the encounter," Elizabeth tentatively added, and as
her gaze swept searchingly over his countenance, Darcy felt heat rising
in his cheeks and his neckcloth becoming uncomfortably tight.

He cleared his throat and cursed himself for blushing like
a schoolboy, as though he had never come across a young couple on
a romantic tryst. It was not the prospect of relating what he had seen
that was to blame for his discomfort. He was not of a mind to speak
of her sister – not when so many other things begged to be said.
The mortification came from his blatant inability to stop himself
from darting quick glances to her lips – and that was dangerously likely
to betray what he had witnessed and, worse still, what he was thinking.
Not that he had lost his senses to the point of yielding to the exquisite
temptation. That was out of the question. For goodness' sake, her
walking companions had barely left them! It was beyond unthinkable
that he should risk her good name and place her in the same improper
situation that her youngest sister had recklessly chosen for herself!

He narrowed his eyes, willing them into obedience, and blessed
his stars – blessed *her* too – when Elizabeth spoke again and broke
his treacherous train of thought.

"I cannot imagine how Lydia might offer an apology for her
unguarded conduct, so pray accept mine on her behalf," she said softly,
which could not fail to elicit his fervent protest.

"You are not your sister's keeper—!" Darcy forcefully began, but she would not let him finish.

"Perhaps I ought to be. Goodness knows she needs one," Elizabeth murmured with a sigh, and thus raised Darcy's unavailing anger at her indolent father and her carelessly indecorous mother. It was for them, not their right-minded daughter, to guard the hoydenish one, prevent her from ruining her reputation and safeguard the others from the distress of having to blush on her account.

He made to say as much, yet held his peace lest he pain her by openly criticising her parents, much as the pair of them deserved it. It was Elizabeth who broke the silence.

"But that is for another day, it seems," she dismissed the awkward topic with some determination. "Now, I doubt that Lydia will retrace her steps to rescue my bonnet – so if I want something done, I should do it myself," she airily concluded, which brought a rueful little smile to his lips.

"I wish I had spared you the trouble," Darcy said, then hesitantly added, "May I accompany you?"

The glance she cast him was delightfully arch.

"Some would say it would be ungentlemanly of you if you did not."

"Indeed," Darcy agreed, but the air of mock solemnity was conquered by a self-deprecating chuckle when he found himself compelled to qualify, "Although all I can offer is my company, for what it may be worth. I am sorry to say that I shall be of no use to you as a guide. I… er… seem to have lost my bearings."

"Have you? Then it is fortunate that I have not. This way, sir," she indicated. "The rotunda is up that slope, and a little to the right."

And with that, she left the path to cut across the grass, and Darcy was all-too-glad to follow.

"So, do you have any tidings of your cousin?" Elizabeth asked while they were sauntering up the gentle incline.

"Pardon?" Darcy floundered, distracted from the guilty pleasure of taking in every detail of her lithe form as she walked nimbly on, a few steps ahead of him. "Oh. Anne. Of course. Yes, I do, as it happens. She was married this morning—"

"Already?" Elizabeth exclaimed in dismay and, with a sudden swish of skirts, she spun round to face him. "I am so sorry…" she whispered, her eyes full of sadness and compassion, and laid a comforting hand on his lapel once he had closed the small distance between them.

Her generous concern and her proximity played havoc with his senses, yet Darcy fought to gather his wits in sufficient measure as to supply a prompt albeit disjointed answer:

"No need. I thank you for your kindness, but you need not fear for her. Nor for her chances of happiness, I think. She is very happy. As for her relations, we are… well… baffled, but relieved. Still quite put out, in Lady Catherine's case, yet I would say that even she is relieved all the same. You see, Anne never intended to marry Wickham. There was someone else – a neighbour's brother, now a seafaring captain. They had been attached for some time, Anne said. Wickham was only asked to assist her in making the arrangements in the captain's absence. That was all."

"Thank goodness!" Elizabeth said with feeling, then gave a breathless little laugh. "Now, that is an extraordinary tale. Who would have thought that your retiring cousin could be so intrepid? Or such a dark horse, for that matter?" she chuckled, and incredulous amusement shone in her countenance, banishing the shadows of sympathetic pity for Anne's supposed sorrows – and perhaps for his.

And yet her hand remained on his lapel.

It was impossible for Darcy to refrain from covering it with his – only to regret his rashness a fraction of a second later, when she lowered her gaze and gasped. It could have signified either displeasure or surprise, but he could not tell which, and it unnerved him. He gave an uneasy sigh as he conceded that, today of all days, he would be wise to err on the side of caution. Reluctantly, but with some determination, he slackened his hold and made to draw his hand away.

He blinked, startled by a fresh surge of hope, when she would not allow it. Elizabeth curved her thumb around his, and raised the side of his hand for a better look.

"How did you come by this?" she whispered.

It was only then that Darcy noticed the trail of dried blood that ran down the side of his fifth finger, and likewise the state of his knuckles – two of them scraped raw.

"Rough bark, I expect," he mumbled without thinking, then cringed. Of all the asinine things to say! He could have claimed that there had been some minor mishap on the journey to Netherfield, instead of giving her reasonable cause to believe him given to violent displays of temper – or unhinged.

What sort of a man vents his frustration on a tree trunk – and then is enough of a dunce as to compound that folly by admitting it?

Yet he was not taken to task. Elizabeth merely said in a wistful murmur, "I wish you had not injured yourself, physically or otherwise. But I imagine it could have been much worse. I would not have put it past you to seek your horse and ride away hell for leather, never to return."

Darcy's first response was a forceful shake of his head. It was the quickest way to let her know that, for all his sins and indefensible misjudgements, he could not have brought himself to leave. Not until she asked him to go, and all hope was lost. But before he could find his voice to say so, Elizabeth spoke again:

"I am relieved that you did not," she said softly, and the uplifting avowal robbed him of the power to form anything more cogent than, "You are?"

His glance swept over her in an anxious endeavour to ascertain her thoughts. Their faces were almost level as she stood before him, one step further up the incline, but that was of no use whatever, if she would not look at him. He could only see her nod, twice… yet she still kept her face averted as she gently rested his hand upon her upturned palm.

A faint breeze swirled around them and toyed with the wispy ringlets that framed her brow – or maybe it was his own breath that made them move this way and that. Yet every thought of swaying ringlets slipped from his mind when her fingertips fluttered in a light caress over his uninjured knuckles, then drifted slowly to stroke the back of his hand.

But for an involuntary twitch of his fingers, Darcy stood stock-still, his throat dry, his heart pounding. It took every shred of common sense that he could command, and every ounce of strength into the bargain, to force himself to remain motionless and silent, and not unsettle her with something wildly ill-judged and overhasty… such as reaching out to clasp her to his chest and crush her lips with his.

Yet the injunctions became harder and harder to obey as he stood there, his every muscle and sinew almost painfully taut and his stare fixed on her slender fingers as they glided back and forth over his skin.

So he took a deep breath – the only movement that he dared allow – and closed his eyes, letting her electrifying touch wash over him and send every fibre of his being into sharp, almost unbearable alertness. He fancied he could hear the rush of blood ringing in his ears, drowning out birdsong and the sound of his own shallow breaths, and the self-imposed blindness was rendering him little short of dizzy. Even so, he did not stir and kept his eyes closed, relishing every exquisitely tormenting moment – until a warm and fragrant puff of air brushed over his face, and he was rocked to his core by the featherlight touch of soft lips on his.

Darcy's eyes flew open, and he forgot to breathe.

She—— She had just *kissed him!*

He swallowed hard and struggled for a ragged breath as his awestruck gaze drowned into hers. Deep brown eyes specked with amber. Smiling eyes that crinkled at the corners, sparkled and shimmered and lit up his world.

Dazed with incredulous wonder, he eagerly searched them – and, of its own volition, his gaze drifted to her lips. They were rosy and full, and curled up into a smile that was engagingly self-conscious, but blessedly unrepentant too. If anything, it held more than a hint of impish daring and no little amusement, as though she mischievously delighted in having stunned him with so much more than he could have possibly anticipated.

He leaned closer then – holding back was utterly unthinkable – and leaned closer still, until there was but a hair's breadth between them. He brushed her lips with his in a light caress that was little more than a silent question: *'What next?'* A cautious question, repeated in another tentative kiss… and another… and another – and all of a sudden, she answered them all by reaching up to weave her fingers through his hair and stood on tiptoe to press her lips to his.

And that was when the world exploded into euphoria, and time lost its meaning. Darcy wrapped his arms around her, and was swept into sweet insanity when he found her responding to his kisses with a fervour that matched and fuelled his.

He could not have enough of her. The taste of her lips, the scent and flavour of her skin, the warm softness of her neck – all begged to be explored with ravenous kisses, and he clung to her, feeding the yearning he had carried within for five months complete.

And yet the yearning only grew, as did the hunger. They spiralled out of control, along with the blaze of passion that consumed him. He burned in the white heat of the flame — and relished the burning. Relished what she was doing to him with her caresses and her ardent kisses; relished each and every one of her responses to awakened passion. And when her lips parted to release a whimper of pure abandon, the white-hot flame seared him and grew hotter still — something which he would not have thought remotely possible before.

It was only then that a glimmer of reason cut through the intoxicating haze that fogged his mind to everything but her. And reason sternly pointed out that this, their heedless descent into unbridled passion, was a far greater impropriety than the relatively minor transgressions he had witnessed at the rotunda. There were no two ways about it: this was wildly improper. Terribly imprudent, too. Downright irresponsible.

Yet such tiresome precepts could not carry the day. They had precious little power over him — nowhere near as much as she — and were silenced in a trice. Because this was as far from wrong as could be. And besides, there was no comparison. Unless Tom Lucas and Lydia Bennet were on their way even then to petition Mr Bennet for his consent, there was no comparison. This was no tryst. It was the deepest truth of his soul, and she… she was everything.

"Marry me," Darcy breathed against her lips, once he had conquered at least some of the sweet insanity and brought himself to draw back by the smallest fraction.

Elizabeth made no audible answer. Instead, she twined her arms about his neck and wordlessly urged him to close the distance he had put between them. Not for a second did he contemplate resisting. And sweet insanity engulfed him yet again.

Chapter 16

"That means yes, I hope," Darcy whispered. Then, lest they outrun their luck and be discovered in wild abandon by whoever else might have gone walking through Bingley's gardens, he saw some wisdom in keeping the tantalising spell at bay with a hint of levity and choked out an arch, "For goodness' sake, how many times must I offer marriage before I receive a clear and satisfying answer?"

"You only have yourself to blame, seeing as the mode of your declaration improves with every repetition. However am I to forgo the next? Past experience tells me it will be even better," Elizabeth returned measure for measure, her lips shaped into an adorable pout. "Although I cannot imagine anything better than this," she added with the warmest smile, the jesting air suddenly abandoned.

Breath caught in his chest at the unreserved admission and the look in her eyes. Darcy tightened his arms around her and rasped, "Nor I," much as he knew that, to some extent, he was disingenuous. He *could* imagine something better, and he often had, in sleepless hours of longing. And the heat of passion they had so easily built with their ardent kisses could not fail to show that his wildest imaginings would be fulfilled. Surpassed, even.

He swallowed hard as he determined that now was not the best of times for mulling over that – and certainly not for sharing precisely what it was that he was thinking. So he was almost glad when she reverted to facetiousness:

"Then we are both in agreement that today's offer was presented in the best possible way, and you can do no better?"

"It would be fair to say so," Darcy replied with a throaty chuckle, safe in the knowledge that he was being truthful this time. There was no room for anything better. Not in a proposal, anyway.

"I see," Elizabeth said, with a return of the enchanting pout as she pretended to consider. "Well then, in that case, there is little joy to be found in procrastinating, so I might as well accept your offer now."

Although by then he had ample reason to hope for a favourable answer, Darcy exhaled in incommensurate relief.

"Thank heavens for that," he said, and claimed her lips again.

It was a while until sense prevailed – the long-ignored common sense that urged prudence and discretion. Even when Darcy forced himself to pay heed, his compliance was insufficient as far as both prudence and discretion were concerned. He still kept her in his arms, and bent his head to rest his cheek against hers, draw the first easy breath in what seemed like an age, and savour his good fortune. It was all over now. Praise be, it was all over: the months of foolish indecision, the troubles that followed. She had pledged herself to him at last. They were engaged. They would be married.

"When is it to be?" he whispered, and this time there was no doubt that it was his breath that made her ringlets flutter.

Elizabeth stroked his hair and whispered back, "Soon."

He straightened up then, so that he could search her eyes.

"How soon?"

"To own the truth, I was rather hoping for a double wedding, so… will a fortnight do?" she asked, her lips twitching in the most engaging manner, and sent his heart soaring with her delightfully unabashed confession, and no less with the promise of a remarkably short wait.

"Yes, that… that will do very well indeed," he faltered, thrilled beyond measure.

"You may well find such haste unsettling and a touch unseemly," she teased, the glint in her eyes a clear indication that she knew full well just how unlikely he was to baulk at it, "but you may wish to know that it was largely Papa's doing. When Mamma began to expound on the joys of many an incursion to the town's best warehouses for Jane's wedding clothes, Papa was quick to point out that one must be mindful of ancient lore. He went so far as to quote old adages, such as *'Marry in the month of May, and you'll surely rue the day,'* and the equally portentous *'Monday for wealth, Tuesday for health, Wednesday is the best day of all; Thursday for crosses, Friday for losses, Saturday for no luck at all.'* So there we have it: Jane and Mr Bingley were persuaded to make do with the last Wednesday in April, and I am pleased to say that your friend was prodigiously accommodating," she said with another impish quirk in her lips. "He has already commissioned his attorney to apply for the licence. I would hazard a guess that your people might easily achieve the same."

Darcy nodded, and forbore to say that, unlike Bingley, he could vouch for his ability to go one step further and procure a special licence, not merely a common one. But that was neither here nor there. The wedding would be held in her parish church, not at some private location or another, and it would not do to boast of his superior standing. Besides, just then he was not in the least inclined to talk.

Yet he was compelled to reconsider when she giggled – a singular response to his exultant kiss. So he drew back a little to rest his brow on hers.

"What amuses you, my love?" he whispered.

"Only the usual fate of sly schemes," she replied, a wry little smile at the corner of her lips. "I expect that Papa will not like it in the least to hear of the unforeseen result of his machinations."

"I say!" Darcy chortled in his turn, and could only wonder if Elizabeth had caught the note of unholy glee when she asked, "Oh? Has he been difficult already?"

"Mmm… testy might be an adequate description. And certainly disinclined to let me know where I might find you. I can only assume he is not too well disposed towards me," he speculated, suitably contrite about the ignoble explanation he had assigned to the older gentleman's reluctance, and far too happy with the changes in his situation since his last encounter with Mr Bennet to openly declare that *'testy'* was an understatement.

"You assume rightly," Elizabeth confirmed with a little laugh. "I daresay he was peevishly seeking to delay the inevitable. Chances are that he would have been more amenable – and liked you better, too – had I not warned him that you would come ere long to spirit me halfway across the country."

"Oh, you have, have you?" Darcy retorted, his smile growing wider.

She gave a faint shrug and nodded with mock gravity.

"You must see that it had to be done. I love my father, and he is not getting any younger, so I thought it only proper to have a care for his health and give him fair warning, instead of exposing him to shocks out of the blue. But I suspect he chose to believe that I was merely sporting with him for my own amusement," Elizabeth continued, a rueful twinkle in her eyes. "Were it not for the testiness you spoke of, I would have said he was still seeking to persuade himself that my warning was in jest. Either way, I fear he will not warm to you for quite some time," she soberly observed, then lightened that prediction by airily concluding, "Still, with any luck, that might come to pass a goodly while before Papa is given the wicked satisfaction of seeing you presented with suitors for *your* daughters."

Despite himself, Darcy gave an uneasy chuckle at the prospect of contending with a cantankerous Mr Bennet for years on end, only to dismiss the unpalatable notion in a flash, once the essence of Elizabeth's words sank in. A future with her, and the sons and daughters they would have. A home. A shared life — which would commence in as little as a *fortnight*. That was more than enough reason to give thanks for Mrs Bennet's rapturous talk of warehouses, and for her husband's crafty use of old wives' tales.

"I should do him the courtesy of speaking to him as soon as may be," Darcy said, making no effort to conceal his eagerness for the endeavour, but Elizabeth chortled mildly in response.

"We were looking for my bonnet, if you remember," she teasingly pointed out, then grew solemn when she added, "As for Papa, it would be an act of kindness to give him till the morrow. Besides, I think it might be best for all concerned if I should have another opportunity to assure him that my warning was in earnest."

There was nothing that he would deny her on this exhilarating day — and for that matter, he thought himself unlikely to ever deny her anything that was in his power to give.

"As you wish, my love," Darcy agreed, and was gratified to find that his complaisance did not go unrecognised. In fact, it was so comprehensively rewarded that, in due course, he felt duty-bound to remind her, "Your bonnet...?"

"Ah, yes. We had better find it before it is blown away. And we should head back," she conceded with a little grimace, "lest Mamma grow too aware of our absence, sniff out the truth and reveal it to all and sundry. I hope she does not, for Papa's sake, and no less for yours. I imagine you would not choose quite so public a betrothal."

"I should not care a whit if she announces it from the rooftops," Darcy replied, and found with no little surprise that he was in earnest, which went to show that love did work wonders after all, if it could reconcile him with the loud and tactless Mrs Bennet.

"I hope you will be able to hold on to that thought," Elizabeth said with a half-apologetic smile. "And on that note, it might serve you well to join forces with Mr Bingley. For safety in numbers, if nothing else," she laughed.

Darcy smiled back.

"There is a great deal to be said for that. So, am I allowed to tell him? This evening, I mean, once we are left to our own devices?"

"I would be exceedingly surprised if you can resist that temptation when left to your peace and your brandy. I know I cannot command quite so much self-restraint. I can scarce wait to tell Jane tonight, as soon as we can speak in private."

So this would be a time of shared confidences and, for some of them at least, there would be brandy. But as he clasped Elizabeth's hand in his and they resumed their walk towards the rotunda and the abandoned bonnet, Darcy knew full well that there would be no peace for him in the hours of the night. There would be elation, and grateful wonder, and restlessness, and the same old yearning. Peace would still elude him. But, praise be, only for another fortnight.

⁂

Happiness had a way of softening even the most unforgiving hearts, and it often made generous-hearted people even kinder, so Mr Bingley was gracious in accepting his friend's apologies, and took the news of Darcy's engagement remarkably well.

The same could not be said of Mr Bennet. Just as she had expected, on the following morning Elizabeth had her work cut out for her when she sought her father in his study to prepare him for the upcoming interview with Mr Darcy – or rather for the moment when her beloved would come to brave the dear old lion in his den and say his piece.

She was sequestered with her father for the best part of an hour, and all the while he endeavoured to impress upon her that fine clothes, fine carriages and any number of glittering jewels *did not* make for a happy union. Moreover, he voiced his disappointment at finding her, his most sensible offspring, in need of being warned against the folly of a rash choice in a matter of such import.

Elizabeth's earnest assurances that, to her way of thinking, she could not have chosen better and could not imagine being united to any other man were met with further pleas to bring her head down from the clouds and open her eyes to the realities of life, not least the soul-destroying evils of an unequal marriage.

This was the closest that Mr Bennet had ever come to openly declaring that he had married in haste and repented at leisure, and would not see his dearest girl err as grievously as he.

Since Elizabeth could not bring herself to malign her own mother, she refrained from an unflattering comparison between her least favourite parent and the man she loved. She could only insist time and again that she knew perfectly well what she was doing – that she had been mistaken in her initial estimation of Mr Darcy's character – that she understood him now – knew him well – loved him – and that he loved *her*, and his devotion was not the work of a day.

"If he loves you so well, let him prove it with a proper courtship," Mr Bennet grumbled. "Bingley is an accommodating sort – too accommodating, if you ask me – so he will suffer the fellow to come and stay. If not, Darcy can take rooms at the *Red Lion* for all I care, or come a-courting from his house in town."

Elizabeth stared. At any other time, she would have thought that her father spoke in jest. But there was no hint of raillery in his manner – not today. So she protested, barely resisting the urge to roll her eyes:

"You do know that the return journey is over fifty miles!"

Mr Bennet shrugged.

"And what is fifty miles of good road? Little more than half a day's travel. That should be nothing to a young man of means, if there is true devotion and firmness of purpose."

A mutinous crease formed between Elizabeth's brows. She made to speak, but her father raised his hand in a request for silence.

"I am a reasonable man, Lizzy," he said, leaning back in his wing-chair and steepling his fingers, "so I shall go as far as to say that he may come and go as he pleases, wherever he is coming from, and he can court you at his leisure. I will give him two months. Nay, four. If he shows himself to be everything you say, in four months' time I shall be ready and willing to revisit the matter of his proposal."

"Four months!" Elizabeth exclaimed in something akin to horror.

"Aye, and not one day less!" her father declared, his mien darkening into yet another scowl. "Who the blazes does he think he is to storm over here and demand that he marry you in as little as a fortnight?"

"Papa!" Elizabeth chided, then drew a deep breath in an endeavour to regain her equanimity. Her voice was low and measured when she spoke again: "He will not '*storm*' over here, I assure you. And I have it on the best authority that he will make no demands in that regard."

"On the best authority!" Mr Bennet spluttered. "Since when is he your best authority on anything?"

"Since the time when I discovered that he is the very best of men, and the only one I could ever love," Elizabeth replied, unwittingly paining her father with the instinctive admission that she now regarded Darcy, not him, as the worthiest man of her acquaintance. "But the authority I spoke of was mine. *I* suggested we marry in a fortnight. I would dearly like to share my special day with Jane."

When her father gave a gesture of vexation as though to say that, in the grand scheme of things, such overly sentimental considerations were of little import, she reached out to clasp and hold his hand.

"I have no need of a four-month courtship to understand my feelings and his, Papa. I will not break your heart with something as hurtful as an elopement, and he is too honourable to abet me in such an underhanded ploy, even if I were so selfish as to contemplate it. But I shall be of age in four weeks and a half. I shall wait that long if I must, but no longer. I *will* stand beside him at the altar as soon as it can be arranged. So I beg you, do not break my heart either, and spare me the pain of marrying without your blessing."

Under her brimming eyes, Mr Bennet's countenance lost the taut lines of anger and gradually sagged, as though he had aged a decade in a matter of minutes. He lowered his gaze to their joined hands, and for a very long time remained completely silent.

The first indication that he was about to conquer himself and relent came when he raised her hand and brought it to his lips. But his voice still dripped with petulant resentment when he asked, "So now you expect me to forgive him for driving a wedge between us? As if it were not bad enough that he would take you away to that estate of his, hundreds of miles from here!"

"The location of Pemberley he cannot help," Elizabeth said, smiling through her tears, then sought her father's eyes and earnestly added, "Nor can he drive a wedge between us. No one can do that, Papa. Except you."

ଈ୧ ୨ଈ

Thus, Mr Bennet's consent was obtained — extracted by means of shameless blackmail, he maintained in his subsequent and oft-repeated grumbles aimed at his second daughter — and henceforth Darcy was afforded the unenviable privilege of witnessing the master of Longbourn turning peevishness and excessive parental supervision into something of an art.

Yet Mr Bennet's spleen, liberally manifested throughout the following fortnight, detracted nothing from the poignancy of the day when he led his eldest daughter and his dearest one to the altar and entrusted them to the devoted care of the men they loved.

When he stepped out of Longbourn Church a married man, Darcy was little short of giddy. Nothing could mar his overwhelming joy. Certainly not Tyndall. The man had lost all power to distress him two weeks ago to the day. Since then, the supposed rival could only inspire sympathy whenever Darcy's reflections had veered towards him. Shamefully, no doubt – but most predictably – that had not happened often. Truth be told, Darcy had not thought of him once ever since Tyndall had chosen to remove himself from Hertfordshire, soon after the news of Elizabeth's engagement had begun to travel through the neighbourhood as swiftly as such things tend to spread and become common knowledge long before they are formally announced.

Thus, Tyndall had not shown himself at the wedding as the only sour countenance in the congregation. That questionable distinction belonged to Lady Catherine – and she was still clinging to it when the assembled company spilled out from the old church to mill about on the gravelled paths.

At least Lord Malvern somehow contrived to appear solemn instead of grimly disapproving. As for his lady, she looked positively buoyant – although Darcy had reason to suspect that Lady Malvern's cheer, pointedly displayed since the Fitzwilliams' arrival into Hertfordshire the previous evening, had more to do with her sister-in-law's discontent than his own happiness. Still, it would be good to have her on his side, albeit for the wrong reasons. It was her own affair if she genuinely rejoiced with him or not. As far as his relations were concerned, it was enough to know that his sister did. And his cousins too, Richard in particular. Lady Malvern could continue to have her sport with Lady Catherine if it pleased her – so long as it worked to Elizabeth's advantage.

With all the generous forbearance of a man in love who had just seen his best dreams fulfilled, Darcy readily dismissed all thoughts of his petty aunts. He was too elated to pay heed to anyone but his bride – and least of all inclined to dwell on Lady Catherine or the fact that, until the blissfully happy day of his wedding, she had been far more difficult to ignore.

She had made an appearance at Netherfield twelve days prior, hard on Georgiana's and Richard's heels, availed herself of his friend's hospitality and resentfully informed him that she had come to see just how low he was prepared to sink, once he had disdained to do his duty by her daughter.

Despite that provoking declaration and the snide remarks that followed, Darcy had steadfastly endeavoured to remind himself that, however sullen, Lady Catherine could lay claims to his compassion. She had just been deprived of her only daughter. There was nothing left for her to do but prepare herself for months upon months of loneliness, and make her peace with the galling notion that, having spent all her adult years seeking to direct the lives of others and influence the most trifling details of their existence, she had been proven singularly unsuccessful where it mattered most. For one of her disposition, this must rankle a vast deal, and pain her far more than the emptiness awaiting at Rosings.

Yet his forbearance had failed him five days ago, while they were returning to Netherfield after a predictably taxing dinner at Longbourn. The large company – far too large for the Bennets' dining room – would have been enough to account for his discomfort, even without the mortification that his aunt had caused him. She had been ungracious throughout, almost as though she had only attended so that she could point out the deficiencies of the Bennets' abode, their servants and their table arrangements. None of the dishes could meet with her approval, much as Mrs Bennet – shockingly, the better-mannered of the two – had sought to be an attentive hostess and tempt her with one delicacy after another. Lady Catherine had continued to sulk and grumble – which, judging by Mr Bennet's countenance, had served to vindicate most if not all of the older gentleman's prejudices against him – so much so that Darcy had seen no other option but to follow the ladies into the drawing room as soon as they had left the gentlemen to their brandy and port, and quietly but sternly insist to escort his aunt to Netherfield forthwith.

It had been a most unpleasant journey – just the pair of them driven back in Bingley's carriage – but Darcy had been glad of his friend's absence, and likewise Georgiana's and Fitzwilliam's, for it had given him the liberty to grimly warn his aunt that she was hurtling headlong for a rupture if she persisted in being so monumentally uncivil to his future wife and her relations.

"You would discard *me*, your mother's only sister, to please an impudent minx who should never have had the effrontery to aim so far above her station? Then you are well and truly brought to heel, Nephew — and serves you right, I say," Lady Catherine had sneered, compounding his vexation. But she had not stopped at that. Full of spite, she had bitterly resumed, "Aye, serves you right for turning up your nose at Anne. She would have brought credit to your name, not to mention a vast fortune. And she would not have presumed to meddle in your affairs, nor dictate your choices. More to the point, had you married Anne when you were first told to, she would not have thrown herself away on Maynard, and would now be out of harm's way in Derbyshire rather than on some confounded ship, preparing to set sail and leave me to fear for her safety. So do not sit there threatening me with a rupture. I flatter myself that I can bear the loss of your society, if I can endure Anne's absence and my apprehensions for her future. Be off with you, then. Go and set up house with that chit, surround yourself with her lowly relations, and see what good it does you. *I* will not pander to the likes of them. Bah! They should count themselves fortunate if I acknowledge the connection."

The arrogant pronouncement had rung a detestably familiar bell. He had once shared his aunt's haughty views. He might not have put them in the same words, but the sentiment had been there. Moreover, there were some mitigating circumstances in Lady Catherine's case. She belonged to a different generation, and she was a bitter old woman who had been dealt a severe blow. Whereas *he* had not had any such excuses.

So Darcy had held himself in check and had not answered as harshly as he had intended, but merely said, "I do not wish for us to become estranged. I would be loath to leave you to your own devices until Anne returns to settle back in England with her husband, and I do not doubt that Georgiana and Elizabeth feel the same. However," he had qualified with understated firmness, "I will protect my wife and her— our relations from unpleasant scenes. And that is all I shall say on the matter."

"Good. For I have no wish to hear another word on that score," his aunt had rancorously replied – and the remainder of the journey had passed in acrimonious silence.

By the time he had conveyed her to Netherfield and returned to Longbourn, the best part of the evening was gone. But there *had* been some consolation – and wholly unexpected, too – when, of his own accord, Mr Bennet had traded places with Elizabeth, so that she could leave the whist table and join him. The gesture had not gained them much; just a few minutes of illusory privacy. Yet Darcy had made a point of meeting his host's gaze and offering a silent nod of gratitude for the kindness, in equal measure reassured and humbled by the notion that Mr Bennet might very well be a better man than he – for, by the looks of it, the older gentleman's good opinion, once lost, was not lost for ever.

Nonetheless, Darcy could not go as far as to describe his new father-in-law's mien as friendly when the garrulous wedding party drifted towards the waiting carriages and Mr Bennet came to shake his hand with a quietly spoken yet ominous, "I trust you will take good care of my daughter, sir."

The brief exchange with Lady Catherine a short while earlier, at the church door, had not been friendly either – not in the common sense of the word. She had not given them joy, but merely offered a curt, "I shall see you at Rosings for Easter."

The terse remark, with its undertones of an imperious command, would have counted as a slight, had it come from anybody else. From her, it was an olive branch – however small and withered.

Darcy would have been relieved to learn that his aunt did not intend to stay on, so she would not mortify him in his absence. Lady Catherine left right after the newlyweds' carriages had rolled away. In her turn, Elizabeth would have been gratified to know that her ladyship had already resolved to make her peace with her beleaguered parson for, after all, she had to have *some* company. As to her parson's wife, she would be reinstated at the same time in Lady Catherine's good graces – such as they were – for Anne, in her kind wisdom, had not revealed anything to her mother about Charlotte's role in establishing the correspondence between her and Mr Wickham.

Unbeknownst to Lady Catherine, one of the occupants of the stagecoach that left the *Golden Cross* at high speed and thundered past her own conveyance, spooking her horses, was the man himself. Mr Wickham was on his way to Bath, to make the best possible use of his well-lined purse.

The generous reward for his exertions on Miss de Bourgh's behalf might have been frittered away as swiftly as the three thousand pounds he had extracted from Darcy in lieu of the Kympton living. But, to Mr Wickham's lasting advantage, he would be favoured with an excellent return for his investments in elegant apparel and sundry trappings, as they would be instrumental in securing him the interest of Lady Dalrymple's daughter.

His personal charm would do the rest. The subsequent elopement would be the last such endeavour that he would ever need to orchestrate, and by far the most successful. Before long, Mr Wickham would be an excessively smug bridegroom returning from Gretna with his new wife, to rejoice in the end of his financial difficulties, and no less in the absence of any family ties to Darcy and Lady Catherine. Another cantankerous dowager, Lady Dalrymple, was destined to have him as her son-in-law and a reviled thorn in her side for the remainder of her natural life.

But Lady Catherine had no way of knowing what was to come, otherwise she might have been grimly satisfied to reflect on Lady Dalrymple's fate, unquestionably worse than hers. Thus, satisfaction was the furthest notion from her mind as she clung to the side of her swaying carriage and inwardly cursed this modern age, when the lesser sort no longer knew their place and presumed to endanger the comfort and safety of an earl's daughter.

At the same time, some sixty miles to the north, the most recent addition to her family could not care less that, to Lady Catherine, she was yet another upstart and a reflection of changing times and declining standards. Sadly for her ladyship, her own nephew had no regard for her views either. Moreover, he had patently lost most of the prejudices of his parents' generation. Blissfully free from any thoughts of prideful self-consequence, Mr Darcy was the happiest man alive as he travelled apace with his darling wife on their way home to Pemberley.

Epilogue

The rising sun sent shafts of light through the tall windows, but it was not their brightness that had awoken him. Darcy had been awake for quite some time, ever since birdsong had begun to signal the start of yet another summer's day. He had always been an early riser. The only difference was that, these days, he was not in the least inclined to leave the bed. So he remained precisely where he was, his wife's sleeping form cradled to his chest, until Elizabeth stirred and stretched with a deliciously sleepy murmur, which gave him more than enough licence to trail his fingertips in a light caress over her skin and feather a host of kisses along her bare shoulder. He would have said that this was the best part of his day, were it not so difficult – well-nigh impossible, in fact – to pick a favourite from the countless blissful moments that made up each day spent beside her.

A gasp and a quiet giggle escaped her when his lips drifted to her neck.

"Now, now," she playfully chided. "This is not the time. We have a houseful of guests to attend to, if you remember."

And so they had. The entire Bennet contingent. Bingley and his wife. Mr and Mrs Gardiner and their children. And, as luck would have it, Lady Catherine, who had descended upon them without notice. Soon to be followed by Miss Bingley, who must have thought it advisable to smother her resentment and retain the rights and privileges of a longstanding acquaintance, for she had sent word through her brother that she very much hoped to give them her best wishes in person, and would like to stop at Pemberley along with Mr and Mrs Hurst, on their way back from Scarborough.

It would be an exceedingly lively summer.

Yet the thought lost the power to vex him when, in blatant disregard of her own warnings against the delights of self-indulgence, Elizabeth turned around and sought his lips, rendering him breathless with her kisses.

"All the more reason to make the most of this time of day, if you ask me," Darcy rasped as soon as he could speak, and brought her closer still, his hands roaming over her in sweeping, feverish caresses as the age-old fever built within.

He made no effort to subdue it. Nor did she, but wrapped herself around him as she drew her lips from his to willingly expose her throat to his hungry exploration and chuckled, "You know full well that your aunt rises at the crack of dawn. She will comment yet again on our tardiness for breakfast."

"Let her," Darcy breathed against her skin, then buried his face in the curve of her neck and inhaled deeply, filling his senses with her exquisite fragrance, which only served to stoke the flames and send them leaping higher. All the more so when she nipped his earlobe, her mischievous whisper a warm tickle in his ear.

"You are becoming a shockingly disobliging nephew. And what is worse, you encourage your blameless wife into the same undutiful behaviour," she teased, yet raised her hand to twine her fingers in his hair and draw his lips to hers – a thrilling sign that, as always, she did not require a great deal of encouragement.

Nevertheless, he matched her teasing with a quiet whisper of his own:

"Mmm-hm… I was rather hoping to."

"Were you?" she murmured, her fingertips leaving his hair to graze the back of his neck and slide down his spine in a slow, tantalising caress. Her other hand came up to cover his over the swell of her bosom and she filtered a sultry glance through lowered lashes, the very picture of an enchantress, as her lips curled up into a smile. "I see. Well then, so much for dutiful conduct. But there is still the question of morality…"

"Morality?" Darcy choked out, his head too full of her to leave much room for coherent thought, and even less for philosophising.

"Indeed," Elizabeth laughed softly, her warm breath brushing over his face and scattering whatever was left of his senses. "For what becomes of it, if we owe our happiness to something as irregular as an elopement?" she asked as she dug her fingers into the small of his back, then lazily stretched to catch his lower lip between her teeth.

An almost feral sound broke from his chest at the delightful and wildly arousing provocation, and Darcy lost the will to pause and tell her that Anne's elopement had been purely incidental. Even if it had not interrupted his monumentally ill-worded first proposal, even if Elizabeth had refused him then, he would have stopped at nothing to make her change her mind. There was nothing, absolutely nothing, that he would not have done to win her heart and her acceptance.

He drew a sharp breath and hazily resolved to say so later — if she did not know it already. For now, he could only rasp, "Morality be damned," and crushed her lips with his.

The End

ABOUT THE AUTHOR

Joana Starnes lives in the south of England with her family. Over the years, she swapped several hats – physician, lecturer, clinical data analyst – but feels most comfortable in a bonnet. She has been living in Georgian England for decades in her imagination, and plans to continue in that vein till she lays hands on a time machine.
She loves to look for glimpses
of Pemberley and Jane Austen's world,
and to write about Regency England
and Mr Darcy falling in love with Elizabeth Bennet
over and over and over again.

You can connect with Joana Starnes on
Facebook: www.facebook.com/joana.a.starnes
Instagram: www.instagram.com/joana_starnes/
Website: www.joanastarnes.co.uk
Twitter: @Joana_Starnes

Or visit
www.facebook.com/AllRoadsLeadToPemberley.JoanaStarnes
for places and details that have inspired her novels.

Printed in Great Britain
by Amazon

40967532R00108